An Excerpt from *At t*

Senth tried not to stare at the slakes along the wall, but their clothing and attitude declared their availability. He stopped to watch a pair of bare-assed male and female slakes bent over a low railing. Androgs handled their bodies like merchandise.

Khyff laid a hand on Senth's shoulder and nudged his chin toward the Androgs. "Comparison shoppers."

Senth frowned up at him. "That's not funny."

"Especially when it's you hanging over the damned railing." Khyff jerked his head to one side. "Come on."

Other than Kin, no one in the place wore leather clothing except Khyff. Kin had a proverb, "To wear an animal's skin, you must take its soul yourself." No one challenged his brother.

Females ruled on the home planet Felidae, and the majority who visited the Ghost had more than one male in their company. A single Kin female at the bar turned and looked Senth over from head to foot. Tall and slender, she wore brown leather the same color as her hair. She slid her tongue seductively across her upper teeth, back and forth between her fangs, and wiggled her cute feline nose. Then she twitched her pointed ears toward Senth.

Khyff grabbed him. "Stay away from her! She'll take you to bed and then eat you for breakfast. And that's not a figure of speech. HalfKin who leave with her aren't seen again."

The female crooked a finger at him. Senth turned and fled after Khyff.

Loose Id®

ISBN 13: 978-1-60737-732-0
AT THE MERCY OF HER PLEASURE
Copyright © July 2010 by Kayelle Allen
Released in e-book format by Loose Id LLC in March 2010 after being substantially re-edited and revised from its original version previously released by another publisher.

Cover Art by Anne Cain
Cover Layout and Design by April Martinez

Printed in the U.S.A. by
Lightning Source, Inc.
1246 Heil Quaker Blvd
La Vergne TN 37086
www.lightningsource.com

ANTONELLO BROTHERS:

AT THE MERCY OF
HER PLEASURE

(A Tarthian Empire story)

Dedication

This book is dedicated to my husband, whose loving encouragement keeps me going during the toughest times.

I wish to thank my friends Barbara Karmazin, Janet Elizabeth Jones, and Jodi Lynn Copeland, the authors who mentored me while I was writing the first edition of this book. To the critique group at para-rom-crit2, thank you! Without your guidance, encouragement, and friendship, the first version would not have been possible.

I dedicate the new version to those readers who, like me, have fallen in love with the Tarthian Empire and its rogue's gallery of inhabitants. My sincere thanks to the members of Romance Lives Forever for their unfailing support. To my editor, Heather Hollis, Therah la hahr— which, translated from the Kin language, means, "You have the heart of a warrior." You need one while traveling through the Tarthian Empire with me!

Chapter One

Tarthian Empire
Kelthia, Miraj City, Crooktown District
Wintresq 12, 4662 Tradestandard date

Sheathed in black, Senth checked left, then right before molding his body into the shadows near a brick wall. The human and feline Kin gangs in Crooktown hunted mixed breeds. At first glance he appeared human, but with his catlike eyes and fangs, no one could miss his feral nature. He tugged the hood of his cloak forward, concealing his eyes. In moonlight, they'd glow like a cat's.

"*Fffffft* this *kkkhh*!" The Kin cuss words hissed past his fangs. *Where are you*? Pressed against the wall, he slipped around a corner and into the alley.

Senth slid into the concealing darkness behind a barrel. His HalfKin senses caught the scent of his quarry before he saw him. He narrowed night-sensitive eyes.

Senth's human half brother leaned against the opposite wall of the rubble-strewn alley, silent and unaware of his presence. Khyffen's blond hair shone faintly in the muted light. A female pinned him, arms around his neck. She tore open Khyff's shirt and ran her hands over his chest, then went to her knees in front of him. Khyff opened his pants.

Yechh. Senth squatted at the base of the brick wall, folding himself into the tight space behind another barrel to guard his brother's back. *Do you have to get your cock out now? If those gangs come down here...* He leaned out from the barrel. Khyff had his fists clenched, eyes squeezed shut, and face lifted to the night sky, mouth open in a silent scream. *Hurry up, Bro.* He rubbed the back of his gloved hand across his brow. *Man, if I had to worry about a perpetual hard-on, I'd never get anything done. We've gotta get you off that drug.* The one Senth's *Sen'dai* gave him had the opposite effect.

A *scritch* near his feet signaled rats. When one ran across the toes of his boots, Senth bared his fangs. He clamped down on a hiss before Khyff could hear it. From down the street the faint sound of a gang chant carried in the chill night air.

Oh kkkhh, they're close. The voices grew louder. *Don't come down here. I get into one more fight this quarter, the Grand Master will take skin off me.*

The whine of a hovercar's engines brought music and female voices. Male voices mixed with laughter, then the sound of doors opening and closing. The car's hum faded as it drove away, leaving silence.

Senth thunked his head back against the wall and blew out the breath he'd held. *Khyff! Hurry up!*

Khyff and the woman walked over and stopped right in front of the barrel where Senth hid. Pulling his hood farther down, Senth leaned back and rested his gloved hands atop his drawn-up knees.

The woman, blonde and beautiful, looked at least forty.

Rich, judging by the material of her jacket and pants, yet something about her felt different. Senth lowered his brows and squinted. Women like her didn't come to Crooktown. Not to mention to hire a slake. She didn't look like the type who paid for men. Surely she knew how Khyff made his living.

"Let's meet again in three days. Someplace safer."

"No." Khyff tilted his head. "You like it on the street, up against the wall in an alley. You like danger. That's why you come to me."

The woman threw both arms around Khyff's neck and kissed him. "You're so right, you beautiful hunk."

"You've had enough for one night." Khyff shook off her embrace and tossed blond hair out of his eyes.

She reached for him again.

"I said no, Liu. Go home. You shouldn't linger in Crooktown after dark."

"Take this." The woman held a silver debit bracelet on the tips of her outstretched fingers, as if offering food to a dangerous animal. "It's a thousand *draks*. You can spend it anywhere."

A thousand? The long leather coat and pants his brother wore only cost a fraction of that.

Khyff tucked a strand of his hair behind one ear. "You already paid me."

Senth bit back a startled laugh. Khyff actually sounded as if he was turning it down.

"You made me happy tonight. Come on, Khyff. Please? Think of it as a little extra tip."

"No way. You know I can only take soft money. You think I want people knowing about us? You think I want your banker knowing you've got a slake?"

Oh, you don't want your prints in her bank's possession. Senth nodded. *Or your master knowing you moonlight.*

"It's debit, not registered. Untraceable. Come on." She jiggled the bracelet. "Let me do something for you. I want to."

Khyff reached out, hesitated, and then took the bracelet. "You carried this kind of money here? Are you crazy? You could have been buzzed. There are thieves everywhere."

Senth suppressed a snicker. *Ain't that the truth. What would the Grand Master say if he knew I passed up a chance at a thousand draks?* He shook his head. *Never hear it from me.*

She ran her hands over Khyff's chest. "You care about me?"

He moved her hands away. "You know I do."

"Oh, Khyff."

"Oh, Liu."

Oh, please. Senth rolled his eyes.

When the woman exited the alley, Khyff's smile flicked off like a switch. He dropped the bracelet into his pocket and patted it like an old friend.

Senth rose to his full height, level with his brother's shoulders. Khyff lunged into him, grabbed him by the front of his cloak, picked him up, and slammed him against the brick wall. His raw, physical power rendered Senth immobile.

With a gasp of recognition, Khyff set him back on the ground. "Sen?" He shoved back the cloak's hood. "You deadlurking me, Bro?"

Senth dusted himself off. "I cozied your back. Peak freaks out there, sniffin' out drugs and buzzin' clinkers. Didn't want them shoppin' you."

"Don't ever cop on me in the dark. Especially if I'm hostin'."

Senth held up both hands. "Sorry I rode your pocket."

"Nah." He slid his fingers back through his hair. "Nah. Junk me. You comin' out of the dark like that. I know you didn't peep me."

Senth grinned. "Which time?"

Khyff narrowed his eyes, jerked a thumb in the general direction of the street, and started walking. Senth fell in step beside him. No shops stood open at this hour, all the windows and doors barred. Clouds covered Kelthia's single moon. Those streetlights unsmashed by gangs cast too dim a glow to banish shadows.

"Why you cozy, Sen? No life?"

"Got a rompin' life. Just cozied your back 'cause you're blood. 'Sides, goin' sly a few days. Wanted to tap you first."

The two brushed their fists together in a quick greeting, as close as his brother got to shaking hands. Khyff raked a hand through his hair. "What you sly for?"

"I got a pull. Grand Master has me facing a buyer tonight."

"Where?"

"The Ghost." The worst club in the red-light heart of

Crooktown, it butted right up against the slakehouse that owned Khyff.

His brother snorted. "I sure you boastin' me."

Senth handed him a piece of paper. "Scope this."

Khyff halted in the middle of the sidewalk and tore the paper in pieces.

"Hey!" Senth grabbed him, but the body under all that butter-soft leather felt like iron.

With both hands on Senth's chest, Khyff shoved him. Paper remnants fluttered to the ground as Senth danced backward to keep from falling.

"I told you!" Khyff raised balled fists. "I told you no one touches me! Not you. Not anybody."

"She touched you."

"She paid for it, Sen. Back off!"

Senth put up both hands and ducked. "I didn't mean to annoy you, Khyff. I'm sorry. It won't happen again."

"It better not. And stay out of the Ghost."

"Can't do that. The Grand Master says you-know-who wants me there." Senth didn't say his Sen'dai's name. No one did.

"Why?" The word came out a plea.

"You think I'm gonna ask *him* why he does anything?"

"The Ghost is no place for kids."

"I'm a legal adult! I'm old enough to join the armada and vote, so stop calling me a kid."

"*If* you were free." Khyff turned on his heel and started walking.

Senth growled low in his throat but followed. "Why'd you...you know? Back there. I thought you hated doing that."

"I do."

"Then why?"

Khyff halted and swung to face him. Senth backed up a step.

"Look, Sen, it's different when you're not forced. Besides, the money's easy, the tips are great, and on the street, I decide how much of my clothes I take off." He pulled the bracelet out of his jacket. "Here. You know where to put this." Straight into the freedom savings account entitled to slaves.

Like all children born into slavery, Senth would be freed at age twenty, in two years. Khyff's time in prison and parole delayed his freedom for at least eight more years, or until he had enough money to buy himself.

Senth stuffed the bracelet in a pocket. "You keep getting tips like this, you can buy me too. She must like you."

Khyff snapped him a look, then chuckled. "Guess Liu does look female."

Senth felt his face flame. "That was a guy?"

"That was a *Chiasma*. An *Androg*. Fully male and fully female. Never seen one that close before?"

"I thought she seemed different."

"Liu's beautiful, huh? They always are, no matter which gender phase they're in at the time. There've been a lot of them at the clubs lately. Liu's fascinated with humans. Drogs can't imagine what it's like being one gender all the time.

They switch every quarter. I make good money catering to them. Especially on the street."

"Does it matter which phase they're in?"

Khyff made a noise halfway between a grunt and a sigh. "Like slakes ever get to pick the menu."

Senth contemplated that for a moment before asking, "Is it true Androgs can make you feel what they're feeling?"

"Sure, when they want to. I'm guessing that's not happening in a dark alley." With an abrupt grin, he punched Senth in the arm. "Come on, Bro. Let's get you over to the Ghost. It's time to put *you* to work for a while."

* * *

As Senth approached, the beefy Kin bouncer at the Ghost put out a hand. "Hold up, kid." She nodded approval at his brother with no more than a glance. Khyff waited while she motioned Senth aside. "You got ID?"

Senth opened his cloak, revealing the unmistakable insignia of the Thieves' Guild, a skeleton key inside a slashed circle, on the lining. *No key required.* He gave his Sen'dai's hand sign.

"Ffffftt!" The bouncer held up both hands and made an apologetic nod. "Sorry. Why didn't you say you were his right up front?"

"*His* shouldn't have to." He brushed a hand down the front of the cloak. "And I'm no kid."

"Sorry, sir." She opened the door for both of them and bowed.

Smiling with envious pride, Khyff chuckled and shook his head. He held out one palm, and Senth slid his down it, hooked his fingers as Khyff did, and with hands clasped, gave one downward shake. "C'mon, Bro." Khyff led the way past the darkened foyer.

Inside, music pulsed like a living entity. The throbbing bass tickled Senth's chest, and he coughed. Drums pounded. Colored lights swept the cavernous room. Strobes flashed across the congested dance floor, highlighting bobbing heads and upflung arms. Light glinted off human bodies slick with sweat. Bared and damp Kin furskin stuck out in points, laden with glitter.

"Stay close," Khyff shouted over the pounding music, standing next to Senth. He headed for the rear and left no chance to argue. They skirted around the crammed dance area. Senth liberated a few loose credit stubs clipped carelessly to belts and stuffed them into the pockets of his cloak.

Senth tried not to stare at the slakes along the wall, but their clothing and attitude declared their availability. He stopped to watch a pair of bare-assed male and female slakes bent over a low railing. Androgs handled their bodies like merchandise.

Khyff laid a hand on Senth's shoulder and nudged his chin toward the Androgs. "Comparison shoppers."

Senth frowned up at him. "That's not funny."

"Especially when it's you hanging over the damn railing." Khyff jerked his head to one side. "Come on."

Other than Kin, no one in the place wore leather clothing except Khyff. Kin had a proverb, "To wear an animal's skin, you must take its soul yourself." No one challenged his brother.

Females ruled on the home planet Felidae, and the majority who visited the Ghost had more than one male in their company. A single Kin female at the bar turned and looked Senth over from head to foot. Tall and slender, she wore brown leather the same color as her hair. She slid her tongue seductively across her upper teeth, back and forth between her fangs, and wiggled her cute feline nose. Then she twitched her pointed ears toward Senth.

Khyff grabbed him. "Stay away from her! She'll take you to bed and then eat you for breakfast. And that's not a figure of speech. HalfKin who leave with her aren't seen again."

The female crooked a finger at him. Senth turned and fled after Khyff.

Two female Betters conversed with each other, ignoring the human males chained to their wrists like pets. The men wore pants, boots, and chain harnesses across their chests.

Enhanced humans with every sense fine-tuned, Betters were bred for intelligence, leadership, beauty, and lust. Khyff had told him they went into heat like animals, and that once you'd had a Better in heat, you couldn't be satisfied with a normal human ever again. To curb potential problems, Betters were not permitted to hire slakers or enter slakehouses. Ever.

Senth walked into a solid wall of muscle, and backed up. "Oh kkkhh!" He flinched, ready to duck.

Khyff glared down at him, arms folded. "You better be glad it was me." His brother grabbed him by the arm and shouldered through the throng with him in tow. "Quit hawkin', Sen." He glanced back. "You want talons in your eyes?"

The noise level lowered when they rounded a corner. To the left, wide marble stairs wound upward. Bouncers stood guard on the first landing, weapons cradled in their arms. Beside them, arrowed signs pointed in different directions. HOTEL. CASHIER CAGE. EXIT TO SLAKEHOUSE.

Senth took one step up and felt a tug on his cloak. He turned and looked straight into Khyff's eyes.

"I can't go any farther than this." Khyff set one foot on the bottom stair. "There's only one place they'd let me go up there." His glance moved left. "My master's here, by the way. I saw him when we came in." Holding a wad of soft money, Khyff moved his hand between himself and Senth. "Take this. He'll pat me down before he puts me to work."

Senth hid the cash in a pocket. For eighteen years he hadn't known he even had family. In the tradestandard month since he'd discovered he had a human half brother, he'd bargained everything short of his soul to buy Khyff's slave contract so they could be together. Leaving his brother, even for a few days, left a gaping, lonely hole in his heart.

"Please." Khyff's misery-hardened eyes implored. "Stay safe. After all these years of not knowing you were even alive—"

"Hey!" He forced himself to focus on the job at hand. "You think you can shirk my cozy without a drip? Man, Bro, yo' cover is for gloom." He stuck up a thumb. "I got you happy." *You can't get rid of me that easy. No one watches your back better than I do.*

Khyff grinned, shaking his head. "Go to work." He

turned and shouldered his way back into the crowded club.

On the hotel level, six of his Sen'dai's private, no-nonsense goons in dark suits and dark glasses blocked the hallway he approached. Senth flashed his Sen'dai's hand signal. With a grudging nod of respect, one of the men opened a door for him and then shut it behind him with a *click.* Background noise ceased.

Without moving, he sized up the room. High ceilings, subdued lighting, heavy furniture, marble-topped tables. No paintings. Two statues, obvious fakes. Dense drapes, deep carpet, wood-paneled walls. The positions of the door and windows, plus the spacing of the panels, meant a hidden safe. No visible security, but nowhere the guild set up a meet lacked it.

A door opened, and though Senth could not see the Harbinger, he felt the man's presence. A native-born Kelthian, Luc Saint-Cyr's dark chocolate skin and habitual black attire made it possible for him to disappear into the shadows.

Though the Harbinger had personally sent for him, his presence was the last thing Senth expected. If his Sen'dai was on Kelthia, this was not the usual grab and go. The man moved one hand into the light and gestured Senth closer.

"Sen'dai." He stepped forward and bowed. Like most people, he avoided looking directly into Luc Saint-Cyr's eyes. The man wore contact lenses that turned his eyes completely black. Raven's eyes, peering, intent. Predatory.

"With me, Senthys." Saint-Cyr led him through the darkened room to a hidden flight of stairs. He paused with one hand on the railing. "How much was it?"

Senth lifted his head. "Sir?"

"Khyffen's tip tonight. How much?"

He cast about in his mind how his Sen'dai knew.

"Of course I know what Khyffen's up to." The Harbinger tucked a finger under Senth's chin and smiled down at him. "You're the finest *Deshai* I've ever trained. Nothing that affects you escapes my attention. You're too important." He started up the steps and halted so quickly, Senth bumped into him.

"Sorry, sir."

"Well, Senthys? How much?"

He held his Sen'dai's gaze, focusing on the centers of the solid black orbs. "A thousand, sir."

"Good." One corner of his mouth lifted. "I told Liu to take care of him."

"Liu's one of yours?" They continued up the stairs.

"Mmm. You know your brother's master and I are old...*friends*." His emphasis on the last word sent a chill up Senth's spine. "I want to help Khyffen. He'd be an exceptional asset to my face business."

For Women Only, Saint-Cyr's private security company and one of the faces for his true business. It offered premium protection services to celebrity female clientele.

"Thank you, sir."

"You offered once to bargain for his freedom." Saint-Cyr stopped, and then turned back. "Are you still open to that?"

Senth leaned forward. "Yes, sir! Whatever it takes."

Saint-Cyr shook a finger at him. "What have I told you

about being too eager?"

"Sorry, Sen'dai." He hung back. "You surprised me."

"Bargains are always a surprise. Keep that in mind."

"Sen'dai." He lowered his head in respect.

"Senthys, you'll be free in two years. Khyffen still has eight. Suppose I were to guarantee his freedom in less than a week?"

Senth tried not to show his glee, but a smile pasted itself across his face anyway.

The Harbinger closed his solid black eyes, head shaking in a way that said, *What am I to do with you?*

"I'm sorry, sir! You've never lied to me. I trust your word."

The black-skinned man gazed down at him for a silent moment. He nodded and laid a hand on Senth's shoulder. "And well you should."

"What do I have to do, sir, for Khyff's freedom?"

"The job we're meeting about tonight will bring in a fortune for us, but it holds extreme risk for you. I don't usually give you a choice, but this time I'm going to because of the job's importance. I'm also offering to buy Khyffen and free him. In return, I want a few promises."

"You know I want this, sir. I'll do whatever it takes."

The Harbinger's mouth lifted at one side. "Never admit *that* to anyone either."

"Yes, sir."

"Senthys, you understand why I've kept you on Shackle?"

While Khyff's master had addicted him to Thrust, which put his sex drive into overload, Shackle did the opposite to Senth. From puberty forward, he'd never known life without it. The drug also controlled aggression.

"Yes, Sen'dai," he answered swiftly. "I never want *that* to happen again."

"Good." The Harbinger tapped a knuckle against his mouth, frowning at him. "You know what they'd do to you if it did, don't you? Where they'd take you?"

"Yes, sir." He stiffened. "I don't want that."

"No, of course not. After five days without Shackle, you'll start withdrawal. Your heart will pound. Your head will feel like it's splitting apart. And for several days, you'll have a semipermanent erection. You understand what that means?"

"Yes, Sen'dai. I'd be as high and strung out as Khyff is on weekends."

"Well put. There's a possibility of stroke if you quit cold. It's extremely dangerous. You must taper off the drug. Do you understand?"

He nodded. "I do, sir."

"This job should take four days, so it's important that you return as soon as it's over."

"Yes, sir."

"I'll dose you before you leave to ensure you have the full five-day effect."

"Thank you, sir."

"The reason I've told you all this is because you'll be working side by side with a Better."

Senth opened his mouth, shut it again, and then mouthed, *Better?*

"Listen to me, my young Deshai. Despite the romantic nonsense you've heard about Betters being extraordinary lovers, their kisses can poison you. If her saliva mixes with yours, she can control your mind. The touch of her hands will drive you insane. There are ancient myths about sirens, women who used their voices to lure men and then slay them. Betters aren't mythical. They're real. If she subjects you to her passion, you'll be at the mercy of her pleasure forever."

Senth swallowed against the tight feeling in his throat and nodded to show he understood.

"This woman is dangerous. I wouldn't normally let any of my people work with her kind, but in this case...I have my reasons. I trust you to obey me. You bring in too much income, and you're personally too valuable to me to lose. I'd never let you take a job where you were at serious risk. Besides, if you come back to me no longer a virgin, I will know. The deal for Khyffen's freedom will be off if you disobey."

"How would you know I wasn't a virgin?" Senth covered his mouth the moment the words escaped, shocked at himself for even asking the question.

The Harbinger gave him a dry smile. "As long as you stay a virgin, that won't be a problem. If you had sex with her, I would know because her pheromones would addict you to her. If that happened..." He paused. "I would not be pleased with you."

Senth reached a foot back, feeling for the next lower

step.

His Sen'dai lowered his eyelids and angled his head toward Senth like a bird of prey sighting its next meal. "You know what happens when you displease me."

When Saint-Cyr put both hands on his shoulders, he flinched and shook his head vehemently. "I wouldn't want to do that."

"No, you wouldn't." He leaned in until the dark, predatory eyes completely filled Senth's vision. "You are my Deshai. You want to obey me, Senthys. You fear me. You will not let me down. I need you, and I want Khyffen. You want to obey me. You know the rules I've set for you, and you *will* follow them. You want to obey me. You feel good when you comply. This job will be a success. Agree."

"Yes, sir. This job will be a success."

"Good." The Harbinger stood up straight and smiled. "My Deshais always want to please me, don't they?"

"Yes, Sen'dai."

"They all obey me. They fear my wrath if they disobey."

"Yes, sir! I would never disobey you, sir. I swear it."

"Excellent." He brushed aside Senth's hair from his brow. "Wake."

Senth blinked and looked behind him. *How did I get halfway up the stairs?*

"Remember, as long as you return in fewer than five days, losing control won't even be an option. Shackle will protect you from her."

Senth raised a hand to his brow.

"Senthys? Are you all right?"

"Fine, Sen'dai. Sorry."

"Good. Come with me. It's time you met NarrAy Jorlan, your temporary partner." A simple hand sign—a fist with thumb down and then up—put Senth on guard. Vigilant silence.

Chapter Two

Kelthia, Miraj City, Crooktown District
The Ghost

Captain NarrAy Jorlan of the All People's Liberation Army leaned against the third-floor balcony railing, counting her blessings that she stood far above the dance floor. Lieutenant Broxus, her human assistant and security escort, had worn appropriate party clothes to the Ghost, but when NarrAy appeared, the staid officer had gone googly-eyed and started stammering.

Maybe this low-cut red party dress wasn't the best choice.

The noise level where she stood felt merely painful rather than deafening. She resisted the urge to plug a finger into each ear. Her other aide, Encie Falehla, moved around down there, lost among the heaving bodies. Encie liked this sort of place. Noisy, jam-packed with people. *More like with sweating males. What's with Kin and the smell of sweat anyway?*

Two Betters posed at the bar and surveyed the crowd. Her kind hid as well as the sun on a clear day. Perfect skin, perfect hair, perfect teeth, perfect bodies. Perfectly lonely lives. Everyone wanted the pheromone-induced lust a Better could provide. Few desired their addictive nature. And since enactment, the Better Laws ensured even fewer dared taste the exquisite pleasure.

Just down from the Betters, Encie turned from the bar to flirt with someone in the crowd.

Please, not another HalfKin. Another disappearance ranked high on NarrAy's avoid-at-all-costs list. The APLA might shelter thieves, ruffians, and even cold-blooded assassins, but not suspected serial killers. Even knowing the truth, NarrAy had sworn she'd fire Encie if it happened again. The fragile state of the fledgling rebellion warranted all due care.

After turning from the railing, she moved back into the room where the Harbinger had agreed to meet. Her aide came to attention.

"Any word, Brox?"

He touched one ear, listening to his comm. "Not yet, ma'am." Broxus refused to meet her gaze.

This dress was a mistake. Too revealing, too short, too red. She suppressed a sigh. "Tell me about the Harbinger."

He glanced toward her feet. "Didn't you meet him, ma'am?"

NarrAy rubbed her arms and shivered.

"I see you did." Broxus flipped open his notereader and tapped the screen. "Luc Saint-Cyr's reputation is more chilling than his eyes. He's been tied to everything but prostitution and homicide, but never arrested. Ops says folks around here won't talk about him. No one even says his name, and they flinch when an outsider does. Creeped me out doing background research, tell you that. I got the impression he's some kind of father figure to a lot of young men, though."

She snorted a laugh. "I have a little trouble picturing him as the daddy type."

"From what we can tell, he looks out for his people. There's no crime in his territory. One thing's for sure"— Broxus turned off the notereader and tucked it into his pocket—"no one crosses him. Police can't get a snitch anywhere close."

"And Senthys Antonello? Anything on him?"

"No, ma'am. The name's known, but that's all. No arrests. No warrants. Rumors indicate he's young, but nobody talks except to say he's the best. Trained by Saint-Cyr himself. Thieves' Guild ranking is advanced interior security, level nineteen, which means he can break into government holding areas."

"That's exactly what we need."

Brox folded his arms across a wide chest. He filled out that plain suit as well as he did his usual uniform. "You know, they say the Thieves' Guild adopts toddlers and rears them to be thieves."

"Well, unless Senthys is underage, I don't care how old he is."

Head tilted, Broxus lifted two fingers to his ear. He nodded to NarrAy, then motioned with his fingers toward the door.

NarrAy turned, tugging the skirt of the tight dress down

a bit more. She held herself more erect. After two knocks, the door opened.

The Harbinger stepped inside, another person behind him.

"Ms. Jorlan." Saint-Cyr made a slight bow.

She clenched her teeth behind her returned smile. The man's whiteless eyes made it impossible to see where he looked.

"Mr. Saint-Cyr." She interwove her fingers behind her hips. The customary handshake of greeting wasn't an option because the Better Laws forbade unnecessary touching.

"May I present my Deshai—that's *protégé* in the guild— Senthys Antonello." The Harbinger gestured to the dark-haired, handsome youth with him. "Senthys, Ms. NarrAy Jorlan."

"Ms. Jorlan." Senth extended a hand. To his credit, his blue-eyed gaze never strayed.

NarrAy ignored his hand.

"My apologies, ma'am." The Harbinger nudged Senth. "Betters don't touch others, son."

The boy glanced up at him with clear surprise. NarrAy had the impression he reacted to the title "son" rather than the belated instruction.

"Yes, sir." He ducked his head. "My apologies, ma'am. I didn't know."

"Quite all right." She motioned to Lieutenant Broxus. "Please show Mr. Saint-Cyr and his Deshai to the door."

Broxus did not hesitate. "This way, sir."

"Ms. Jorlan?" The Harbinger turned his head from her to Broxus and then back. "Is something wrong?"

"I contracted with you for a professional, not a child. He can't be a day over fourteen."

Senthys grunted with exasperation and threw up his hands. "I am *not* a kid!" He turned to the Harbinger. "Sen'dai, please tell her my qualifications and how old I am." He turned toward NarrAy and clasped his hands behind his back, his shoulders straight.

"My Deshai has more credentials and experience than three-fourths of his peers—of any age, and as for his youth?" Saint-Cyr shrugged. "He has a baby face. He's eighteen."

NarrAy scrutinized the Harbinger. Had she just seen *him* obey an order? *There's more to this boy than I thought.*

Senth took a step forward. "Believe me, Ms. Jorlan, I can accomplish whatever your contract requires. I've spent the last fifteen years learning my craft. How many years have you studied yours, whatever it is?"

With a smile, NarrAy nodded. "Point well taken." She made a slow perusal down his lean yet muscular frame. Huge, pale eyes the color of a dawn sky, with the feline pupils of a Kin. Nothing else catlike about—*Ooh, look at those irresistible little fangs.*

A riot of loose, dark curls fell to Senth's shoulders, the way she preferred. He had dusky skin and symmetrical features not unlike a Better's, yet muted. With his young face, his masculine beauty seemed gentle, but she sensed an inner and physical strength she hadn't noticed at first. A physical presence and leashed energy.

And he doesn't fear Betters. Well, well.

"Come, Senthys." Saint-Cyr touched the youth's arm. "Ms. Jorlan does not—"

"Wait." NarrAy spoke to Senthys. "Do you have gloves?"

"Yes, ma'am." Senthys started to pull them on.

Broxus lurched forward, but NarrAy stopped him with a lifted hand.

Saint-Cyr stretched out a hand to stop Senth. "I don't think that's a good idea, son. It's against the law to touch a Better."

Again NarrAy caught Senth's faint look of surprise. She flashed a look of irritation at Broxus, who backed away.

The young thief smile widely. "The law's never stopped us before, Sen'dai."

Saint-Cyr frowned but moved aside.

NarrAy offered her hand. She'd practiced this with her father as a girl. "*A gentleman doesn't try to overpower a lady's hand, NarrAy. But he isn't afraid to be firm either.*"

She held his gloved hand between both of hers. "I can see you're a gentleman, Mr. Antonello."

His cheeks reddened. "Just Senth, ma'am."

"Senth it is, and I'm NarrAy. Never Ms. Jorlan, nor ma'am. Not on this job." She gave his hand a squeeze. "Understood?"

He met her gaze. "Does that mean you want me?" He blushed again and glanced down at their still-joined hands. "For the job, I mean."

She bit back a laugh. *What a little innocent you are.* "So

long as we're clear on who's in charge."

"When it comes to theft, I am. For everything else, you are, in every way."

You have no idea. She grinned at him. He had never once tried to look at her body. *Maybe this dress will be okay after all.*

"Come sit." She gestured toward an adjacent room. "Let's talk business."

* * *

NarrAy crossed her legs, exposing a good portion of her skin under the short dress. If she'd been sitting opposite Senth, the length might have been welcome. But the Harbinger lounged in that chair, and Senth sat beside her on the couch. Her position put her a little closer to him.

"Destoiya murdered my parents," NarrAy continued her story, "as surely as if she'd actually been the one who shot them in the back. They were scientists working on secret technology. When rumors got out that they were planning to give their findings to the rebellion, the Conqueror had them killed and then confiscated everything, including their personal belongings. There was a locket my mother inherited from my grandmother, which my grandmother inherited from her grandmother. It's mine, and I want it back."

She met Senth's penetrating gaze and held it. She heard rather than saw Encie enter the room and take up a place near the door. Broxus moved to stand beside her. NarrAy couldn't take her gaze off Senth. *How did I ever see him as a boy?*

He had a man's hands, well-groomed nails, and sinewy forearms that revealed power and strength. Biceps bulged when he gestured. Angular jaw, a firm mouth with lips made for kissing. A hot flutter rose within her, and she tamped it down at once, refusing to let her pheromones get the upper hand.

"Let me see if I have this right," Senth began. "You're hiring a level-nineteen thief and transporting him to another world to break into a government building and steal back a locket with sentimental value."

NarrAy nodded, her mouth dry. His proximity heightened her desire. He smelled clean, fresh, and ruggedly male. An image rose within her of Senth sliding into her feminine heat and rocking against her, holding her tight against him as he thrust deep. A tingle signaled the imminent letdown of her pheromones, and she clenched her hands into fists, fighting to calm the spike of lust flickering through her like a torch about to combust.

Senth watched her, gaze narrowed, head tilted.

He asked me something. Damn it, NarrAy! Pay attention to business and not your body. She sat up straighter. "I'm sorry. Would you repeat that, please?"

Senth's faint smile revealed nothing, but he lifted his head, sniffing the air. Kin could smell emotion and desire. Could HalfKin?

NarrAy swallowed and forced a bigger smile onto her face while she waited for him to speak.

"What I said was no one spends that kind of money and effort on a trinket. Especially one in the custody of the Conqueror. What's it really worth?"

"It's a priceless *heirloom*." She set a hand against her bosom.

Senth didn't follow her hand movement. Instead he tilted his head a bit as he leaned back against the couch. "I'm smarter than you are beautiful, NarrAy, and that's saying something. Tell me the truth."

She felt warmth in her cheeks. When was the last time she'd actually blushed over a compliment? Especially one as offhand as that? Still... *He thinks I'm beautiful. Mmm. How delightfully promising.*

"If you want me to take a job stealing from the Conqueror, you have to be after something more valuable than your mommy's jewelry." Senth turned over one hand, palm up. "What's the locket's true value? I have no intention of marketing it, but I need to know what kind of real security I might be up against."

"Market...?"

"Fence." The Harbinger steepled his fingers.

"Oh." She turned back to Senth. After a long pause, she let out a sigh. "Very well. It is an heirloom, but an inscription inside leads to a numbered account holding my inheritance. The Conqueror has no idea I want that piece. Our intel says my family's property is being held in a government warehouse on Tarth. It has no higher security than any other warehouse. That account is a fortune, and I want it back."

Senth passed a hand across his mouth, casting a glance at the Harbinger.

The man remained immobile except for tapping his

steepled fingers together twice. Some kind of signal? A code? NarrAy bit the inside of her cheek.

"Okay. I can see that as a reason. Where's the building?"

She motioned to Lieutenant Broxus, and he gave Senth a notereader.

He opened it, thumbed through several screens, withdrew the stylus, and made a few notes. "It's in one of Tarth City's outlying districts, sir." He handed the reader to the Harbinger. "A Vassindorf?"

Saint-Cyr read for a moment, then gave it back to him. "No doubt."

"A Vassindorf is a kind of security system, NarrAy. The company upgrades them frequently. I'd need to train on certain protocols before we arrive."

"I don't understand why a level-nineteen thief needs training."

"It's standard procedure for any job over a specific skill level. I'm more than qualified. If someone else were doing this job, I'd probably be called to train them. Certification is insurance against getting caught between software and security upgrades. I could be certified by noon tomorrow."

"All right. I guess I see why you need the training. Keep those notes. When can we leave?"

"Around two in the afternoon."

"I'll be the one picking you up." NarrAy stood. "Where should that be?"

Senth stood and held out a chip for a debit bracelet. "Meet me here. We'll have a final briefing, sign a contract, and be on our way."

When she reached for the small chip, he held it up before him, causing her to meet his gaze.

"You don't have to worry about my ability. I can and will do exactly what you hired me to do." He dropped the chip into her outstretched hand. "We'll get your locket and be back here within four days. Five, at the absolute most."

"You're sure?"

"Oh yeah." Senth flashed a look at the Harbinger. "Count on it. Grab and go." He snapped his fingers. "Just like that."

Chapter Three

All People's Liberation Army Ship Jalane
Officers' Quarters

After her debriefing, NarrAy returned to her cabin. She locked the door and set the privacy indicator to full block, then kicked off her high heels and took off her red party dress. The liberation movement had spent a tradestandard month raising funds for this mission, and she couldn't waste one drak of it. But even the combined cost of their party clothes, flying to Tarth via an empire-class sleepliner, reserving the finest suite in the biggest hotel, ground transportation, and the flight back hadn't come close to what they'd paid to hire Senth.

She laid a hand against her chest. "Please let him be worth it."

Wearing only a pair of the red thong panties Encie had purchased for her as part of the mission, she hung the dress inside her bagbot and stuffed the shoes into their cubby. She stepped back and took in the meticulously arranged articles of clothing, hung according to length and grouped by color—most of them red—and nothing she'd ever pick for herself. One of the drawers had panties and bras folded and placed with their cups tucked into one another, each bra lying beside the others in neat rows. Thongs were grouped by color. The smaller drawer held an array of cosmetics, none of which she recognized. Beyond her preferred fragrance-free soap and moisturizer, the rest belonged to the persona she'd display during the mission.

NarrAy chuckled. "I *know* Encie did all this." The plain white cotton briefs NarrAy wore under her uniform were conspicuously absent. No doubt still crammed into her top drawer and mixed with white bras and gray uniform socks. No one inspected drawers or closets in the officers' quarters. The ship's droid staff laundered and pressed her uniform, cleaned her entire cabin, and made the bed. She'd long since given up any pretense of personal organization anywhere but in her work, and she had an aide for most of that.

What mattered were results, and results were what she was known for.

She toed the drawers shut, slipped off her panties, and stepped out of them, leaving them on the floor. She glanced back at the bunk and then tossed herself onto it. She rubbed one foot against the other, hands linked behind her head. The high heels had no arch supports, made her feet ache, and put stress on her shoulders and lower back. Yet women wore them routinely so they could walk around on tiptoe for the purpose of attracting men.

All I have to do is enter a room and my pheromones grab them by the nose. She chuckled. *Among other parts.*

She drew up one foot and began rubbing the arch. Encie had painted NarrAy's toes a light red to match her fingernails. Supposedly the special *glossrylic* applied to her nail beds guaranteed they wouldn't chip or peel, and changing color was as easy as touching a wand to a color sample, which then transferred to her nails with a single tap on each.

She arched her foot, lowered it, and then massaged the other for awhile. The tight dress had left a mark across her chest, and a thin line still showed against the fair skin of her bosom. She slid one finger along it, then applied more pressure with her thumb. The organic process of a firm touch, even of her own skin, stimulated her pheromones.

Her breasts tingled with the initial release, her nipples tightening into hard buds. NarrAy gasped at the unintended arousal. The mingled scent of vanilla and butter made itself evident. In such a confined space, the effect of the sugar-cookie scent was instantaneous. The scent of other Betters had no effect, but her own sent her into bliss. Her feminine parts warmed and became instantly wet. She writhed against the cotton blanket, its texture stimulating her even more.

"Damn it! I hate when my body does this to me." She got up and took two steps toward the private head within her cabin for a cold shower. *No, that would hurt before it helped, and my pheromones are still going to be in the room. Even the ship's ventilation can't remove them all.* She turned and set one knee on the bed, opened a drawer tucked into a panel, and grabbed the egg-shaped toy on top of the other items. *I never have to rummage through drawers for this little baby. I use it way too often not to know right where it is.*

She sat, felt for the remote under her pillow, turned on the tiny screen, and chose her preferences. *Let's see—Penile size: Kin. Diameter. What? This setting isn't on the human penis size. Are Kin that much bigger? How do you calcu—* Screw that. She chose *Circumference* instead. *Bigger than I can get one hand around, so that would be...* She hesitated and then tapped the Six key. *Wait. This is Tradestandard inches, and Senth's a HalfKin.* She changed it to seven. *Length.* NarrAy chuckled, tapping the Nine key. *Hey, a girl can dream, can't she? Movement.* She keyed through her choices. *Thrusting, Vibrating, Rotating, Half Rotations, Custom.* She chose the last and then clicked *Thrusting* and *Vibrating.* It wouldn't actually move. A weight inside the toy would plunge against the rounded tip and then roll back. The last option was *Speed.* With a grin, she selected *Slow. Oh yeah. Gonna do a Kin, gotta make it last.*

She reclined on the bed. While she'd been setting her preferences, the egg had warmed itself to her body temperature and begun secreting lubricant along its surface. She drew back one knee, reached down, and inserted the toy.

The silent instrument activated at once. It lengthened and widened in smooth increments, soon filling her. NarrAy relaxed her body and allowed the toy's sensations to overtake her. Its gentle vibration made a constant thrum against her G-spot. The feel of a cock thrusting into her made her moan.

Feels so real. So good. Mmm. So so good.

She cast aside the remote and placed her feet wide apart. Most nights a quick session with this toy and a little clitoral stimulation were all she needed, no fantasy required. Tonight, with the memory of Senth fresh, she reached between her thighs and stroked her wet opening, then slid the thick lubricant up and around her clit. She reached her other hand across her chest and took a nipple between her first finger and thumb. A gentle twist and tug wouldn't do it tonight. She pinched her nipple and tweaked it. NarrAy hissed as she sucked in air through her clenched teeth. The mix of pain and pleasure linked nipple and clit in a direct line.

Closing her eyes, she brought Senth's image to mind, picturing him as he'd looked at the Ghost, minus the overbearing Saint-Cyr and the audience of her aides.

*"Mmm, hell-*loh, *Senth." Standing naked before him, she slid one hand up the front of his shirt. "Can I interest you in a sugar-cookie snack?"*

He leaned forward, bending down to kiss her, his dark, curly hair a cloak around them. The hesitant brush of his lips against hers made her press up against him, capturing his kiss.

She pulled back enough to speak. "Hold me. Please, Senth, hold me. No one ever touches me. I'm so alone."

Senth drew her fully into his arms and embraced her, fitting the entire length of his body against hers. "I'll touch you anywhere you want, NarrAy. Everywhere you want." He slid his fingers through her hair, his smile revealing fangs. "Let me kiss you again."

NarrAy gripped his jacket with both hands and drew him down. The wet heat of his mouth against hers brought another crest of pheromones.

Senth slid one hand down her body, cupped one of her breasts, and then bent to suckle her. His rough, catlike tongue against her sensitive skin triggered a line of heat straight to her core. Moisture seeped onto her thighs.

Senth inhaled. "Mmm. You smell so good." He slid his hand down the front of her body and pressed his palm against her outer lips. He slipped one finger between them. "You're wet." He lifted his hand to inhale her fragrance, then licked his finger. "Sweet." He went to his knees before her, his pale blue gaze lifting to hers. "May I taste you?"

She shook her head no, but her mouth said "yes." She leaned back against the wall of her cabin and widened her legs.

He paused, looking up at her as if for permission.

"Please," she whispered.

Senth lapped and curled his tongue along her labia. She hovered on the precipice. Senth hummed, and she pitched over the top into ecstasy. A third crest of pheromones released in a gush of wetness between her thighs. Tears streaked down her cheeks.

Shaking, she fisted her hands in his long hair. "Again. Please, Senth! I want your touch."

Senth used his fingers to spread apart her lips, then licked the tip of her clit with tiny strokes, teasing her into another orgasm within moments. The vaginal quake rocked her so hard, she tossed her head. He used the widest part of his tongue and changed his stroke.

With a cry borne solely of lust, NarrAy arched her back, her body stiff. Wave after wave of pleasure coursed through her. She gasped for breath, unable to speak, unable to think past the drenching heat of her body.

She came down from the sexual high a little bit at a time, so slowly it took a while before she became aware that she was alone. She patted around herself for the remote, found it, and flipped the vibrator to Off. She sat up. Near her knees, the egg glistened with her wetness. She'd squeezed so hard during her orgasm, the thing had rocketed out of her.

NarrAy stifled a laugh at the thought. She grabbed the toy and went to clean it, but paused to pick up a flatpic of her parents smiling at one another, sharing a moment of mutual joy. They'd taken a series of pics the day they found out they'd been approved to conceive a Better. Her.

Smiling, she set it down and went to wash the egg. Once finished, she stepped into the shower. To wet her body, she cycled the water, turned it off, and soaped up. She cycled the water once more to rinse. She dried off with a thin, army-issue towel, gray, like everything else in the APLA.

"You have to keep your mind on your mission." Her reflection didn't look convinced. "You don't have time for an affair. Especially with someone you'll be around for several days." Her past lovers, few and far between, had been one-night quickies right before she was reassigned or transferred. She hadn't had to stay and deal with the feelings of being attuned to a lover. No emotional roller coasters every time their feelings cascaded over hers. No panic attacks when her sexual partners were in danger. Any fun she had with Senth would have to wait for their last night together, if then. Besides, what if the mission took longer than the four days they'd planned? What if something went wrong? She'd had Encie pack enough for ten days, in case.

"Oh yeah. Grab and go." NarrAy snapped her fingers,

copying Senth's last words to her. "Just like that. And don't I hope that's how it happens." Her sigh fogged the mirror. She swiped a hand across the wet glass. "Somehow I have a bad feeling it won't."

* * *

Kelthia, Miraj City, Central City District
Thieves' Guild Headquarters, Training Room Seven

Senth rubbed the back of a gloved hand over his damp brow. The Vassindorf, a duplicate of the complex system he'd face in the government building, might as well have been an iron wall. The featureless structure showed no signs of access. Other faceless models by the same manufacturer lined the room where he practiced, all of them guaranteed to react like the real thing.

He'd worked at it all night, but the complicated interior mechanism of the Vassindorf reset every time Senth's lockpick engaged the system.

Nearby at a conference table, Flea and Gnat watched him practice. Sylk, their four-year-old Deshai, sat between them. The two Kelthians had trained Senth at that same young age. With white hair and saintly smile wrinkles, they hardly seemed like professional thieves, yet each held the rank of arcane master, the highest in the guild, and had for more years than anyone could remember.

Senth made another try with the Vassindorf, and the alarm sang out again. *Fffffct this! I need a break.*

He set the fat, stylus-shaped lockpick on a chair and

pressed his palms together, placing his hands before him as if in prayer. Closing his eyes, he cleansed his thoughts, talking himself down to a lower state of anxiety. The words his Sen'dai had taught him rolled through his mind and brought peace, tranquility, and reassuring calm. He let out a long breath and rolled his head, stretched his arms above him and then lowered them, flexing his fingers.

Okay, Senth. Be one with the lock. He opened his eyes, mouth twisted. *What does that mean, anyway?* He snatched up the lockpick.

He reset the instrument and tuned it to the new Vassindorf codes downloaded from the guild that morning at great cost to his Sen'dai. *First, aim.* Senth used the lockpick's pinpoint light to target the portal's safeguard zone. *Second, activate.* He thumbed the pick and felt the unit hum within his grasp. When initiated, it would release a pulse, disabling security codes. *If* it was programmed and aimed correctly.

Come on, you lousy piece of kkkhh. Work this time. He crossed mental fingers. *Third, initiate sequence for—*

The alarm wailed.

"Oh fffffft!" Senth gripped the lockpick in his fist, so tempted to hurl it on the ground, he had to force himself to set it down. He turned toward his coaches. "Flea, I've been trying for hours. What am I doing wrong?"

"You tell me, son."

"Flea!" Gnat put in. "What kind of answer is that to give the boy?"

Little Sylk did not pause in his play. Gnat had given the dark-haired child ten padlocks to open, and he worked a manual lockpick into the last one. The other locks already lay opened on the table.

"Senth is just nervous." Flea angled the padlock for Sylk. "He's under pressure. He needs to calm down."

"Then don't ask him what's wrong." Gnat pushed back his chair and leaned forward, his elbows resting on his knees while he watched Sylk's hands. "That's like saying, 'Be one with the lock.' Like that means anything."

Huh. Senth smiled. *So it is nothing but kkkhh!*

Gnat guided Sylk's right hand, steadying it. "Tell Senth what's wrong, Flea."

"But he already knows the answer. He only needs to see it for himself."

Sylk's lock sprang open. The boy beamed at Flea and then Gnat.

"Good job, Sylk." Flea ruffled his hair.

"Good job!" Gnat bent and kissed him on the head. "Want some more to play with?"

The boy nodded solemnly. His pale skin was stark white compared to Flea's and Gnat's, as if illness plagued him. Rumor had it he'd never spoken.

Gnat dug around in a bag he'd set on another chair. "If Senth knew what he was doing wrong, then why would he ask the question?"

The master thieves turned toward him. Sylk looked from Senth to Flea and then Gnat. Both men folded their hands and placed them on the table in front of them. Sylk plopped his there too.

Senth rolled his eyes. "Maybe I'm nervous. I'll try again."

"Good lad." Gnat pushed aside the open locks and set a different type on the table in front of Sylk. "Here you go, son. Try these."

Senth stuffed a few loose curls under his cap and went back to work. He smoothed his gloves, tightening them over his fingers. He brought the back of one hand up to rub his nose and caught the scent NarrAy had left, triggering senses that flooded him with memories. A shiver ran over him.

Oh, man, that red dress! Even taking Shackle, I had to work to keep myself from looking at her body. Khyff is right, though. Not focusing on a woman's body makes her curious about you. I know for damn sure her breasts would fill my hands. Her lips were dark. I wonder if a woman's nipples are the same color as her lips. I'd like to take a good look, maybe lick 'em. No, she'd prolly take the same kind of look at my fangs and scratchy tongue and say fffffft that. She's gorgeous! Those gold-colored streaks in her hair look like captured sunrays. Oh, I've got it bad! If Khyff could hear me thinking this stuff, he'd laugh his ass off. I wonder why she wears it up? Those sparkly pins sure were pretty, though. I bet it's long. I wonder if it'd tickle if it fell over my—

"Senthys?"

He jumped at his Sen'dai's voice and hid both hands behind him as he whirled to face the man. "Sir!"

Saint-Cyr frowned. "Are you all right?"

"Um, yes, sir." His cheeks blazed.

Saint-Cyr's whiteless eyes narrowed at him like he read every forbidden memory of NarrAy's luscious beauty skulking through Senth's mind. "How's it going?"

"He's doing fine," Flea answered.

"Except for a little trouble," Gnat added.

"Trouble?" Saint-Cyr frowned at Senth. "What kind of trouble?"

"No trouble," Flea insisted. "He's doing fine."

"Fine," Gnat echoed. "Except for not being able to break into the system."

"You can't get in?" Saint-Cyr stalked closer. "Why not, Senthys? What are you doing wrong?"

"Nothing, sir. I can do it." Senth took a step back, spreading his hands. "It's just…" Flea, Gnat, and Sylk were watching him. "Um, it's just…"

"That he hasn't done it yet." Flea nodded. "He will, though. In time."

"Time is something he doesn't have." The Harbinger pointed toward the door. "It's nearly noon. Ms. Jorlan will be next door at the cafe in two hours. Senthys, do you mean to tell me you haven't gotten into the Vassindorf even once?"

What if he hands over the job to someone else? What if he lets another thief work with NarrAy? Senth folded his arms in defiance. "No!"

Saint-Cyr raised his eyebrows.

"Er…" Senth lowered his hands to his sides. "I…I mean… Not yet, Sen'dai. It's complicated."

"What's complicated, Senthys? The system, or your excuses?"

Flea pushed back his chair and stood to walk around the table. "The system, Luc, of course. Senth's doing fine."

Senth had never heard anyone but the Grand Master, Flea, Gnat, and Wulf Gabriel, his Sen'dai's lover, call the Harbinger by his first name. Senth had given up trying, even in fun. One glare from the man's whiteless eyes held more threat than the risk was worth.

"That security system is far from impossible. Hell, Senthys, you broke into the one I had under my house when you were barely fifteen. Why can't you get into this one? What's so hard about *this* Vassindorf?"

Senth opened his mouth to answer, but Gnat tsked at him. "Luc, my boy, the Vassindorf's nothing. Sylk could get into that."

The little boy lifted his head, looking from Gnat to the Vassindorf and back.

Saint-Cyr steepled his fingers and tapped them against his mouth. "Is that true, Senthys? If you can't do this, tell me now. I don't have time to waste finding a replacement."

"No, Sen'dai, I can do it. All I need is—"

"Vassindorf security breached successfully," the guild's training computer announced. "Resetting."

Everyone's gaze followed Sylk as he handed Senth the lockpick, went back to the table, and climbed up into his chair. He stuck a pick into a lock as if nothing unusual had happened. Gnat leaned over and kissed Sylk's dark hair.

The Harbinger stared at the boy, the Vassindorf, Senth, then back at Gnat. "How old is he? He can't really be a child."

"Sylk." Gnat pointed to the Harbinger. "Tell him how old you are, son."

He held up four fingers.

"You're sure? Senthys could never do anything like that when he was four. Hell, he's having trouble with this one at eighteen."

Senth crossed his arms, mouth tight.

Flea gestured to the boy. "Sylk's incredible. He opens everything we give him. We don't know how he does it."

Senth wagged his lockpick. "But how could he breach a Vassindorf?"

"That's your lesson for the day, Senth." Gnat rocked back in his chair, hands behind his head. "Never think about the importance of a lock. Just pick it."

* * *

Kelthia, Miraj City, Central City District
Miraj City Bakery Café

Senth draped his cloak over the back of an empty chair and sat at the café table.

The Harbinger took the seat beside him, cup of coffee in hand. "Ms. Jorlan is due any minute." He sipped his coffee, set it down, and smiled. "You opened the Vassindorf ten times in a row. Good job."

He wished he could see the man's real eyes. Read him for once instead of guessing. "Thank you, sir."

"Once you saw a four-year-old could do it."

Senth thunked an elbow on the table and leaned his chin on a fist.

The Harbinger patted his arm. "Don't take it so hard. That boy's amazing. And with those two as his teachers, no doubt he'll reach arcane master one day."

"You think I could?"

His Sen'dai leaned back as if appraising him. "Do you want to?"

Senth stared into the unfathomable, ravenlike eyes. "More than anything."

"Then keep working. I chose you out of that orphanage because I saw a spark of brilliance in you. At age three, having had not one bit of training, you picked my pocket without me feeling a thing." He leaned forward. "People were amazed at you when you were that age." With a pat he added, "They still are."

"Thank you." Praise came so rarely, he basked in any he received.

"That wasn't meant to make you feel good. It's simply the truth." Saint-Cyr reached into his pocket and laid a notereader on the table. "There's something you need to know. Khyffen was injured last night."

Senth sat up straight. "What? How? What happened?"

"His illicit street activities caught up with him when a client went to the slakehouse and recognized him. The client had never visited before. Apparently, Khyffen's master put two and two together and took a whip to him." Saint-Cyr clamped his hand on Senth's arm when he tried to rise. "Sit down. You need to hear the rest."

Senth sat, his teeth grinding so tightly, his jaw hurt.

"Another sex worker called the police. In the end they

arrested Khyffen for parole violation and Stalkos for abuse. Your brother was treated for lacerations on his back, legs, and arms."

The Harbinger gripped Senth's arm more tightly. "Sit down."

"Sen'dai, please! I need to see him."

"I went to see him myself while you were practicing, and I assure you he's fine. Now sit down."

Senth clenched his fists but obeyed.

"You need to focus. Khyffen's freedom is riding on your completing this task."

He nodded, wetting his lips. "Yes, Sen'dai. What's going to happen to him?"

"Right now he's in jail. He didn't fight back when he was beaten, which will go in his favor, but they've got him for violating his license by working the street without permission. Stalkos is threatening to sue his illicit clients for rape."

"Rape!"

"He's within his rights. Having sex with a slake without a master's permission can be construed as such."

"As if addicting him to Thrust and then selling him to the highest bidder isn't."

The Harbinger picked up his coffee and blew on it. "Of all the deeds I've had my dirty fingers in over the years, prostitution was never one of them. Train a child to steal? Yes. Train a child to be a sex slave?" When Saint-Cyr sighed, the steam from his coffee faded. "Never happen to one of mine." He sipped the drink.

"Sen'dai, we have to stop him. Khyff's been putting every drak in his freedom account."

"I'm more than aware." He patted a pocket. "I have the deposit note for the money you gave me this morning. He's reached a substantial balance. And don't worry. Stalkos would have to name Khyffen's clients first, and I doubt any will come forward and confess. I've already contacted the guild's lawyers. One or two owe me favors."

"Thank you, sir."

"Don't thank me yet." Saint-Cyr glanced toward the door. "She's here. Now"—his hand tightened on Senth's arm—"remember our deal. I'll take care of Khyffen. You do your job safely and get your ass back here."

"Yes, sir."

They both stood when NarrAy approached. Saint-Cyr pulled out a chair for her while Senth kicked himself for draping his cloak over the seat closest to him. She sat facing him.

"You said we'd have a final briefing." She folded her hands on the table. "I'm ready if you are."

Saint-Cyr slid the notereader toward her. "Final contract. Read it, imprint your thumb, and tap Send, and we're official. The guild copy will be permanently archived once Senthys returns safely and you're satisfied with his performance."

She dropped her gaze and looked back up at Senth under her lashes. "I'm sure his performance will be wonderful."

Senth's cheeks warmed as he considered the double meaning of those words.

"Which reminds me." Saint-Cyr withdrew a silver tube from an inner pocket. "Senthys, take off your jacket and bare your arm, please."

He sent a pleading look his Sen'dai's way.

"There's no help for it. You're like a son to me, and I can't risk your involvement with a Better. Now bare your arm."

Eyes closed, Senth bit into his lower lip. How could he bear to face NarrAy once she knew what his master did to him?

NarrAy extended a hand. "What are you doing?"

"Giving him Shackle."

"I assure you, Mr. Saint-Cyr, my being a Better does not mean I intend to seduce your son."

"This isn't about you, Ms. Jorlan; it's about Senthys. He's more than a son to me. He's a major source of income. And a slave."

"I can't condone—"

"Please!" Senth yanked off his jacket and pulled up his sleeve. He turned his head. "Get it over with."

Knowing NarrAy watched while his Sen'dai emasculated him stung worse than the all too familiar scald of the drug racing through his veins toward his heart. He chewed his lip and bounced one knee, but air hissed over his teeth anyway because of the pain. Senth stood, shoved his sleeve back down, and pulled on his jacket, refusing to rub away the ache.

NarrAy set her thumb against the notereader and tapped it once. She shoved it at Saint-Cyr.

"This is your copy." Saint-Cyr handed her back the reader and stood when she did.

"Let's go." Senth snatched up his cloak. Everything he needed for work was in its myriad pockets. He aimed a remote at the squat bagbot waiting near the door, and the automated suitcase rose on stubby wheels.

Senth gestured NarrAy ahead of him and followed her to the door.

"Senthys."

One step from exiting, he halted at his Sen'dai's voice. NarrAy waited outside. His face burning, Senth turned back and tried not to glare. "Sen'dai."

The Harbinger's eyes were unreadable as ever. "Good luck, son." One corner of his mouth lifted. "Especially with the Vassindorf."

Chapter Four

Tarth, Tarth City, Palace District
Imperial Palace, Stable Wing

Her Majesty Empress Rheyn Destoiya awoke to the feel of lips kissing the backs of her knees and neck. She sighed with pleasure, stretching into the pairs of hands caressing her.

Her two newest Jades, Rudolf and Sander, moved to lie on either side of her on the wide bed. The human Rudolf, with his exotic piercings and limber body, had danced his way into her stable of pleasure slaves, shedding his clothes one piece at a time. The Chiasma named Sander captured her attention with his sharply defined beauty and dual sexuality, but his nimble mouth secured it. She and Rudolf had kept the tireless Androg busy all night. What he could do with that tongue...

What *phe* could do, she corrected herself.

The Conqueror soon forgot the niceties of Chiasmii pronouns when her Jades made her moan aloud.

She turned on her side and took Sander into her arms, dragging him closer for a kiss. She wanted that mouth again. He slid a hand between her legs and lifted her upper thigh as he pulled it toward him, opening her for Rudolf. She arched back against Rudolf and welcomed the exquisite sensation of his pierced cock. He parted the lips of her pussy from behind and plunged deep inside.

"Yes, like that. More."

She laid her head back against Rudolf's shoulder when he thrust harder. Wrapping her leg around Sander's waist, she clung to him with both hands.

"More," she demanded, her voice husky. "More mouth."

Sander laved her throat, nipped her skin. Using his teeth, Rudolf tugged at her earlobe. Destoiya shivered at the heat of Rudolf's breath, the coolness of Sander's mouth, both moist against her skin.

Sander flattened his palm against her mons, and when he cupped his fingers between her labia, she nearly arched off the bed. Searing heat flooded her body and took her breath.

Sander was using his *Empas* to absorb her lust—and Rudolf's—and was pinpoint feeding it back to her. The desire of three, magnified, aimed, and delivered with precision. She half expected to combust.

The moment Sander's fingers probed inside her rear opening, she climaxed. She hunched back against Rudolf, screaming her release, sobbing with it. Sander clamped his mouth over one breast, the tip of his tongue battering her nipple. She moaned again, her mouth wide. She gripped Rudolf's upper thigh and rode him, thrusting back while he ground himself into her.

His cock twitched and jumped inside her while he cried out his pleasure and shudders racked his body. His gasps heated her neck.

Sander thrust inside her the moment Rudolf withdrew.

The change between lovers only hurled her faster over the top. Frenzied by Empas-inspired lust, she panted. Mewling cries escaped her throat.

"Wet," Sander murmured against her mouth. He drove the full length of his cock into her, fast and hard, just the way she loved it. "So lush and hot."

He dipped his tongue into her mouth, curled it against and around hers.

Rudolf reached between them and took her nipple between his finger and thumb, twirling it roughly. He set one hand in her hair and pulled back her head. Rudolf grazed her throat with his teeth, licked the back of her jaw, and circled her ear. The metal studs in the middle of his tongue tingled against her skin.

Destoiya turned her face to capture Rudolf's lips.

When Sander cried out his climax and arched his back, Rudolf splayed a hand across her clenched buttocks and shoved her hard against Sander in counterpoint to the Androg's ramming thrusts.

She moaned into Rudolf's mouth.

The two slaves eased her back down to a manageable level of ecstasy, petting and stroking her while she shivered and shook between them. Her chin quivered. Chiasmii calm spread over her.

Destoiya recognized Sander's influence at once. She had no composure of her own. When she could finally draw a breath without shaking, she willed her body to relax.

Sander stroked her hair, settling her against his shoulder as Rudolf drew covers over the three of them and cuddled her.

Snuggled between their warmth, she pulled Rudolf's arm around her waist, hooked one leg over Sander, and let herself drift.

"Your Majesty." The deep voice yanked her rudely back to awareness.

Destoiya opened her eyes. Her android guardian stood a short distance from the bed. Dark skinned as a Kelthian, with midnight hair and darker eyes, he stood with his hands behind him, his cool gaze regarding her.

She heaved a sigh. "Damn it, Prentice. What is it?"

"A token has been moved."

"Sander, Rudolf." At her tone, both Jades left her bed at once. They bowed and remained in that position while they backed away. When they reached the required distance, they straightened and turned to go. She admired their naked backsides all the way across the room. At the door they turned in tandem, and finding her watching them, each blew her a kiss.

Returning her attention to Prentice, she punched a pillow and dragged it under her head. "This had better be worth what you interrupted."

"I waited until you were finished."

"More like they were. They earned their keep last night and this morning. See to it they're well rewarded today."

"I'll relay your orders, Your Majesty." He bowed.

She harrumphed and folded her hands behind her head.

"Talk."

"Captain NarrAy Jorlan signed a contract today with the Thieves' Guild on Kelthia."

"Finally! Some action. Any details?"

"Senthys Antonello, level nineteen, advanced interior security, has been contracted to retrieve an item of undisclosed nature sometime within the next four days."

"Excellent. Now we'll find out where the Jorlans hid their data. I knew they stashed it among their personal effects, and only their daughter had any idea what the form of the information was. You were right, Prentice. Patience is a virtue." She chuckled. "And I need every bit of virtue I can buy."

* * *

Kelthia, Miraj City
Central City District

NarrAy allowed Senth the privacy of his thoughts while Lieutenant Broxus loaded Senth's bagbot into the trunk of their hover.

Senth held the door of the rented car as she climbed into the roomy interior. He and Broxus entered from opposite sides and slammed the doors.

"Starport," Broxus told the driver.

The car bumped as it rose into the air.

NarrAy took the time to introduce her coworkers. "Senth, this is Chad Broxus, my assistant, who was with me last night."

"Call me Brox. Everybody does." The men shook hands. They sat side by side, facing the rear.

"And Encie Falehla, my friend."

Senth reached diagonally across NarrAy and shook Encie's hand, then quickly withdrew.

"You remember me, I see." Encie folded her arms. "We saw each other at the Ghost, NarrAy. I was ogling him, and he seemed interested for a moment."

A blush stole across Senth's cheeks. He kept his head down.

"Until some pretty thing in black leather talked him out of it."

So that's who you were flirting with. NarrAy arched a warning look at her aide and silently mouthed one word. *Mine.*

Encie lifted a brow but turned her gaze out the window.

NarrAy turned hers to Senth, who still hadn't lifted his head.

"Encie runs an underground railroad for HalfKin. You didn't really need to know that, but I can tell you've caught wind of her reputation."

NarrAy made a gesture at Encie, freeing her to talk.

The Kin female settled back against her seat. "You ever come up against prejudice?"

"Every day." Senth nodded. "All it takes is for someone to see my eyes or for me to open my mouth." He pulled back his lips, revealing extra-long incisors alongside his human teeth. "The rest of me is totally human. Well, pretty much, anyway. I'm as strong as a full blood."

"My people hate the way humans have swarmed onto Felidae, polluting it, spoiling the rivers, and hunting. Being human can get you killed for breathing."

"So do you help HalfKin get off world?"

Encie nodded. "Every HalfKin's different. Some appear completely Kin; others are more like you. But all it takes is one human trait on Felidae and you're an outcast."

"And only one *nonhuman* one here." Senth rubbed his arm. "People think you can't control yourself. It makes me mad."

Like people thinking I'll spray pheromones all over them if they get too close. To avoid the Better stereotype, NarrAy purposefully wore clothes that covered most of her body. Today she had on a dark gray conservative pantsuit that didn't show so much as an inch of flesh below her neck. It was Encie's only concession to NarrAy's insistence on some of her mission wardrobe being sensible and modest.

She crossed her legs, sliding a foot down Senth's leg in the process. "Sorry."

Beside her, Encie coughed the word "not" into her hand, earning a glare from NarrAy.

Senth kept his head down.

Encie fiddled with the window controls. "So, Senth. How'd you end up a slave?"

"More of that prejudice you talked about." He drew his folded cloak over his lap. "My brother says when I was born, the *tzesar* declared me anathema, or *cursed*, took me away from my mother, and ordered me killed. An elder took pity on me and sold me to slavers instead." He shrugged. "At least I'm alive."

"Your mother was Kin?"

"Human."

"What clan was it?"

"Ruh."

"The Ruh clan being nice to humans. There's a switch."

"You call what they did to me nice?"

"To your mother. If Ruh slit the throats of Kin who breed with humans, imagine what they do to the humans."

NarrAy leaned her head back, taking in the exchange between the two. Brox seemed engrossed in something on his notereader, but she knew him well enough to know he missed not one word or gesture.

"The Ruh probably weren't nice ever again. My brother says he had pneumonia and could barely breathe, and my mother was pregnant and homeless, so one of the clan elders took them in and nursed my brother back to health. After I was born and sent off to be killed, the Ruh tzesar threw my mother and brother out."

"Where are they now?" Encie crossed her legs.

"My mother—she..." He shook his head. "Dead. Brother's here on Kelthia. A slave like me. Different type." He picked at a button on the cloak. "Human."

"So a half brother."

He nodded.

"He the one who dragged you away from me last night?"

Senth bit his lower lip and nodded again.

"You're close, huh?"

"Very."

"That pretty thing in leather have a name?"

He glanced up at NarrAy as if asking advice on whether to answer. She nodded. Senth turned his pale blue gaze on Encie. "His name's Khyff."

"Antonello, like you?" She drummed her fingers on her thigh. "Nice looking for a human."

When NarrAy poked her with an elbow, Encie gave her a look that said, *What?*

"Our cover, Senth," NarrAy put in, "is a group of friends on vacation. We have a luxury cabin on the sleepliner. Empire class on the ship and on Tarth. One day out, one day back, one to work. One extra if we need it, so enjoy the trip. You can have anything you need."

"And most likely, anything you want."

"Encie—"

"Well, kkkhh! Excuse me for giving the man the facts."

NarrAy forgave her when she saw how Senth preened at the word "man." If it cheered him, she'd forgive Encie anything.

They arrived at Starhaven Leojnimaj, and Senth turned in his bagbot at security. When they tried to take his cloak, he opened it to show them something, and they waved him off with an apology.

"What did you show them?" NarrAy took his arm and walked beside him, careful not to touch any bared skin.

"I went through hell to earn this cloak." He pulled back its edge, revealing the Thieves' Guild symbol. "Levels from cloak up are exempt from search."

"Cloak is a level?"

He tossed the garment across one arm. "You'll see more later, but yeah. Cloak is level fifteen. Once you reach that, you can sign contracts and hire out." He smiled down at her. "Don't worry. It's protocol for the guild, and we do it all the time. While working under contract, we can't be arrested. My having a cloak won't draw undue attention."

"You read my mind."

He tossed back his curly hair. "Comes from knowing how to read a mark."

She squeezed his arm and laughed, leaning against him. "Remember, we're here to have fun. Or appear to, anyway."

"Was I wrong not to pack my cloak?"

"Not at all." She tugged his arm, drawing his gaze. "But it's wrong not to smile at me."

"Now that"—he flashed those adorable fangs—"I can do."

* * *

Tyran Sleepliner Ceroman Hethen

Empire-class Berthing, Suite Alpha

Senth refused to give the porter his cloak and went to hang it in the closet himself. He stood before the open door.

NarrAy came over to him. "Something wrong?"

"No. Sorry." He draped the cloak over a valet stand. "This closet is about the size of my bedroom at home."

"One of the luxuries of empire class." She leaned against the wall. "Hungry?"

"I get pretty jumpsick."

She nodded toward Encie. "Kin seem to love jumping."

"They probably always land on their feet when they fall too. I prefer being out cold."

"One of the other benefits of empire class is good jumpdrugs. Brox will fix you up."

She walked away, the gray suit hugging her in all the right places. *What a body! Nipped waist, rounded bottom, long legs.* He rubbed his arm, cursing his Sen'dai's insistence on Shackle. His mind knew what he wanted, but his body refused to cooperate. *Four days with NarrAy, and not a chance in the worlds anything will ever come of it. I'll be a virgin forever.*

Each of the four traveling companions had a cabin within the suite. In his, Senth flung himself down on the bed. His bagbot had delivered itself, and he aimed the remote to deploy it into closet mode. Practically all the clothes in it were new. Traveling empire class warranted a suitable wardrobe. Saint-Cyr might not splurge on day-to-day needs, but he knew how to make an impression.

Senth was changing clothes when Broxus tapped on the door. He let the man in. "I was dressing for dinner. Let me grab a shirt."

"No, don't bother yet. NarrAy asked me to give you some Holiday."

"Do what?"

"The jumpdrug." He pointed to Senth's arm. "What are you taking?"

He covered the bruise on his inner elbow.

"Sorry, but I need to know in case it reacts with Holiday."

Senth grimaced. "My Sen'dai has me on Shackle."

Broxus whistled. "Must have been one hell of a dose to leave a bruise like that."

"No more than he always gives me."

"You're kidding. May I?" Broxus bent to examine the bruise. "I've seen plenty of Shackle marks, and I can tell you, you shouldn't get a bruise like this. Did it sting?"

"Like a son of a bitch."

"He's overdosing you. It shouldn't hurt, and it shouldn't leave a bruise. Sorry to tell you, but he's likely giving you that much to keep you under his control, not to prevent aggression or make you focus like they all say Shackle's good for. That much reduces the will and negates the libido. He ever hypnotize you?"

"No." Senth lifted his arm, the bruise purple and yellow. "How would I know?"

"You might not. Fortunately"—Broxus produced an air syringe—"it won't interfere with the Holiday." He pressed the syringe against Senth's upper arm. "Done. No sting, no pain, and no barfing up your toenails. Except for the jump alarms, you won't know we jumped, and your stomach will be fine. No sickness at all."

"Thanks. Do we dress up for dinner, or down?"

"With Encie in charge of accommodations?" Broxus rolled his eyes. "Definitely up. Man, I hate putting on all that fancy stuff."

Senth pulled a white shirt out of the closet and tossed it on the bed. "I've always liked it." He set out a tie and diamond cuff links.

"I should have known. The one time I get to work with another guy…"

Senth grinned. "It's not so bad. You need help?"

"You know how to do those flat collar things?" He pointed to the black tie on the bed.

"Sure."

Broxus stroked his jaw. "Maybe you'll be all right after all. If I let Encie do it"—he stuck his thumb toward the door—"she'll have my collar so tight, I won't be able to breathe."

Senth laughed.

"Gotta tell you, man"—Broxus gripped the doorknob—"the lady likes you. If you weren't on Shackle…" He shrugged.

"Are you serious?"

"Sure am." He opened the door. "She hasn't stopped talking about you since you left the room."

Senth pumped a fist in the air. NarrAy liked him!

"You want me to say something?"

"No! Yes. No." Senth winced. "You think it's a good idea?"

"Why not let her know?" Broxus winked as he went out

the door. "You'll like her. Encie's quite a prize."

The door shut behind him.

Senth felt the blood drain from his head. "Encie?" He clapped a hand to his brow. He jerked open the door and went after Broxus.

The two women turned toward him when he entered the main cabin, their gazes flicking over his bare chest. Both had changed into evening attire. Encie wore green. NarrAy wore another red dress to haunt his memories. Sleeveless, strapless. A long, slinky, shiny, scarlet red dress that looked…wet.

He tore his gaze away. "Brox," he whispered hoarsely.

Broxus turned back, a question on his face.

"Um, about that"—Senth moved a hand to his face, lowered it to his chest, and half turned aside—"that…thing…we discussed."

Broxus nodded.

"Uh, better not do that. It would be the wrong one."

"What would be wrong?" NarrAy asked.

"Oh," Broxus began. "Uh, it's…a type of tie. Senth was suggesting what type of tie I should wear with my shirt."

"Yeah," Senth agreed. "I'll come show you."

He hurried past the women, following Broxus into his cabin. He leaned against the door once inside.

"It's not Encie!"

"I gathered that." Broxus set his hands on his hips. "You realize NarrAy's a Better?"

"Duh!" Senth rubbed his temples. "In that dress, how

could you not know?"

"I guess you'd have to be an idiot. Sorry. Encie…" He held up a hand. "I won't start down that trail. It doesn't go anywhere you'd want to be. Afraid you're on your own with NarrAy. If she's interested, she'll make it plain enough. I assume you also realize, with as much Shackle as you're on, it won't matter."

"I know." He covered his face with both hands. "I know." He took a deep breath and blew it out. "And it'll be two years before I'm free."

A knock on the door startled them both.

Broxus opened it, with Senth standing behind it, out of sight. "What is it, Encie?"

Senth pressed up against the wall.

"NarrAy wants to go to dinner, if you're done playing with your tie."

"Be right there." Broxus shut the door in her face. He yanked a tie out of a drawer. "Here. Help me with this thing."

Senth looped it around Brox's neck and deftly flipped it a few times. "There."

Broxus looked in the mirror. "That's perfect. How'd you get good at doing this?"

Senth smiled. "Scams."

"There's a tie scam?"

He laughed. "No. Dressing to look the part during a scam." He tapped the backs of his fingers against the man's chest. "I gotta go get ready."

When he exited the room, NarrAy and Encie both eyed him. With a blush, Senth inclined his head and swept back to the safety of his room.

NarrAy bit out a curse and folded her arms.

"What?" Encie sidled closer.

"He likes Brox."

"Senth?"

NarrAy motioned toward his door. "Why else would he look so embarrassed? And come on, helping him with his *tie?* Since when did Brox ever care about that? It's obvious they wanted to be alone together."

"No way."

"What makes you so sure?"

"Look at them!" Encie gestured, palm up. "Slabs of testosterone on two legs, both of them."

"Like that has anything to do with it."

"Well, Brox is so *not* interested in his own gender."

"How would you know?"

Encie wiggled her eyebrows.

"You and... No." Brox's door remained shut. NarrAy squinted. "When did this happen?"

"Before we came to work for you." Encie waved off the importance of it. "We're long since over each other."

"So you don't think—"

"I know Brox isn't."

NarrAy tapped her fingers against her lips. "Good."

Encie leaned closer. "There's one way to find out."

"Oh, I know there's going to be trouble when you get that tone in your voice." NarrAy couldn't help but smile. "What are you suggesting?"

"He's on Shackle, right? Seduce him."

NarrAy shook her head. "That wouldn't be right."

"You've been flirting with him since he got in the car back in town. Don't even try to tell me you don't like him." Encie set a hand on her hip. "You told me 'mine,' remember?"

"Oh I do. Believe me. He's the hottest thing I've seen in weeks. Did you see the abs on him? Mmm. I almost swallowed my tongue."

"So get him into bed."

"I'm a Better. I can't risk addicting him. Besides, he's on Shackle. He can't do anything."

"He can use his mouth and fingers, can't he?"

"Encie!" She moved back.

"We're friends on vacation, remember? Just friend-to-friend advice."

NarrAy paced the room, her pulse heightening.

"Come on," Encie urged. "What do you have to lose? You'd only be testing him so you know for sure if he's interested and what kind of woman he likes." When NarrAy didn't answer, Encie added, "In case."

"In case," NarrAy repeated.

Senth's door opened, and he came out dressed in immaculate black-and-white evening attire. Shoes glossy, black tie against his throat, loose curls brushing his shoulders. The suit accented his wide shoulders, narrow waist, and firm behind.

Yum.

Those big, pale blue eyes focused on her, causing NarrAy to tingle all over. Moist heat spread through her, throbbed between her legs, made her wet. Even her eyes burned.

He lowered his gaze shyly and adjusted a cuff.

Senth's untutored vulnerability and restrained sensuality lashed at her senses like a whip.

Have I ever made love to a virgin before? Senth was an innocent bundle of sweetness and charm, waiting for the right woman to awaken his passion. *You're going to find that woman very soon, Senth, and she's going to be me.*

Swaying her hips, she strolled across the room.

Chapter Five

Tyran Sleepliner Ceroman Hethen
Empire Class, Promenade Deck

I can't believe this is happening. Senth caught the reflection of himself with NarrAy on his arm. *Her. With me.* His image grinned so big, he wondered why his back teeth didn't show. *Oh wow.*

She'd focused on him all through dinner at the ship captain's table. Tablecloths, crystal, gold-embossed china. The flatware was for show—his thief training let him recognize that—but the ambience and the opulence of the food had not failed to impress him. Neither had NarrAy's interest in everything he said. And now they were walking arm in arm on the promenade deck. Just the two of them. Unfortunately, in this case, two equaled four because Brox and Encie trailed them like watchdogs.

With NarrAy leaning her head against my arm, who cares if they tag along? Is this what love feels like? Words Flea and Gnat had told him a few years ago came to mind. "*How you tell the difference between love and lust, Senth, is that lust can't wait to get, but love can wait to give.*" *But getting feels so good!*

A bell pealed. He clutched his stomach.

"Oh, we're about to jump!" NarrAy clapped her hands. "Let's go watch."

"That's okay. I—"

"Come on." She took Senth's bare hand in hers and led him toward the transparent wall ahead. "Have you ever seen a jump before?"

"Never." Her hand felt warm where she touched him. His skin tingled.

She released his hand and touched the window. "Watch. See that bright light off to the left?"

"Mmm," he agreed, seeing nothing but her. *Her hair has those sparkly pins in it again. I wish she'd pull them out so I could watch her hair fall around her face, all soft and—*

"Here it comes."

As if a liquid sun swallowed the ship, light swept over the hull. So bright, it hurt to watch. Senth threw a hand in front of his eyes. Utter darkness followed. No stars, no nebulae, no visible illumination at all. He staggered back from the window.

"Frightening, isn't it? This is the real reason most people sleep during jump. Even though they don't get the sickening gut twist if they're drugged, when they see this the first time, most never want to see it again."

"Where did everything go?" Senth reached blindly for her, unable to wrench his gaze from the utter blackness outside.

She slid an arm around his waist. "Theory has it that we're outside of time."

"Theory?" At her disturbing words, he swallowed. "They don't know?"

"No. We use the technology, but no one knows how it works."

"Someone has to know."

"When you go into your room, you flip a switch or say 'lights on,' and the lights come on, don't they?"

Senth frowned. "Yeah. Sure."

"Do you know how that works?"

"No, of course not. It's not the same thing."

"Sure it is. Everything exists to build the ships, so it gets done, but no one knows for sure how jumping works. The Tyrans thought they invented jump technology. After the Conqueror jumped into their system and invaded their world, their engineers got together with human engineers to compare notes and found they both used the same basic systems. Why do you suppose that is?"

He considered it a moment. "What do you think?"

"My parents were jumptech scientists, and they thought it was because all of it's based on the same history as well as the same science."

The Tyran captain and his first officer, with their horns and hooves and angular faces, came to mind. "You're talking about the Sower theory—that we all came from humans and were transformed into nonhuman races."

"Betters are humans transformed in the womb. It could have happened that way." She shivered.

He shrugged off his tuxedo jacket and wrapped it around her shoulders. Its large size made her look even more fragile and delicate.

"Thank you, Senth." She hugged him.

Joy shot through him like fireworks. With the darkness beyond, their reflections showed all the more, and the sight of NarrAy hugging him brought that inane grin back to Senth's face. He couldn't force it away. He racked his brain for something intelligent to say.

"So if we're outside time, does that mean we're time traveling?"

"In a way. When we arrive at Tarth, one day will have passed for us, when it should have taken years to make the trip. Of course, if you believe *all* the old legends, it used to be possible for a single person to jump without a ship at all."

"Like that could ever happen."

They both laughed.

NarrAy gave herself a mental slap. *What was I thinking telling him that? Thank goodness he laughed it off.* Her parents' esoteric experiments in personal jump for the armada's Forgotten Technologies Arena was what had got them killed. No one outside a select few even believed in the FTA's existence, let alone its secrets.

"Senth." She stepped back and took his hands, letting her smile woo him away from the subject. "Ever gone dancing in lo-grav?"

Without waiting for a response, she led him by the hand and walked toward the inner part of the ship. Passing Encie and Broxus, she said, "Don't wait up," and followed the words with a pointed look.

Whatever protest Broxus might have made went unheard. Encie's laugh followed them out.

She and Senth were shown to a table in the darkened XO's Lounge. NarrAy noted with amusement that for once women were not glaring at her. They were staring at Senth.

In the black light of the lounge, his eyes glowed like a cat's at night. His physique could have turned heads even without the well-tailored clothes. *Especially without.*

She squeezed his hand. The music was too loud for any Better's liking but far more bearable than at the Ghost. She hung Senth's jacket on the back of her chair and took his arm. "See how the colored lights under the dance floor make concentric rings?"

He nodded.

"The outside light blue part is normal gravity. The darker blue it gets, the lower the gravity." A slow song ended, and older people left the floor as a song with the steady pound of drums began. A younger, more energetic crowd surged onto the round pad. "The purple near the center is about one-eighth normal g, and the red area in the bull's-eye is just under one-fourth. You can pick up your partner and fling them across the room if you're not careful."

"I never knew you could turn off gravity."

"The jump engines produce a varying field naturally. Humans discovered it, but the Tyrans figured out how to make money with it. They can reproduce it anywhere it's wanted. They're brilliant scientists." She bit her tongue. *I sound like my parents.* "In empire-class berthing, you can control gravity in sleeping areas. You get a great night's sleep in lo-grav. Especially after dancing in heels. You should try it tonight."

He chuckled. "I'm not ready to try dancing in heels."

She swatted him playfully. "Low-gravity *beds.*"

"That, I might go for."

You bet you will.

She could sense Senth reacting to her on more than one level. His body might not be aroused, but his attention was. The mind behind those sparkling eyes was fully engaged and focused solely on her.

She squeezed his hand. "Ready to try it?" She didn't wait for an answer but led him onto the dance pad.

Time to get our money's worth out of this shimmery red dress. When she lifted both arms in a graceful arch and undulated her hips, Senth went glassy-eyed. *Oh, honey, that was all too easy.*

She didn't dare release her pheromones here; she didn't want a mob frenzy. A half hour of dancing, brushing against him, teasing him with the slow rock of her hips, and he'd be hers anyway.

The next two songs were fast, and she enjoyed watching Senth move. Whatever schedule Saint-Cyr kept him on, it was clear he'd found time for fun. When he laughed, the bright dazzle of his light blue eyes and bouncing dark curls worked its own magic on her. She feasted her gaze on his sensual mouth, the way his fangs glimmered, so wet and sharp and ready to bite. Would he sink those teeth into one of her nipples when she took him? An image flashed into her mind of rising over Senth in bed, a breast pressed against his open mouth, his curls flung against her pillow.

Heat flared between her thighs, a delicious ache she longed to satisfy—with him.

She danced closer, sidling against him, remembering the body she'd glimpsed that afternoon. Smooth chest, unlike a Kin. The moment she'd seen him half-naked, she'd had the urge to touch him. Taste the texture of his skin with a long, slow lick.

She danced behind him, rubbing her back against his, sliding up, and then easing down with a shake of her hips. She flung back her head, all too aware of her desire. She wet her lips. In her present state, pheromones would release whether she liked it or not.

Too fast. Too fast. Need to get him somewhere private.

The rhythm changed to a slower one. NarrAy knew better than to put herself in Senth's arms in public. Unless she *wanted* a riot. His body against hers meant passion, and passion meant pheromones.

She led him off the floor, grabbed his jacket on the way to the door, and entered one of the elevators. He didn't question her, allowing her to lead without protest. Once the doors closed, she leaned into him, pinning him against the wall, arms around his neck. She closed her mouth over his. Senth kissed back, opening his mouth when she licked his lips.

His tongue felt exactly like a Kin's. Exactly as she'd fantasized.

He is so hot. She felt her pheromones release their first wave. Her breasts tingled with it. NarrAy rubbed up against Senth, drawing him down hard against her body. He wrapped his arms around her waist, fitting her along his length.

"Touch me, Senth. Hold me. I want to kiss you." She tangled her fingers in his curly hair and drew him down for more kisses. She nibbled his lower lip, licked his chin and jaw.

He let her kiss him, resisting nothing, allowing her intimate touch. She ran a hand over his chest, yanked his shirt up out of his trousers, and fit her hand underneath.

"*Nnnhh*, Senth. I love your skin." The elevator doors opened. In the corridor she palmed the door lock, and it opened to their suite. She half dragged Senth into her cabin and locked the door behind them. Tossing his coat over a chair, she advanced on him.

He stood there, a haunted look about him.

Without pause, she opened his shirt and pushed it off his shoulders.

He made a small move to stop her when she reached for his trousers, but she brushed his hands away.

"Have to have you, Senth." Her second wave of pheromones hit the air. By now he should be trembling from the rush the way she was. When the third overtook them, he'd do anything she asked, long past the point of saying no. She unfastened his pants and pushed them down along with his underwear. When she stepped closer, he moved back, stepping out of his shoes.

"NarrAy." He put his hands in front of him. "Not like this."

"I know about the Shackle. I don't care. I want to hold you."

"But I—"

She ignored his protest and took his penis into her hand. She couldn't close her fingers around him. "Once you're hard, you'll be huge."

"But, NarrAy, I can't. I—"

"Shh...I don't care." She fondled him. His eyes were open all the way, his innocence shining out of them. "This part of you isn't human, baby doll. This part is big as a Kin." She growled, low in her throat. "I love it." She set her hand against his chest and pushed. He bumped into the bed and fell onto it.

"NarrAy..." He tried to get up but stopped when she pointed at the other end of the bed.

"I want you! Get under the blankets."

While he complied, she set the grav controls. You needed only a bit of gravity to cling to each other, but not so little you bounced away.

When the gravity faded, he sighed. "Didn't know how tired I was."

She reached behind and unfastened her dress. It fell at her feet. She peeled off her red thong panties and climbed into bed beside him. The lo-grav made her feel light. She rested on her side next to Senth. His eyes were closed, a peaceful expression on his face.

"Feels good, doesn't it?" She brushed back his hair.

"Mmm." He didn't open his eyes. "Up all night, practicing." His face relaxed.

"You'll sleep well tonight, sweetheart. I promise." She leaned over and kissed him. No response. She kissed him again. Nothing. "Senth?" She rose on her elbow over him. "No!" She patted his cheek. "Senth!"

Out cold.

With a groan, NarrAy threw herself onto her back, fists clenched. "Saint-Cyr, I know you did this to him. I don't know how, but I know you did." She glared at the ceiling. "I'm going to get you for it."

She drew a deep breath, forced it out, and then did it again. As her pheromone level dropped, so did her anger. Guilt took its place. She scrambled out of bed, refusing to look at the sleeping youth.

He's seven years younger than me. Barely a man. I almost raped him. NarrAy covered her face with both hands. *How can they call us Betters?*

She grabbed her robe and pulled it on as she fled the room.

Chapter Six

Tyran Sleepliner Ceroman Hethen
Empire-class Berthing, Suite Alpha
Wintresq 13

Senth woke in darkness and fumbled for his clock until it dawned on him he was in NarrAy's room. Breath held, he patted the bed. Alone. He flung off the covers, felt around for his clothes, and yanked on his pants. The memory of NarrAy stripping him returned with complete clarity. Shame scalded his face. He bolted toward the door. Listening, he opened it a crack and scanned the common area.

Empty. Good! He tiptoed to his room, entered silently, and leaned against the door. *How could I let things go so far? Khyff. Have to think of Khyff.* He visualized his brother in the alley, forcing himself to endure while Liu used her mouth on him. At that time Senth hadn't known whether Khyff felt anger or pleasure. In retrospect the tightly closed eyes and clenched fists screamed anguish. He pictured the Ghost and Khyff hanging over the establishment's railing with his pants down. *Can't let this happen again. Can't let Khyff down.*

Not bothering with the light, he climbed onto his bed.

Onto lower gravity. And a body. Firm hands slammed into the middle of his chest and shoved. Senth yelped. Arms windmilling, he fell backward into full gravity. The floor came too fast, with a rude *thud*. The body landed on top of him. Hard. The wind whooshed out of him. Someone pinned his arms to the floor.

The lights came on when the door banged open. Broxus charged in, a gun in his hand. "What the...?"

Senth sucked in air as his breath returned.

NarrAy was the one pinning him. She climbed off, affording Senth a great peek at her long, incredible legs and the lack of anything beneath her short gown.

"I thought I heard a scream." Broxus put the gun out of sight.

"That was Senth." NarrAy wrapped herself in a robe and turned away. "I scared him."

"What?" Senth rolled onto his side and sat up, bracing himself on his hands. "You didn't scare me! I wasn't scared."

"What's going on?"

"I wasn't scared." Senth gestured to himself. "That was a Kin sound. I yelped."

NarrAy paced near the end of the bed. "I was sleeping in here. Senth is in my bed. Or he was."

"Why was he in your bed?"

At that, Senth leaned one arm against the bed and hid his face against it.

Broxus cleared his throat. "Do I want to know any of this?"

"I heard a scream." Encie's voice sounded in the doorway.

"I didn't scream." Senth turned toward her and pushed hair out of his eyes. "I yelped. It's a Kin sound. Kin yelp."

"What's going on, Brox?" Encie ignored Senth. "Why is he on the floor?"

Senth moaned. *I wanna crawl under the carpet.*

"It's handled, Encie. Sorry to have disturbed you, ma—um, NarrAy."

The door clicked shut. NarrAy stooped beside him. "I'm sorry, Senth."

He lifted a hand and waved it in a dismissive motion. "It's okay."

"No, let me help you up. I shouldn't have hit you so hard." She touched his shoulder.

"Gee, thanks." He refused to meet her gaze. "Way to make a guy feel good. I'm fine."

"No, you're not. Please, let me—"

"I'm *fine*, NarrAy." He raised his head, still not looking at her. "Could you please just go?"

"Sure." She stood. "I'm sorry, Senth. For everything."

He heard her footsteps. The door opened and closed.

Senth slumped on the floor. "Fffffft fffffft fffffft!" *Could I embarrass myself any more tonight?* He rolled onto his stomach and slammed a fist into the floor. *No no no. Don't even ask.*

* * *

Tarth City, Starport District
Empire Central Starport

NarrAy walked beside Encie and behind Brox and Senth as they entered the starport's ground transportation mall.

The sounds of the starport careened around in her head. Voices echoed off walls and hard floors. Machinery whined and hummed. Thousands of feet stomped, dragged, and tapped. She winced at the inhuman pitch of bagbot wheels. Squeaky rubber shoes shot up the decibel level when a trio of uniformed port workers sprinted past them. Sun filtered through opaque ceilings, and she squinted against it until she found her dark glasses in a pocket.

"*Like having a permanent hangover,*" Brox had said when she described her normal world. "*I wouldn't want it.*" Neither did she.

Especially not now, coming down from a pheromone high, with her senses still peaking.

Senth's kisses attuned her to him. The myth about Betters controlling others through a kiss was that—a myth. It worked the other way around. She heard his heartbeat even from here. No, not heard. Felt. Indescribable sensation, being attuned. Like having him inside her. Living, breathing, existing. Dominating her thoughts, ruling her desires.

And all because she gave in to goading from Encie. A moment's impulse on the dance floor. A kiss stolen in an elevator. Senth's warm skin against her hands. So innocent. So simple. So life changing.

Never do that again. What was I thinking? How am I

going to work right next to him? She'd kept no previous lover long enough to worry about it. She was gone the next day, or they were. Lack of proximity limited effect. *Three more days next to Senth. I'm going to die from this.*

"You okay?" Encie's voice intruded on her thoughts.

NarrAy adjusted her glasses. "Fine. A little tired."

Encie leaned closer. "Did you—"

She held up a hand. "Don't take that road. The bridge is washed out." She raised the hand a little higher when Encie made as if to press the point.

Her aide shrugged.

Senth glanced back at them as he exited.

Could I have made this any worse? She shielded her eyes from the sun. *No, you idiot. Don't even ask.*

The groundcar and driver met them at the curb, and the smooth trip along Conqueror's March Boulevard brought them down through Tarth City Park, past the massive Destine Pietan Stadium, and into the Imperial Business District. Just inside the Royal District sat the luxurious Royal Arms Hotel, shaped like a giant arrow being driven into the ground. Tyran engineering at its finest. Like their suite on the ship, the empire-class suite sported a common living area and four bedrooms with private baths.

NarrAy's corner room had a breathtaking view of vast Tarth City, showcase of the empire. Impossibly tall spires drove through the clouds. Steady shuttle traffic climbed into the sky to the west, near the starport. The wide swath of Tarth City Park divided the metropolis in half all the way to the horizon, and the Cyr de Typhin River meandered through it, bright blue water glinting in the sun.

She directed her bagbot to its place against the wall. While it deployed into closet mode, she went back to the common area and waited in a wingback chair for the others.

A few minutes later, a sock-footed Senth went sliding past her on the dark wood floor. Arms out for balance and holding a shoe in each hand, he slammed up against the wall and laughed.

He tossed the shoes on the floor and shoved his feet into them before launching himself across the back of the burgundy leather sofa. And kept going, sliding right off its slick surface and onto the floor.

Senth jumped to his feet and dusted himself off, noticed her, and turned bright red.

"I...um...I was getting..." He gestured toward his room and hit the large glass lamp next to him. Senth made a grab for it, righted the shade, and set the lamp back on the table, only to step back and stumble over a potted palm. He danced sideways and bumped into Broxus as the man entered.

"Ready to go?" Brox steadied Senth.

"Yeah." He didn't turn back toward NarrAy. "I'll get my cloak." He hurried toward his room.

NarrAy clapped a hand over her mouth and shook with laughter. *What a cutie.*

Senth returned shortly, wearing his cloak, his expression somber. He barely glanced in her direction.

"Okay, people." NarrAy clapped her hands. "Time to go sightseeing."

In the car Broxus hired, she sat next to Senth so they

didn't have to look each other in the eye.

The Imperial Armada Military Storage and Weigh Facility Tarth-F took up a city block in the Namalia District. Across from it, in one of the oldest restaurants in the city, NarrAy eased into a seat beside Brox and across from Encie. Senth headed for the warehouse.

NarrAy picked over the appetizer tray of green Tyran cheese cubes and sliced *m'jaj*, an egg-shaped, fuzzy green fruit from the Chiasmii homeworld. She drank liberal amounts of green tea with honey, trying to settle her nerves.

She tried not to watch the door, but every time it opened, she glanced up. Even as slightly connected as they were, when Senth's heart raced, so did hers. Every time he held his breath, she caught hers. She knew when he scaled the building. Her adrenaline rush announced it.

If I'd done more than kiss him, I'd be having a heart attack right now. She shook her head, forcing the thought away.

Brox watched her. One signal and he'd be up and after Senth. She would not order it. Despite the excitement Senth broadcast so plainly, he also felt emotions that settled and calmed her: pride and absolute confidence.

They had already ordered dessert when Senth sat down beside NarrAy's aide. He set his cloak between them.

"Just coffee," he told the waiter and leaned back when the android left. He played with a fork on the table.

NarrAy sipped her water, showing a calm she did not feel in any part of her body. Having him safe and within her sight made her ridiculously happy. "Did you enjoy your walk?"

"Yes. It's a beautiful day outside." Senth flashed his fangs in a self-confident smile. "It's perfect weather for a walk."

She sighed in relief at hearing the code words Senth had given her earlier. He'd scoped the place and was satisfied. Everything was a go.

* * *

Tarth City, Royal District
Royal Arms Hotel, Suite 1221

Senth ran both hands across the inside back of his cloak, smoothing the surface against the table. NarrAy and Brox watched from the opposite side. Encie, in charge of comm-gear, prepared equipment in another room.

Senth captured NarrAy's gaze, then turned to Broxus. "You two are about to see why we don't let these cloaks out of our sight. Please remember this is classified to our guild, as much as the military has its secrets."

He pulled on a pair of dark gloves and swept them across the inside surface of the cloak. An image sparkled into view.

"This is the layout of the storage facility." Senth stroked a fingertip down the right side of the picture, activating a menu. "By our intel, we want the third floor." He chose options. "New arrivals. Household. Security level would be at least a three. Date. Um, NarrAy?"

Broxus answered for her. "Her parents were murdered the first week of Sumertsag."

"After the first, then." Senth tapped in the date. The image shimmered and clarified into a floor plan with one section highlighted.

Broxus rubbed his hands together. "I like your toys!"

"Thank you." Senth touched the highlighted section, and it zoomed in to show individual containers, one of which glowed red. He tapped it once. "This is ours, right here. Three twenty-three. These aren't rooms, of course, but huge metal crates. Getting into those is a snap. It's the doors leading into the warehouse that are the problem."

"Which is why we hired you."

Senth met NarrAy's gaze. "Exactly." He passed his fingers across the menu, and the picture changed to the outside of the building. A few taps and a rear entrance filled the small screen. "The Vassindorf is one of the finest security systems in the empire. It looks like part of the wall, but it's connected to every lock in the entire structure. The newest upgrade means that one picked lock, one misstep, one wrong passcard anywhere on any floor, and it alarms. You can't go around it, can't destroy it. It's foolproof."

NarrAy and Broxus flicked glances at each other. She cleared her throat. "And you're smiling, why?"

"Because it has two tiny design flaws. First, they were so certain it couldn't be compromised that they don't even scan its access points. I could walk right up to one of them and bounce a ball off it for thirty minutes without triggering one alarm. Second, once I do breach the Vassindorf, it'll let me in anywhere else in the building."

Broxus grinned. "You can do that?"

Senth turned off the image. "As you put it, that's why you hired me." He slipped his arms into the cloak and sealed the front of it.

Broxus came forward and felt the cloak's collar. "What else does this thing do?"

"The cuffs at my wrist provide access to the info you saw on the back panel. I can't talk about other things. Proprietary. It's made of nightstealth. It makes me all but invisible on routine scans. Not even copbots can read it."

"I've heard of stuff like that, but when they upgrade cop sensors all the time, how well does it work?"

"Oh, it works great, Brox. We upgrade our cloaks too."

Broxus pulled a face. "How do you upgrade what amounts to a fancy coat?"

They always ask. Senth adjusted his cuffs. "I'll tell you what they told me after I joined the guild. You'll find out at level fifteen."

The man gave Senth a grudging smile.

"Okay." Senth turned to NarrAy. "Let's get the comm-gear. Time to go to work."

* * *

Tarth City, Namalia District

Imperial Armada Military Storage and Weigh Facility Tarth-F

NarrAy clung to the shadows of the building while Senth worked. The first door opened as if he had a key for it, and they entered a darkened hallway. He motioned her to an alcove and held a hand to his lips, then pointed up and right. She glimpsed a green dot of light.

Spyware.

Senth disappeared into a shadow.

Squinting, she could just make out a darker outline against the blackness. His cloak absorbed light. Like Broxus, she wished for a few of Senth's toys. *Even more, I'd like to toy with him.* Shaking her head at the direction her thoughts took whenever Senth was involved, she focused on the matter at hand.

When he moved again, he motioned at her to stay and went to work on a door. Seconds later, he gestured for her to join him.

"That was fast," she whispered when they walked through the door.

He flashed a smile. "Don't be impressed yet. The Vassindorf's next."

Around another corner, the security-system access point came into view.

Even she recognized it as formidable. Aside from the word *Vassindorf* engraved on the upper-right corner, nothing on the outside indicated what it was. Not a seam, knob, or opening. No controls or pads. It might as well have been a wall.

Hell, it is a wall. NarrAy clutched her stomach. *We'll never get past that.*

Senth tilted his head and studied the entire structure before stepping forward. He took out what looked like a fat stylus or data pen, made an adjustment to it, and held it out at arm's length.

I hope that's a magic wand, because we're going to need one with this thing.

A panel opened in front of Senth. Before NarrAy could tell what he was doing, he was turning back to her and the panel was closing.

She clenched her fists. "What happened? What's wrong?"

He cocked his head. "Nothing." He put the stylus in his pocket. "It's disabled. We're in." He swept a hand forward. "Shall we go to work?"

"That's it?" The iron giant appeared unchanged. "You're done?"

He frowned. "What did you expect? I told you I was a professional. But it's not over yet, you know. You still have to find the locket."

With one more glance at the Vassindorf, she followed him up a set of stairs beside the device. "I guess I'm more impressed than I thought I'd be."

He smiled down at her. "Thanks. I think." On the third floor Senth stopped. He tightened a hand around his wrist and appeared to be listening.

"Are you reading intel from the cloak?"

"Shh." He nodded, then motioned to the right and headed that direction.

The numbers on the enormous containers increased: 320, 321, 322, 323.

"This is it." Senth worked his magic on this door too, and

it swung open on silent hinges. He stepped back to let her enter.

She clicked on her flashlight and shone it around. "Um, Senth? Problem." Her voice sounded hollow in the metal crate.

He flipped on his light and swept the beam from side to side. Empty as a politician's promise.

Chapter Seven

Tarth City, Palace District
Imperial Palace, Conqueror's Offices

Empress Rheyn Destoiya clasped her hands in front of her, fighting the temptation to stroke the fair skin of her personal assistant, Alitus Vivaldi. The blond had been a Jade in her stable of men until he proved his mettle during an attempted coup. He served her now as a free man. Or as free as a Better ever was from his lover. His addictive pheromones worked both ways, addicting her to him and him to her.

The vid presentation he'd prepared for her cabinet meeting was excellent as always, but she could not give it the attention it deserved. Not when they stood so close, she could feel the heat of him all along the length of her body. She reached up to run her fingers through his silken hair and down over the short hairs on his nape. When long, his golden hair used to trail across her breasts while he pleasured her. Alitus had let it tickle down her body. He had teased her with it while he nibbled and licked ever lower. She'd loved having it draped across her thighs while he brought her repeatedly to orgasm with his mouth and tongue.

Intelligent and loyal, he'd been acquired when he was fifteen. She'd protected his virtue by having him educated far out of her reach and, the day he turned eighteen, brought him into her stable. Now, at twenty-one, he was fully in his prime. Making love with him was more than lust. It was fire and wine and smoke and mirrors. Pure magic. Those long, powerful legs and skilled hands did things to her none of her Jades dreamed of matching.

And his pheromones. Mmm. She clenched her fists, forcing her awareness away from him with supreme effort. "I've seen enough, Alitus. It's perfect. You always know exactly what I want." His ability to satisfy her made him her all-time favorite. *When he thrusts into me...* She tightened her jaw, reining in desire. "Send it out in the morning."

"Yes, Majesty." He loosened his shirt collar, having left his jacket at his desk. "May I do anything else for you?" The low pitch of his husky voice fired her blood.

She took a deep breath. "Oh, Alitus." The chamber outside her office was full of petitioners, and it was night already. She stroked his cheek. "There's not nearly enough time for what I really want from you. There are still so many people I have to see."

"It's past office hours, Majesty."

Pausing, she canted her head to regard him. "Meaning?"

One corner of his mouth tilted up in a naughty grin. "I sent everyone home before I came in. So...if you want anything more..."

"In that case, strip out of those clothes right now."

He ducked his head. "As you wish, Majesty, always."

Opening his white dress shirt, he flirted with her from under long golden lashes, his teasing eyes the pure dark blue of Trien's virgin oceans.

"I could get lost in your eyes." She touched his lips.

He sucked her finger into his mouth and twirled his tongue around it.

Nearly coming from that simple touch, Destoiya panted, her gaze riveted on his lush mouth. A Better's pheromones were in every part of him: blood, sweat, saliva, semen, tears. Contact with any part of Alitus—even breathing the same air when he was aroused—brought her close to orgasm.

He slid the shirt down his arms and onto the chair behind him, took one more lick of her finger, released it, and pulled his T-shirt over his head. He tossed it after the shirt, baring a smooth chest. His skin gleamed with a bronze luster, but when did he find time for sun? He spent his life at her beck and call. He stepped out of polished shoes, cast off the socks, and then took a half step back, opened his black pants, and let them drop. Nothing lay beneath other than the finest cock in the empire. Thick as her wrist, a dusky rose with a darker head, his cock rested against his thigh, rising in response to her gaze. Nude, he stepped out of the pants, lifted her right hand, and placed it against his chest.

His heart hammered beneath it.

"May I release my pheromones, Majesty?" A Better's heart suffered if he didn't release them. Each Better had his or her own scent, and although simply being near one was enough to affect a normal person, the actual release of pheromones wrought dynamic changes, even influencing the mind. Alitus never misused his pheromones and never lost control. He released them fully only at her will.

"Do it," she whispered. Her mouth went instantly dry, as if the peach-and-apricot scent had channeled all the moisture in her body straight to her pussy. "Wet, Alitus." She dragged her fingers down his chest and hard abs. "You make me so...wet."

"I can smell your cream. Is it seeping down the insides of your thighs?" He knelt before her and gripped the hem of her skirt. Looking up at her, he licked his lips. "May I mouth-worship you, Majesty?"

She nodded, past speaking.

Alitus pushed her skirt to her waist, wrapped his hands around her bare hips to support her, and leaned in to inhale her arousal. "You're soaking wet. Mmm. Is this all for me?" He smiled up at her.

"Damn it, Alitus! You know it is." Destoiya arched toward him, widening her stance.

"Good." His sassy grin flashed, revealing perfect pearly teeth. "I love you, My Conqueror." His whispered words cast warmth across her skin. He scattered kisses across her mound, his mouth gentle.

The feel of his tongue between her desire-swollen lips drew a gasp. Though it was he who serviced *her*, it was *she* who gave up control. With only a few kisses and two licks, he had her trembling. Still bracing her hips, Alitus lapped deeper between her folds, sipping at her cream.

She jammed a fist against her mouth, trying not to cry out, not to yield so swiftly, until he curled his tongue around her clit and all pretense of resistance shattered. A climax shot over her from anus to clit and up the front of her trembling body, out across her breasts, rushing heat along her throat and into her cheeks. A keening sob left her.

Alitus released his second wave of pheromones, driving her straight to the peak of a second climax. Breath caught in her throat, and she threw back her head, blinded by pleasure so intense, it bordered on brutality.

She gripped Alitus's head with both hands and held him against her. "Alitus. Fingers. Please!"

He stretched her sheath open using two fingers. He thrust his tongue deeper, pulled it back across her labia, and flicked her clit with its tip. She wagged her hips, trying to increase the erotic licking. Fire burst forth everywhere his tongue touched. Alitus licked up and over her clit, down one side of her labia and back up the other. Destoiya widened her knees, pushing herself against his mouth, arching toward him. He twisted his fingers in and out but lightened the pressure of his tongue.

Heat rose out of control. A flashover of passion ignited inside her. She bit her lip, trying to stop her cries. Her knees buckled, and Alitus caught her, lifted her into his arms, and as he stood, slid her down onto his cock.

She quivered inside, filled with his magnificent warmth. Stretched wide, stuffed full, she wrapped her legs around his waist and rested her brow against his shoulder as another orgasm swept over her. Pulses of heat traveled over his hard length, gripping him, pulling his cock inside her. She sucked in air, shuddering, dizzy with lust. Unable to speak, she let herself be carried toward her desk.

Alitus seated himself on the edge and helped her shift

her legs so he could lie on his back, cock still inside her. "Use me like your favorite plaything, My Conqueror." He spread his arms wide, surrendering his control. "Ride me any way you like."

Kneeling over him, she took in his rumpled hair and his blue, lust-filled eyes wild with untamed hunger. My Conqueror, he called her. Even when scratching an informal note, he capitalized both words as if that was her formal title. He called her his personal empress, and yet it was he who first abbreviated Your Majesty to simply "Majesty." Not until asked would he call her by name.

"Say it." She lifted her body, leaving only the head of his hard shaft inside her. "You know what I want to hear."

"I love you, Rheyn."

"Oh, Alitus. Yes, like that." She knew herself as Destoiya the Conqueror, but with this man, she longed to be Rheyn the Woman. A quick flutter of her sheath drew a gasp from him.

He arched his throat as if baring it for a bite.

She took her time, lengthening the agony of his desire by feeding her own. She rubbed the drenched mouth of her sex against the base of his cock.

He gripped her waist with both hands and held her still. "Tell me who owns your heart."

"You do, Alitus." She rocked against him. "Only you."

"Good. Good." He gripped the edge of her desk, a hand on either side of her. "Now, pleasure yourself with me. Take my body, Rheyn. Use me." Eyes half-closed, he stretched out beneath her. "Use me until you use me up."

She arched her back, shuddering, her slick pussy quivering with unsatisfied lust. Destoiya felt his cock jerk within her. His face contorted in a mix of ecstasy and pain.

"Beautiful, Alitus. You're beautiful like this. Erect, hungry, pleasing me. I love seeing you beneath me." She nipped his chin.

The usual piercing intellect of his gaze dulled with passion. His chest rose and fell as he panted. He blew out a long breath and calmed himself. "I—Oh!" His cock twitched. He swallowed, closing his eyes a moment before opening them again. He wet his lips. "Rheyn. Rheyn, I love you."

She rose up the length of his exquisite cock, hesitated, and then, circling her hips, slid back down. Alitus groaned, head back. Destoiya kept it up, teasing him with slow strokes that made him gasp and shiver. Having this splendid man beneath her in the building throes of orgasm shoved her libido over the top. She rode his shaft faster, trying to quell the heat coursing through her.

Alitus gripped the desk. "Come for me, beloved. Now."

His words triggered a flash of heat. Destoiya ground her hips against his groin. "Yes, Alitus. Oh!"

He gripped her waist with both hands and held on to her while he arched beneath her, pumping into her with abandon, mouth open in a silent scream. The feel of his cock inside her, the heat of his climax, his release inside her body drove coherent thought far from her. Her body peaked, soaring through another pheromone-induced climax.

She panted, supported by Alitus. He flinched beneath her, rocked by the aftershocks of her orgasm. When she had recovered enough to think, she peeled off her uniform jacket and threw it aside, opened the front of her blouse, and lay down atop him, skin to skin. Their mingled sweat reinforced the addiction they shared.

She lay still, playing with his golden hair. "You are incredible."

He kissed the top of her head. "You're a natural phenomenon. Relentless. You tear down all my defenses and leave me helpless in your arms."

The empress braced herself on her hands and smiled down at him. "Are you insinuating I'm stormy?"

With one fingertip, he traced the line of her mouth. "Hurricane Rheyn batters the Alitus coast. Flooding imminent."

Shaking her head at his playful words, she bent to give him another kiss and then eased up enough to let his softening cock withdraw. She climbed off the desk, opened a drawer, and withdrew two soft cloths. She handed one to him and used the other on herself.

Alitus turned on his side. "Will you need me for more, Rheyn?"

Destoiya leaned down to kiss him. "I always need you, my love. But I'm good for now. How about you?"

"I'm already thinking of holding you in my arms tomorrow." Heavy-lidded eyes lowered demurely. "I'll dream of you tonight."

"And I of you." She neatened her shirt and pulled down her skirt to cover hips and thighs. When Alitus had cleaned up, dressed, and refastened the last button of his shirt, she circled her arms around his neck to bring him down for a kiss. "You still taste of apricots and luscious peaches. I could kiss you for hours."

Her towering android, Prentice, strode through the double doors. Alitus had the grace not to pout when she dismissed him with a flick of her fingers. He pursed his lips and blew her a kiss as he drew the doors after him.

Destoiya set both hands on her hips. "You're in time to spoil my fun, I see. Who knows what might have happened next?"

"Really?" Prentice picked up her jacket from the floor and dangled it. "Looks like I didn't spoil it entirely." He shook out the jacket and held it for her. "Will you never free him?"

She slid into the jacket. "He's free. He refuses to leave me."

"He's a Better. Only separation allows a Better to free himself from his lover."

"I'm not holding him here. He's always been free to go." She flipped a hand through her curls, tossing her head. "Besides, he's special to me and always will be. Of all the levels I've established in my stable, the one called *Lover* was never intended for anyone other than Alitus. I don't have to tell you to protect him, do I?"

"Certainly not. I owe him that. He's single-minded in his loyalty to you. That alone earned him my respect. Of the hundreds of young men who've served you over the centuries, none have been as loyal as he."

"You care for someone other than me."

"Are you surprised? Because we androids label ourselves

'iron' doesn't mean we're made of it."

"As you say, Prentice." *So he cares for Alitus. When has he ever shown any of my favorites one bit more devotion than expected? Hmm.* She perched on the edge of her desk. "Well, get on with it. Why the grim face?"

"NarrAy Jorlan is in the warehouse as we speak."

Destoiya stood and picked up her gloves. "Is everything on schedule?"

"Yes. Switching the container numbers should delay them long enough for us to trap them inside."

"Excellent. That's almost worth missing a hot half hour with Alitus." Slapping the black leather gloves against her palm, she paused beside Prentice as he held the door. "Almost."

* * *

Kelthia, Miraj City
Miraj City Central Correctional Facility

"Khyffen."

The male voice jerked him out of a daze of waking nightmares. Which jailers had come to assault him this time? He started toward the bars of his cell, fists clenched.

"Back for more, you rat-faced—Oh!" He tucked his hands behind him. "I'm so sorry, sir. I never intended…"

Saint-Cyr flipped a hand. "Don't apologize. I tend to provoke that response for some reason." The Harbinger smothered a yawn while a guard unlocked the cell and let him inside.

Khyff couldn't help but smile. "I'm glad to see you, sir. Thank you for coming."

"It's nice to be wanted." Saint-Cyr held out a hand.

Khyff shook it and withdrew a step. He made his living by knowing how to read people, but the Harbinger's whiteless eyes personified enigma. *What brings him here again? Is it my being Sen's brother, or does he want something else?*

Saint-Cyr gestured to the single bunk. "May I?"

"Please." Khyff clasped his hands behind him. "I hope you'll understand if I don't join you. I'm trying not to lean against anything."

"Still hurts, does it? How have they been treating you in here?"

Khyff grimaced.

"I see. That," he added, lowering his voice, "will be taken care of."

No one had to tell him that tone meant trouble. "How's my brother?"

"No word yet. Did no one tell you you're due in court in an hour?"

Khyff ran a hand through his hair. "No, sir! What do I do?"

"Not to worry." Patting the air, the Harbinger motioned for calm. He leaned back a bit, looking past the bars. "I've arranged for representation and something besides that yellow prison jumpsuit."

"You got me a lawyer?"

"No." Saint-Cyr bared his teeth in what might have been a smile. With those unreadable eyes, one could only assume. "I got you myself."

"You, sir? You're representing me? You know the law?"

"Know the law?" The Harbinger laughed, obviously enjoying himself. "Son, I've been breaking it for so many years, I know it better than any of those high-paid courtside braggarts. Besides, none of the lawyers I contacted had enough clout with the judges. Ah, finally." He stood when a guard showed up with several boxes. "About time. I brought you a passable suit, son." He snapped his fingers at the jailer. "You! Put those on his bunk and be careful with them; then you can go."

Khyff waited until the guard was out of sight. "He's not going to make it easy on me after the way you treated him, sir."

"Understand something, Khyffen. When I finagled you a fair and impartial judge, I had no intention of letting you stay in here."

Oh, that *kind of fair and impartial*. Khyff cracked the first true smile in two days. "Thank you, sir."

"You can thank me later. Prison clothes make for a bad impression, Khyffen, and we need you as impressive as possible." Saint-Cyr opened boxes and pulled out business attire and shoes. "Get out of that ghastly garment, and let's get you into some decent clothes. We have a case to win."

* * *

Namalia District

Imperial Armada Military Storage and Weigh Facility Tarth-F

Senth stepped back and shone his light on the digital number: 323. A fast check of data from his cloak read the same.

NarrAy turned off her light. "This is the wrong one."

"Nice guess." He tucked his light in a pocket and touched his earpiece to contact Broxus. NarrAy joined the conversation.

Advised of the situation, Broxus checked another data source. "Senth, the third floor has to be right." His voice sounded as clear as if he were in the same room. "The others have military supplies. Three is the only one with civilian goods. Maybe the crates are misnumbered."

Senth tapped the fingers of both hands together. "What do you suggest, Brox? That we open them all and rummage for something familiar?"

NarrAy blew out a harsh breath. "Why are *you* being sarcastic? I'm the one whose stuff is missing."

"Sorry. That was out of line." He held out a hand. "What do you want me to do, NarrAy? We've got twenty minutes before the Vassindorf resets."

"Twenty minutes!"

"You told me you needed no more than five."

She fumed. "Fine! Let's try another one."

"Why not?" He pulled out his lockpick and went to the

next in line.

NarrAy crossed her arms, foot tapping. "I knew this was too easy."

"Easy?" Senth let go of the opened lock. "You think shutting down that Vassindorf was easy? Do you know how—Never mind." He turned back to the job at hand. *Focus, Senth. You're doing this for Khyff, not you.* He opened the door and stood back.

She shone her light inside. "Nothing."

Touching his ear, Senth waited while NarrAy and Brox went over details. Again. The warehouse was full of identical containers. "Wait a minute. Brox?"

"Copy."

"After the stairs, is container three twenty-three a sharp right or a gradual one?"

"Sharp."

Senth pointed with the light. "We went by the numbers on the containers, not by their locations. We should have gone hard right. Brox, how many crates over from the door?"

"Twelve."

Senth paced them off. "It should be this one." He opened it.

NarrAy turned her light into the room. "This is my folks' stuff. I recognize things!"

"We're in," Senth told Broxus. "NarrAy, I'll keep watch while you search. We can't risk being locked inside. Hurry."

He waited in the dark, hearing muffled *clinks* and *thumps* from inside the cargo area. It reminded him of waiting in the alley for Khyff. The same urgency nipped at his patience, but with NarrAy, a whole different set of emotions set him on edge. Emotions surfaced that he'd never had before.

He kept seeing her in that red dress on the dance floor. *She moves like water. Her arms over her head and her hips swaying back and forth. And her breasts—Well, how can I describe those in lighter gravity? They don't bounce exactly. No, they're buoyant. Like in water. Yeah, water. Floating. All wet and—*

"Senth?" Brox's voice in his ear brought him to attention. "NarrAy. You there?"

"Copy," he and NarrAy said together. Five minutes had passed. *Damn it! Focus, Senth! What's wrong with you?*

"Status?"

"It's a mess in there. Everything's jumbled together."

"Hurry."

"I am, Brox!"

Senth heard her grunt. A dull scrape from inside said she'd moved something heavy. He took a few steps away, listening for other sounds. His trained gaze took in the sheer quantity of containers in the warehouse. *Oh, the possibilities. Wonder what's inside all these?* He let his light travel over the closest. His neck tingled suddenly, as if every tiny hair had stood on end. *Digital.* He swept the area overhead, assuring himself once more that no active spyware watched. *Oh fffffft!*

"Got it!"

NarrAy's voice right next to him made him jump.

He took her arm. "NarrAy, these numbers were changed."

She clutched the locket she'd hung around her neck.

"Say again," Broxus demanded.

"The numbers on these crates are digital. There's no way we misread data or the layout."

"Get out!" Broxus ordered. "Go! Go!"

They ran for the stairs and down them.

Headlong in flight, Senth heard the fire door below them slam open. He and NarrAy halted, started to climb back, and heard the one above slam too. The *clang* and *pound* of hard boots on metal stairs ricocheted around the concrete stairwell.

"Halt!" The shouted order boomed off the walls. "Hands behind your heads! Don't move!"

White light flooded everywhere. Blinded after the darkness, Senth squinted. He linked his hands behind his head. Beside him, NarrAy did the same.

"Brox," she whispered. "Taken. Go silent."

A dozen golden-skinned Kin in black uniforms advanced on them. Pinpoints of red light from their multibarreled guns swept the stairs.

Senth went rigid, sure of death as those red points flashed across his face and targeted his forehead. The laser sights cast a scarlet aura across his view of the soldiers circling them. Golden fists emblazoned on each uniform marked them as more than simple armada soldiers.

This was the elite squad assembled to enforce the Conqueror's will, selected for their consummate ability to kill with any weapon. To rip apart the enemy with their hands or their claws. Or their teeth.

The Praetorian.

Chapter Eight

Kelthia, Miraj City
Miraj City Central Court

Taking the Harbinger's advice, Khyff made limited eye contact with the Honorable Judge Alderon, but he felt the judge's gaze on him. Blond like all Androgs, Alderon glowed like an angel in the judicial white robes of the Chiasmii court.

Glad for his fine suit of clothes, Khyff sat still, hands resting on the arms of the chair. As Saint-Cyr had coached him, Khyffen was careful not to react to Master Stalkos's tale that Khyff had robbed him of clientele by working outside his license. Stalkos gestured grandly, jabbing a finger in Khyff's direction at every opportunity. The man's permanent sneer twisted an already cruel mouth into a deeper expression of hate.

The Harbinger, with his quiet authority, dark clothing, and whiteless eyes, appeared menacing even when smiling. Stalkos came across as simply mean-spirited.

When it was Saint-Cyr's turn to question the man, the Harbinger directed his testimony in an entirely different direction. "How many scars did Khyffen Antonello have when you agreed to monitor his parole?"

Stalkos snorted. "I have no idea."

"Twenty-seven." The Harbinger picked up a notereader, which he handed to the judge. Stalkos's attorney switched his copy on and began flipping through it. "As required by law, all sex workers undergo a physical examination when purchased. Khyffen Antonello had twenty-seven scars. Two on each wrist and ankle, nine across his back, and seven on his buttocks. Three on the knuckles of his right hand. Your Honor will find pics of these scars within the notes."

Khyff tightened his right fist. Self-defense in prison. The judge was thumbing through the screens, not looking his way.

"The eight ankle and wrist scars are from being restrained. Khyffen doesn't remember which are from restraint during punishment and which came from rough bondage sessions."

At that, the judge looked straight at Khyff but addressed the Harbinger. "Mr. Saint-Cyr, how old was your client when these scars were made?"

"Begging your pardon, Your Honor. Which ones?"

"Wrist and ankle." His gaze slid toward the Harbinger.

"He was fifteen at that time, Your Honor."

"Fifteen?" His expression became shuttered. He lifted a hand. "Continue."

Khyff gripped the armrests.

"Master Stalkos?" The Harbinger stood in front of the man. "How many scars did Khyffen have before you beat him the last time?"

Stalkos fidgeted. "I'm not sure."

Khyff chewed the inside of his mouth to keep from smiling and loosened his death grip on the chair.

"Sixty-one." Saint-Cyr gestured to the notes. "The current pics are included, Your Honor. Section two. Adding the twenty-four lashes Master Stalkos inflicted two days ago, six of which will leave scars, he has a total of sixty-seven scars. Khyffen Antonello has been subjected to frequent and rigorous beatings over the entire two hundred and seventy days this man has held him captive."

"Objection." Stalkos's lawyer stood. "Antonello is a slave. He cannot be held captive."

"Sustained. Please rephrase, Mr. Saint-Cyr."

"Yes, Your Honor. Khyffen Antonello has been subjected to frequent and rigorous beatings over the entire two hundred and seventy days this man has *enslaved* him." He made a polite bow to the lawyer, who ignored him. "Your Honor," the Harbinger continued, "based on this type of abuse, I move to have all charges against Mr. Antonello and his as-yet-unnamed clients dropped."

"Objection!" Stalkos's lawyer stood again. "Antonello is a slave. Master Stalkos is within his rights to apply up to ten lashes as necessary to instill discipline."

The judge set down the reader. "The law also states that no discipline by a master shall leave permanent marks or scars. Are you implying that these scars came from bondage sessions? Do you have the required invoices for service and documentation from a physician to prove they resulted from that?"

The lawyer looked at his notes, leaned toward his client, and conferred in whispers. "We do not, Your Honor."

"So the scars are from disciplinary action on the part of Master Stalkos."

More conferring. Khyff turned his head to hide the smirk he couldn't wipe away.

"It would seem so, Your Honor." The lawyer sat down.

"One moment." The scratching of a stylus was followed by the judge's chair squeaking as he leaned back. "By my calculations, Mr. Antonello would have had to receive a whipping serious enough to leave a scar an average of once every seven to eight days. This sounds like a serious discipline problem."

"That's right, Your Honor," Stalkos answered.

Khyff braced an arm against his stomach.

"Odd." Judge Alderon picked up the notereader. "I find no evidence you ever reported him as unruly to his parole officer. Your financial reports indicate he's your highest source of income on weekends. Hardly sounds like the problem you make him out to be. How do you reconcile your written statements with your testimony here today?"

Stalkos and his lawyer exchanged meaningful looks.

Khyff clutched the chair, a surge of wild hope flaring in his heart. He saw the subtle hand sign the Harbinger gave him and obeyed it. He looked right into the judge's eyes and let him see his fear, waiting to answer the question Saint-Cyr had assured him would be asked.

"Mr. Antonello." Judge Alderon braced his arms against his desk. "Do you have anything to say in defense of these charges?"

There it was. A chance to reveal the one thing that would land Stalkos in jail and keep him in taxpayer hell for years. He took a deep breath. "Yes, Your Honor. Master Stalkos forces me to work without pay and doesn't report the income."

"That's a lie!" Stalkos jumped to his feet. "Khyff! You're a damn liar! You son of a bitch!" His lawyer grabbed him and sat him down again.

"Bailiff," the judge ordered, "set a guard on Master Stalkos. If he makes another outburst like that, escort him from the courtroom."

"Yes, Your Honor." The bailiff cast a harsh look in the slave master's direction. A guard moved to stand behind the man's chair.

Judge Alderon motioned to Khyff. "Continue, Mr. Antonello. Pay no attention to Master Stalkos. He cannot harm you for what you say here today. I guarantee your safety on that."

Khyff had gone too far to be intimidated now.

"Thank you, Your Honor. I'm not lying. Stalkos does it to all the parolees at the slakehouse. If we refuse, he uses a cane or a whip on us. On top of that, he's addicted all of us to Thrust. If we won't do what he says, he withholds the drug until we beg for it. I started working the streets so I could fill my freedom savings account and get out of there. When he found out the first time, he started chaining me to my bed and threatened to have my parole officer send me back to prison."

"You said 'the first time.' You've worked the streets without permission before?"

Saint-Cyr had drilled him on what to say. "Yes, Your Honor, every chance I got. Every drak went into my savings so I could get out of there."

"I see no notes from your parole officer about abuse. Why didn't you tell him what was going on?"

"He knew about it, Your Honor. Stalkos paid him a fee to get new parolees for his house and gave him free use of any slake he wanted once a week."

The judge gestured to the bailiff. "Have the parole officer arrested."

"With pleasure, Your Honor."

"Anything else I should know, Mr. Antonello?"

Khyff glanced at the Harbinger and received a nod. "Yes, sir. About a month ago, I was reunited with my brother. I'd been told he died at birth. Finding him again..." His voice had gone all squeaky. He paused to clear his throat. "I knew if I ran, I'd get thrown back in prison and lose out on seeing my brother altogether. So I stuck it out with Master Stalkos. My brother's been helping me save for my freedom. I wasn't trying to cheat my master out of anything. I just wanted to be with my family, and I don't..." Saint-Cyr had warned him about talking too much.

The judge waited a moment before prompting gently, "Go on."

Khyff schooled his face into passivity before continuing. "I don't want to be a slake the rest of my life." He added hastily, "Your Honor."

"While I applaud your desire to improve yourself, Mr. Antonello, I must ask you to remember that sex work is considered an honorable profession in the Tarthian Empire."

He barely breathed. "Yes, Your Honor."

"Still, I would not want to do it myself." Alderon smiled at him. "I see ample reason why you would seek to purchase your freedom by any means available. In fact I commend you for your considerable restraint in remaining in such deplorable working conditions. This demonstrates to me that you have more than learned to abide by the law. I find, therefore, that your parole is no longer necessary and terminate your original sentence."

Terminate?

The Harbinger lifted an eyebrow and nodded.

Khyff grinned. *Yes!*

"Bailiff, take Master Stalkos into custody for failure to comply with his parole-monitoring license. I also order an inquiry into the treatment of slaves in his employ. Master Stalkos, you are hereby ordered to pay restitution for abuse. Bailiff, find the price of Mr. Antonello's slave contract. Restitution shall be set at one and a half times that amount, payable in full into Mr. Antonello's freedom account. Master Stalkos will pay for all scar removal and physical restoration of normal skin. Funds in Mr. Antonello's freedom savings account will be released to him immediately. This case is dismissed. Mr. Antonello, please stand and remain a moment."

The gavel sounded.

Malice gleamed in Stalkos's eyes as the bailiff marched

him past Khyff and out of the room.

Judge Alderon stood. "Khyffen Antonello, by the power vested in me by the empire of the Tarthian people and Her Majesty, Empress Rheyn Destoiya, I publicly declare you a free person. Congratulations." He leaned over his desk and stretched out a hand.

Khyff shook it, smiling into the judge's friendly eyes. Alderon left the bench.

"Yes!" Khyff pumped both fists into the air. He shook hands with Saint-Cyr. "Sir, I can never thank you enough! I'd do anything for you."

"Don't say that, Khyffen. You don't know what I want."

The chill of those words splashed over his soul, dampening his joy. Try as he might, Khyff could not interpret Saint-Cyr's expression. Resolved to honor his word, he tamped down the fear that made his stomach quiver.

"I mean it, sir. Thank you." He dropped his hands at his sides and lifted his head, quietly offering himself. "I will give you anything you want."

"I believe you would." The Harbinger took Khyff's face between warm hands. "I know the courage it took to offer yourself, and I'm deeply honored. But I'll never think of you in that way, Khyffen. I want you to never let anyone own you again." Saint-Cyr clasped his shoulders. "You're a free man. The next time you surrender your body, make sure your heart goes with it." He released him.

"Yes, sir." Khyff grinned. "I will."

"Well now. We should celebrate your good news." He hung an arm around Khyff's shoulders as they walked.

For the first time Khyff could remember, having a man touch him didn't fill him with disgust. Saint-Cyr was the first man other than Senth who'd proven worthy of his trust.

"This is so amazing. I'm free! I can't believe this is happening."

"Neither can I," Saint-Cyr agreed. "I'm going to owe your brother a lot of money."

"Sir?"

Saint-Cyr patted him on the back. "Never mind. Thinking out loud. What do you say we find a nice place to eat and then get thoroughly drunk?"

Khyff tossed back his head and laughed.

* * *

Tarth City, Namalia District

Imperial Armada Military Storage and Weigh Facility Tarth-F

I can't believe this is happening. Senth kept both hands behind his head as he and NarrAy were prodded into one of the empty storage containers he'd opened earlier. *At least they didn't shoot us. Yet.*

The metal door clanged shut behind them, trapping them in total darkness. A bar scraped shut on the other side. In the confining space, their breathing echoed.

Senth reached out in the dark and found NarrAy reaching for him. "I'm sorry."

She wrapped her arms around his waist as he pulled her

close. "Not your fault, Senth. I should have known this would happen."

"Brox and Encie. What'll they do?"

"They have orders to leave me behind if I'm caught."

"Great. So we're totally screwed."

"I'm sorry!" She pressed against him harder, hugging his waist. "I should never have got you into this."

"Don't be silly. It's not like you forced me." He rested his chin on the top of her head. "I had a choice."

"Did you?"

"Yes." But now what would happen to Khyff? "Anyway"—he drew his fingers through her hair—"I'm glad I can be here with you. I'd hate to think of you in here alone."

"Oh, Senth." Her hand felt warm on his cheek.

When he moved his head, he brushed his chin against her mouth. Bending to kiss her, he swept his tongue inside, savoring the sweet taste he hadn't been able to get out of his mind since she'd kissed him in the elevator.

She lifted her arms up around him, holding herself against him as she pressed up into his kiss.

They broke apart at the groan of metal against metal. The high whine of a motor kicked in, followed by the *clank* of chains across a concrete floor.

"Hold on!" Senth clutched her. "We're being moved."

The truck-sized container jarred on its foundations and tipped. Senth and NarrAy flung out their arms. The crate skidded across the metal floor and into the wall. A warning beeped, and a whistle sounded. The unit tilted again and lifted into the air. They huddled together on the floor. Senth braced his feet and helped NarrAy sit between his thighs and up against his chest where he could keep her safe. He wrapped her in his arms as the unit began to lower. It landed with a *thud-scrape-thud* and settled hard. Chains rattled on the outside again. More beeping and whistles. A different motor—this one with the deep thrum of a transport truck. A hiss of air shrieked under the truck, and they felt the unit jolt up off the ground.

"We're moving. Where do you suppose they're taking us?"

"You saw those uniforms."

"Praetorian. Does the Conqueror want that locket?"

He heard her sigh, felt her shoulders lower as she leaned against him. "Remember I said it held the key to my inheritance?"

"Yeah. I take it that's something she wants."

"My parents left me data on an old technology they unlocked for her. From before The Barrier was erected, before the First Cycle of Wars."

"I thought all that stuff was a myth."

"It wasn't to my parents. They saw it."

"They saw The Barrier? It's real?"

"They said it was."

"Wow." Senth leaned his head against the wall. "Did they say what it looked like?"

"It resembled a fishing net made of navcapsules cast into space. Beams between the trillions upon trillions of tiny capsules spread across parsecs. Apparently it was intended to scramble navigation. It also broadcast a warning."

"Do you have any idea how much that would've cost? The technology alone—Never mind. Someone must've thought whatever it was supposed to protect us from was damn well worth it, otherwise why would anyone build such a thing? What the hell were they trying to keep out?" He shivered.

"My folks said it kept people on the other side from crossing to ours. My dad's theory was that it worked the way magnets do, pushing against opposite poles. It made ships turn away on either side. Of course, nothing can really stop people from going in either direction, but finding the edges of The Barrier takes time. It's been done, but there's no way of knowing what's out there or what the risks are. Parts of it have broken down, though. It's at least ten thousand years old." She moved her head against his shoulder. "At least that's what my father thought." She rested her hands against his thighs. "He said it was coded with a quarantine warning."

"What kind of disease do people on the other side have?"

NarrAy linked her hands with his. "The warning mentions genetic damage during unprotected landings. Here's the odd part. It isn't beaming the message toward us."

Senth frowned. "What do you mean?"

"The warning is aimed at people on the other side. It warned *them* not to come *here*. It warned them against contacting *us*."

"What? What the hell is wrong with u—" He broke off as images rose in his mind of the fierce Kin with their catlike fangs and furskin—especially the ones who'd surrounded them moments ago. The Tyran, who had goatlike legs and horns on their heads, and the Chiasmii, who were male and female at the same time. Chiasmii telepathy and empathic abilities permitted few secrets. "They couldn't have been worried about Betters, because your people hadn't been created yet, and it can't be HalfKin, 'cause humans didn't even know about the Kin."

"Unless maybe the people on the other side of The Barrier did."

Senth released NarrAy's hands and cuddled her closer. "What if there are other, more dangerous species on our side that we haven't discovered yet?" Both of them shuddered.

Buzzzzz! Pting! Buzzzzz! Pting!

Senth ducked at the loud report of shots ricocheting off the metal container. The vehicle came to an abrupt stop.

"Down!" NarrAy twisted and grabbed him. He felt her warmth and the strength of her body as she covered his with her own. Shouts outside. More weapons fire. A scream of agony.

"What's going on?"

"A firefight." Through his fingers on her neck, he felt her pulse beat as wildly as his own.

"Are we being rescued?"

"I don't see how. Brox and Encie are the only ones who know where we are, and they don't have the firepower to do anything about it." She took his hand as she rose to her feet. "Come on."

He followed her to the door. "What are we doing?"

"Get down, right here." Her hands guided him. "Do you

have claws under your nails like Kin?"

"Sorry. Eyes, fangs, good hearing and smell." He stooped beside her near the door, to the right of the latch side. "Not as good as a full blood, but better than human. I might not have claws, but there's nothing wrong with my fists."

"Can you use them?" Her warm breath heated his cheek.

"Hell yeah." He smacked one into his palm.

"Good, because when that door opens, we're fighting our way out of here."

Outside, the metal bar across the door screeched on its way up.

Chapter Nine

Namalia District

Imperial Armada Military Storage and Weigh Facility Tarth-F

NarrAy leaned her body weight against Senth. "Let me go first, and if you get a chance to run, take it. No heroics. I can always find you."

"What? No way!"

"Senth, listen to me. It's for your—"

"If you're going to say *my own good*, save it. I get enough of that from my Sen'dai. I'm not leaving you, and that's final." He wrapped a hand around the back of her neck and pulled her up close for a kiss.

For one heart-melting moment, she savored the taste of his mouth, smooth as a lick of vanilla ice cream on a hot day. It was all she could do not to kiss him deeper.

The screeching metal stopped. Two taps against the door, then one. All clear. A signal everyone knew. NarrAy readied her fists.

"Chocolate," a man's voice announced on the other side.

"Chocolate is good," she responded.

"Chocolate and sex are better." The APLA security code of the day. She had to smile. How could she not?

"Friendlies!" She leaned into Senth, and they stood.

The door swung outward. The sight of two Kin Praetorian in full riot gear brought NarrAy to an abrupt halt.

The one on the right snapped her a salute. "Lieutenant Stealth Keheyl, Captain. Newly recruited to the All People's Liberation Army."

NarrAy motioned to Senth, and he jumped down with the silence of a cat. He held up a hand to her and helped her down. A stiff breeze caught a few tendrils of dark curls not tucked under his cap. He stuffed them back and pulled the cap tighter. She grabbed his hand.

"My aides?"

"Already picked up, ma'am." Keheyl gestured to one side. Paper litter blew across the bodies of dead Praetorian. "We're in a hurry. This unit has backup on its way. Follow me, please." Keheyl trotted toward the front of the transport.

Wide swaths of burn marks scorched the side of the container. The driver hung out the door, a quasi-burn rifle slung over one lifeless arm.

"You two did this?"

"Had to, ma'am. They wouldn't see it our way."

A scoot squatted ahead of them, looking like a pregnant dragonfly perched on the ground. Above it, blades pulsed, pushing silent air. Once in space, alternate flight surfaces would take control. NarrAy hung back when she saw the Conqueror's golden-fist insignia on the side. She pointed at the logo and sent Keheyl a questioning glance.

"The Conqueror's personal scoot, ma'am." His grin showed Kin fangs. "We steal nothing but the best."

Senth tugged her arm, looking for reassurance. She nodded, motioned him ahead of her, and climbed in behind him. Keheyl and the other Praetorian piled in afterward. She barely fastened her belt before the fat little vehicle shot straight into the air.

It came to a dead stop at the top of the atmosphere and went backward at a ninety-degree angle.

The contents of Senth's stomach went in the other.

Once they'd cleared the planet, the flight crew tended to the mess as if it were an everyday occurrence while Senth sipped at a bottle of water and kept his head down. NarrAy drew Senth into her arms and kissed his brow, settling him against her shoulder. Close together, they could talk privately. The cabin noise was minimal in a luxury scoot like this.

"You've never flown in a scoot before, have you?"

He lifted woeful eyes. "You can tell, huh?"

She smiled at his attempt at humor and stroked his cheek. With her other hand, she removed his cap and played with his hair. She turned to Keheyl. "Lieutenant?"

"Yes, ma'am?" His fingertips touched his helmet in respect.

"We'll debrief once we're aboard the *Vandal*."

He nodded and turned away.

Senth was staring up at her when she turned back. "I'm sorry, NarrAy."

"Don't worry about it."

"But this scoot—it's beautiful inside. Look at these seats! They're leather." He ran a hand over the surface. "The carpet's so deep, you sink in it, and I puked all over the place."

She set her forehead against his. "Think of it this way. It's the Conqueror's."

"Not really helping me that much. You're part of the rebellion, aren't you?"

No reason to hide it now. "I am. Does it make a difference?"

He ran his tongue over his lips.

She went on playing with his hair, letting him think.

He shook his head and smiled. "No. But tell me something."

"What?"

"Does it matter to you that I'm not free? That I can't be free for two more years? Am I imagining a connection between us?"

She gazed down into his beautiful blue eyes. Darker blue outlined his oval pupils. This close, tiny flecks of yellow glowed in the interior light. True cat's eyes.

"No." NarrAy wound one of his curls around a finger. "We just met, but I'm drawn to you far more than a Better would experience if it were only an addiction."

His shy smile widened, turned bold as he gazed at her. "You like me, then? The way I like you. Enough to overcome the fact that I'm a slave?"

"Are you asking me for a commitment, Senth?"

"I'm telling you it may be that long before my Sen'dai lets me act on what I feel for you."

His honesty surprised her into silence.

Senth nuzzled her jawline. "I wanted you to know because I care about you. If you care about me too, I want to take it further."

NarrAy cupped a hand under his chin and lifted his face. *You adorable man-child. I could eat you up.* She pressed her mouth against his cheek, not daring to kiss him here. Not after those endearing words. Her pheromones would wreak havoc in such an enclosed space. "Yes," she whispered. "I care more than you know."

Senth shifted on the seat, one arm around her waist from behind as he snuggled closer and shut his eyes. NarrAy set her cheek against the top of his head and hugged him with both arms.

She wished for words to express what she felt, but what could she say when she'd never felt this way before? This innocent virgin in her arms was so young, yet in every way a man. He'd so completely captured her body that she could hardly bear to be separated from him.

And now he'd captured her heart.

* * *

Kelthia, Miraj City, Holding District
Ran's Ranch Steakhouse

Khyff rested his head against the high leather seatback

and closed his eyes. The booth sat all the way in the rear of the restaurant—the kind of secluded, dark corner most of his clients preferred. Except this was not a client, and he would never again have to perform any kind of sex act under the table in a booth. A genuine smile of pure happiness made itself comfortable on his mouth.

"How are you feeling?" The Harbinger was cutting steak; Khyff could hear the *clink* and *scrape* of knife and fork.

He didn't open his eyes. "Content."

More scraping and clinking. The sound of a glass being moved. "How long has it been since you were good and drunk?"

Khyff turned his head toward the voice and opened his eyes. Luc Saint-Cyr's whiteless gaze glittered over the rim of the wineglass. *Is he watching me or the door?*

"Drunk? I'm never drunk." Khyff shrugged. "But I'm always good."

The Harbinger laughed.

"What is it?" Khyff remained still.

He set down the glass and patted his lips with a napkin. "What do you mean?"

"What is it you want me to do?"

"You think I brought you here to ask a favor?"

Khyff set a hand over his full stomach. "I make a living reading body language."

Saint-Cyr took a bite of meat, chewed it, and swallowed. "I have a feeling Senthys is going to need our help."

Khyff's time on the street had taught him never to show

fear. Instead he quieted, alert to impending danger. "Senth's in trouble?"

"I'm sure of it."

"How do you know?"

The Harbinger circled one finger around the edge of his wineglass. "I sense these things."

"He said that about you." Khyff sat up, reached for his coffee, and drank it. "Tell me what you want me to do."

* * *

Tarth City, Namalia District

Rheyn Destoiya took in the six dead Praetorian on the ground and the one in the door of the transport. The shipping-and-storage container hung open, the inside empty. The acrid smell of charred flesh marred the humid air.

"How did they escape?"

Lieutenant Dhia Ruh, her new senior Praetorian, bolted to attention. "They used your scoot, Your Majesty."

The Conqueror turned to her. "What did you say?"

Ruh fidgeted slightly. "They commandeered your personal scoot, Your Majesty."

"Who let this happen?"

"We found the flight crew dead and the guards chained to their posts with their mouths taped shut."

"That won't save them, Ruh. I want them questioned. I want to know who did this."

"Already done, Your Majesty." The Kin female extended a hand. The paper in it bore the same crimson stain as her fingers. Ruh was efficient. "There was another note."

Swearing under her breath, Destoiya opened it gingerly. *Thanks for the use of the scoot.* The words bore the unmistakable slanted writing of the head of the rebellion, leader of the All People's Liberation Army, the bane of Destoiya's existence—the Sleeper.

Chapter Ten

All People's Liberation Army Ship Vandal
Officers' Quarters

Though still carrying the marks of an armada cruiser, the *Vandal* and its crew had switched sides.

Senth followed NarrAy down a narrow corridor. "Why is everything lit up with red?"

"It's on night ops. Red makes it easier for the eyes to adjust to darkness, and you can still distinguish everything. Let's see, cabin number... Ah, here we are." She unlocked a door, and he followed her inside. "This is our room."

Encie and Broxus had brought Senth's and NarrAy's bagbots with them, and both bots waited in the room, inactive. The tiny cabin sported a chair, a drop-down desk, and a garment rack with a few cubbyholes under it. A mirror covered the back of the door. One bed—a double.

Senth's cheeks burned in remembrance of the last time he and NarrAy were alone near a bed. "We're...um...both in here?"

"Mmm hmm." NarrAy backed him against the door and set a hand on either side of his head. "This cabin is for accompanied officers."

"A-accompanied?" *You need a mind slap, you idiot! Say something intelligent.* Unsure where to put his hands, Senth put them behind him.

"Accompanied." She traced a finger across his chin. "Meaning *with* someone."

"Oh." *Something intelligent, kkkhh face!* But nothing came to mind, and the only thing in sight was the bed. Or her. Right there, up close, next to him, breathing the same air. *Oh fffffft! The way she's looking at my mouth. It's like—Fffffft!* His throat almost closed. *I am feeling soooo…naked.*

NarrAy put one of her feet between his and leaned against him. Body to body. All the way from his calves up to his waist. Even through his clothes, her warmth soaked into him. And her scent. What was it?

Sugar cookies. That's what she smells like. Vanilla and butter and—oh fffffft.

NarrAy pressed her fingers against his lips. Senth held his breath as NarrAy watched the progress of her fingers. She drew them from his mouth to his chin, down the front of his throat, and stopped where his cloak fastened.

He gulped.

NarrAy looked up at him. Her burnished amber eyes were heavy-lidded. He couldn't catch his breath. Her dark blonde lashes fluttered like butterfly wings on a hot summer afternoon. Slow, lazy, indolent, and inspiring sheer fascination.

Senth sucked in a shallow breath.

"I have a debriefing, my tiger, but I'll be back afterward."

NarrAy took both his hands and drew him away from the door. "Then we're going to talk about that commitment you wanted. You get some rest." She put a kiss on her fingertips and pressed them against his mouth.

Too dazed to say anything, he simply stood there as she swept past him and out. When the door shut, he stared at his reflection a moment before realizing he was standing there with his mouth hanging open. He shut it.

"Yes!" Senth pumped both fists in the air. "*Fftt-fftt sha kee*!" He did a slide-step dance across the floor, whirled around on one foot, and danced back. He whipped off his cloak and tossed it across the bed. He danced with his reflection, arms outflung, head back, and then spun around and laughed aloud.

"*My tiger*." He grinned at the mirror. "She called you her tiger. Oh yeah, fftt-fftt sha kee, brother. You've got it."

He danced over to his bagbot and flicked it on. The little bot clicked, a stabilizer shot out at the base, and the top unfolded to its full height. The front panels separated and retracted, creating a makeshift closet with drawers. He chose a black turtleneck sweater and pants, changed, and brushed his hair, settling it over his shoulders. Satisfied with his appearance, he dropped onto the bed to rest.

Eyes closed, one ankle crossed over the other, he folded his arms across his chest. Thirty seconds later, he opened his eyes and drummed his fingers. He tapped a foot.

What was I thinking, asking her to wait for me? He tossed himself off the bed and paced the three steps it took to cross the room. *I can't make a commitment. My Sen'dai will kill me.*

"Stop." He sliced the air with his hands. "Stop. Deep breath. Deep breath, Senth. Calm down." Fingers pressed against his temples, he closed his eyes to shut out distractions and released a long, cleansing breath. *That's right, Senth. Be the lock. Okay, in, out, in, out. Remember your guild training. Relax.*

He clenched his fists until he was shaking.

"Oh ffffftt! This will never work!"

Three steps forward. Pivot. Three steps back.

I can't get involved with her now. And what about Khyff? How could you forget about your own brother?

Pivot. Three steps. Stop.

I can't do anything on Shackle for five days, and I'm going home tomorrow. It's only been three fffffting days, and I have to go home.

Pivot. Three steps. He shook his fists. Senth snarled deep in his chest, a tiger's lament.

Idiot! What were you thinking? He faced the mirror on the door. *Why'd you have to ask her to wait? What is it she's supposed to wait for? A slave? You? He set both hands on the mirror and stared at his eyes. A half-human thief? Forget about waiting two years, kkkhh face. What are you going to do when she gets back here—tonight?*

With a groan, he thunked his head against the door.

* * *

All People's Liberation Army Ship Vandal
Captain's Ready Room

The aide to Colonel Somnoll O'Venna saw NarrAy to the colonel's door, opened it without knocking, and announced her in a whisper. The aide turned back and set a finger over her lips as she gestured NarrAy inside.

Destoiya ranked him a desperado and the number one terrorist threat to the empire, but the man before her was slight of build and had a gentle face and shaggy blond hair. The desperado sat behind a desk piled with documents, notereaders, and vidchips. He held a sleeping child on his lap, her head cradled against his shoulder. Wrapping the girl in his arms, he gestured to NarrAy to close the door.

She shut it quietly and snapped him a salute. "Sir." She kept her voice low. "Captain Jorlan reporting."

"At ease, Captain." The Chiasma officer leaned across the sleeping girl and extended his hand. The APLA disregarded most Better Laws, especially the one about not shaking hands. "Glad to have you on board. Please sit down."

The Sleeper had gained his moniker because of his first name, Somnoll, and his reputation in always catching the Conqueror unawares.

When he swiveled his chair a bit and turned out a bright light over his shoulder, NarrAy caught a glimpse of a braid down his back, woven with a bright red ribbon. One of the oddities of having Androgs in the military was having different dress codes on different days for the same person, but NarrAy felt fairly certain none of the allowances included ribbon or braids.

Colonel O'Venna drew a blanket closer to the girl and tucked it around her.

NarrAy shook off the urge to question him about the child and decided on a different tack.

"Er, excuse me, Colonel, if I may, is 'sir' appropriate when addressing you? I don't wish to offend."

"No offense taken, Captain. Human military tradition provides that male and female officers are addressed as 'sir' when on duty. Chiasmii never joined the military until recently, so it's never been an issue until now. But thank you for not assuming."

"You're welcome, sir."

"Never served with a Chiasma before, I take it?"

"No, sir. It's never been my privilege."

"Nor mine to work with a Better, until now. You've been debriefed, have you?"

"Yes, sir."

The girl whimpered and stirred in her sleep, and O'Venna cooed assurances, adjusting the blanket. She had Kin ears, but they were on the side like a human's instead of near the top. They almost disappeared from sight in her tangle of blonde hair.

A HalfKin like Senth. NarrAy's heart leaped. The Better Laws forbade her to bear children, and a HalfKin could never sire one. What would one of theirs have looked like?

I actually had thoughts of bearing children with Senth? That's a first.

"Was the item recovered, Captain Jorlan?"

"Yes, sir. Lieutenant Keheyl took delivery."

"Excellent! Now a few things you need to know. The

first is about Stealth Keheyl. Do you realize who he is?"

"I believe his family promised him at birth to Ruffhaus Fasra, Destoiya's top Praetorian. I heard talk on the way up here she'd—"

A swiftly upheld hand stopped her. "Been relieved of duty and arrested?"

NarrAy nodded.

"More than true. Stealth and Ruffhaus have been lovers since they were teens. He followed her into the armada and became her right hand. In the short time you've been on this mission, the entire structure of the Praetorian Guard has crumbled."

NarrAy moved to the edge of her seat. "What happened?"

"To phrase it politely, the Conqueror demanded Ruffhaus hand over her brother." He nodded toward the sleeping girl. "He was this little one's father. The Conqueror wanted him for her stable of pleasure slaves, but Ruffhaus refused. When Destoiya tried to force the issue, Ruffhaus stepped in to defend her brother. Before it was over, the Conqueror had arrested Ruffhaus and sent Praetorian to her brother's house to fetch him. They raped and killed his human wife, killed him when he fired on them, and set fire to their house."

NarrAy clutched a hand over her heart.

O'Venna nodded toward the child in his arms. "This is their daughter, Talyn." He gestured for NarrAy to come closer and pointed to the floor behind his desk.

She stood and leaned over to peer down and gasped. A

younger child lay sound asleep on a pallet at his feet.

"Who is this?"

The Sleeper met her eyes. "Onys is the only Chiasma test subject who survived the Sabbath Experiment."

Stark anxiety roiled NarrAy's stomach. She sank back down in the chair.

The Sabbath Experiment. A code name for research that exploited Chiasmii gender phases by intrafertilizing individuals with their own sperm and egg. It created genetically balanced fetuses that, when altered, produced a step beyond Betters. So they said. Arson started by protesters resulted in a catastrophic loss of life, the destruction of countless viable embryos, and led directly to the cessation of all genetic experiments in the empire and the outlawing of Betters.

"I didn't know someone survived the Sabbath Experiment, sir."

"*No one* survived, Captain Jorlan." He looked pointedly at her.

She nodded. "My mistake."

"Stealth and Ruffhaus were assigned there. Stealth rescued O's *tavi*—his mother—who died shortly after reaching Felidae. I barely delivered O from the womb in time to save him."

"You delivered him?"

"No choice. His tavi had died with him still in the womb. I had to act fast."

"Is he like me? Genetically enhanced?"

"Because he's been hidden, he's never been properly

evaluated. If Destoiya had known he survived... I don't have to tell you what his life would have been like."

Tested, prodded, trained, judged, assessed. Pushed to exceed yesterday's accomplishments. Pressed to perform longer, harder, faster. Better.

"No, sir, you don't. I understand completely."

"I thought you might. We hid him from Destoiya by keeping him with Ruff's family. My change in political convictions separated us, but I'd been Ruff and Stealth's friend for years before that. Now they've seen I was right about Destoiya."

"So these little ones are in your care?"

"O was reared with Talyn, so they're both homeless. I've known them most of their lives. Where else would they go?"

"I'm surprised to see an officer of your rank with children literally underfoot." She smiled.

"A Chiasma can father one child and give birth to the next, Captain, so caring for children is part of who we are. All our workplaces are geared around childcare first, then business. My office will need some refitting, it seems." He looked around.

"Quite a challenge."

He nodded, fondly gazing at the child on the pallet. "An incredible challenge. O thinks like a HalfKin, not a Chiasma. I'm not sure what to do with him. He doesn't know how to use telepathy or any of his empathic senses. And Talyn..." He sighed and leaned back in the chair, then grinned widely. "She'd been aboard less than one day when she convinced a fighter pilot to take her up backseat and teach her to fly against the empire. I had to discipline him, but I have a feeling it won't help. The crew's adopted her as their own."

NarrAy had to laugh. "She's a leader, then."

"And a troublemaker, just like her aunt. Ruffhaus will join us soon. Stealth and those Praetorian now on our side hope to free her within a day or so. Destoiya will spit venom when she finds out."

"You expect Ruffhaus to join the resistance?"

"Ruff has no reason to trust Destoiya and every reason to hate her. She can win us our freedom."

"You have a lot of faith in her."

"That is a massive understatement. I'm staking my life on her. More than that, I'm staking the future of the empire." He tucked the blanket under Talyn's chin. "I believe once Ruff's on our side, she'll become the leader of the rebellion. It's time I stepped aside. To that end, Captain, once your mission is completed…" He paused. "Which will be when?" He waited.

"I'll return Sen—Mr. Antonello—to Kelthia and be back within a day, sir."

"Good. When you return, you'll be Ruff's aide. Show her the ropes. That's a lateral move for you, but it will work into a hefty promotion later."

"Thank you, sir. I'm honored."

"Congratulations on a job well done, Captain. I've taken the liberty of assigning your aides elsewhere for a few days. I need their expertise on a private security matter. When they return, they'll report to you. I'll expect you to hire a staff and train them."

Talyn twitched and cried out in her sleep. Crooning softly, O'Venna rocked her in his arms.

"Nightmares." He glanced up. "Small wonder. Thank you, Captain. That will be all."

"Yes, sir." Smiling, NarrAy rose and clasped the Sleeper's hand between hers. "Thank you, sir. I wish you well with the children." She stepped back and saluted. At the door, she paused and turned back.

O'Venna was smoothing one of Talyn's curls.

"Sir?"

He looked up.

"Permission to speak freely, sir?"

"Of course."

"I couldn't help but notice your ribbon."

With a smile, the Sleeper reached back and pulled the long blond braid over his shoulder. "This ribbon is for the Conqueror, Captain Jorlan. She's made a point of saying I'm the primary target in her war against domestic terrorists, which is what she calls anyone who resists her power. I've answered that tyranny cannot and will not rule any person free at heart. So this"—he tossed the beribboned braid over his back—"is to make sure Destoiya can spot me in a crowd."

* * *

All People's Liberation Army Ship Vandal
Officers' Quarters

NarrAy unlocked her cabin and entered.

"Senth?" A darkened, empty room greeted her. She set a hand over her chest. Tight. Hard to breathe for a moment. She shook off the feeling. *Guess Senth went for chow.* She headed back into the corridor.

"Warning. Weight limit exceeded."

NarrAy stopped. The gender-neutral, robotic voice sounded as if it had come from inside her cabin.

She poked her head back inside. The tightness in her chest increased. "Senth?" His bagbot had been activated; its lights were blinking. She entered the room and shut the door behind her. "Lights on full."

Ambient lighting went to bright.

"Warning," the bagbot announced again. "Weight limit exceeded. Please remove items until optimum weight condition achieved."

NarrAy approached the bagbot. "What the..." It swayed like a drunkard.

"Mmmph!"

"Senth!" NarrAy grabbed the retractable doors and forced them apart.

He fell out of the bot and collapsed onto the floor, gasping for breath.

She helped him to the bed. "Who did this to you? What happened? I'm calling security."

"No!" He clutched her arm. "NarrAy. Sorry." He took shallow breaths. "My fault."

"What happened?" She picked up a booklet from the desk and used it to fan him. "Are you all right?"

He grunted and turned on his side, doubled over.

"I'm calling sick bay. You—"

"No! NarrAy." He shook his head and took a deep breath. "My fault. I was trying…test. To see if…if…" His hand tightened on her arm as he looked away from her. "So stupid."

"I don't understand, Senth. What happened?"

"I was bored, so I…" He pushed his face against the bed, avoiding her gaze. "I break into bagbots all the time. I thought I'd try breaking *out* of one."

"You did what?" She sank to the floor beside the bed at eye level with him. "Senth, you could've been killed!"

"Once I got the doors closed, the bot kept trying to compact itself."

All at once she glimpsed the future she'd have with Senth if she pursued him. Her wild missions paled compared to the thought of a life full of stunts like this one. Finding him locked inside some bagbot or cabinet or safe. Having him risk his freedom for the sake of a few rare coins or an old locket like the one he'd stolen for her. Thievery commonplace in her life? Her parents would never, ever approve.

Which was why she had to give that future a chance. "So I'm sure I understand, tell me again. You did that for fun?"

He nodded, peeking at her through his lashes like a little boy caught with a cookie before dinner.

"And was it?"

"Well, yes, until I got overheated in there and it ignored my command to open and kept telling me I was over its weight limit." He breathed a long sigh. "I thought you'd never get here."

Her heart stuttered as pheromones crested in a swift tide of elation like the prelude to an orgasm and felt as good as chocolate and silk and whipped cream all rolled into one. All over her body at the same time. No man had ever made her feel like this *before* having sex.

NarrAy set her chin on the edge of the bed, her nose next to his. "Senth, what am I going to do with you?"

"My Sen'dai says the same thing."

His shy smile made her crest again.

Two crests and I haven't even kissed him.

She arched against the hot spasms of pleasure making her quiver inside.

"Senth." She leaned over and took his mouth in the way she wanted him to take her. A long, drugging kiss, heady with lust.

He turned onto his back as she climbed onto the bed and over him, both of them fully dressed. She didn't care. She had to have her mouth on his.

"NarrAy, I—"

"Shh…" She placed light kisses all around his mouth. "It's okay. Please, Senth. Hold me. Let me kiss you."

She fisted both hands in his hair and held him in place while she ravaged his mouth. She fed on his sweetness. Licked his chin, his jaw. She scraped her tongue over his fangs, flicked the tip of it against them.

When he pushed his tongue against the roof of her mouth, it scratched her. "I want that rough cat tongue on my nipples, Tiger. I'm on fire for you. I want your tongue spreading me open, licking my clit until I scream." Knees on either side of his hips, she rubbed herself from side to side across his body. "Hold me, Tiger. Hold me hard."

He tugged her down against him.

The third crest hit. She threw back her head.

"Senth. Oh, Tiger." No man had ever made her this hot this fast. She bent down for more of his lips, almost bruising them in her rush to taste him. "Palm here." NarrAy guided his hand between her legs. Her clit throbbed and burned. Her panties were soaked. "Oh yes. There, Senth. Hard."

She rubbed against him, yanked up his sweater, bared his chest, and splayed one hand across his smooth skin. Her palm brushed across a rigid nipple.

You're reacting. Good. I'll get you past this Shackle yet. A vibration started in his chest. *Oh. Oh, Senth...*

He was purring.

An orgasm shuddered through her. She cried out hoarsely, rocking atop his hand in a frenzy of lust. Shivering, gasping for air, she draped herself over him in contentment, repeating his name in hushed whispers.

He drew her head down against his chest, shushing her, bringing her fingers to his mouth for kisses. "NarrAy."

She lifted her head and brushed away tears. "Senth, you truly are my tiger."

His pupils had widened, the blue gone from sight. He smiled. With one finger, he traced the curve of her cheek. "Did I hurt you?"

"No!" She kissed him. "It was so good. So precious." She

sniffed. "It made me happy."

"I'm glad I could give you what you wanted."

"Oh, Senth!" She kissed him. "I wanted you. Only you." She nestled her head against his shoulder, arms wrapped around him.

Pounding at the door made them both jump.

NarrAy wiped her eyes. "Who is it?"

"Colonel O'Venna, Captain. Open up. Hurry!"

She and Senth shot to their feet, rearranging their clothes as they did. They exchanged a look of relief the knock had not arrived moments earlier. NarrAy opened the door.

"Here." The Sleeper handed her a slip of paper. "This is what the cryptographers deciphered from the locket you retrieved. Do you have any idea what it means?"

Sugar is sweet. NarrAy laid a hand over her heart. "But I thought the locket held a key to their technology. Their formula. Their secret."

"Instead"—the Sleeper tapped the paper with a finger— "it's some riddle. Does this mean anything to you? Anything at all?"

She read it aloud. "'Sugar is sweet.' I have no idea what it—Oh no. No." She sank onto the bed. "She wouldn't have. Surely not."

"Captain." O'Venna's voice carried a warning. "If you know anything…"

"What is it, NarrAy?" Senth stooped beside the bed. "What's it mean?"

"There's a holopic of my father right after my folks found out they'd been approved to conceive a Better." NarrAy lifted the paper with a weary hand. "Mom had this corny poem microetched on the bottom of it. 'Sugar is sweet. Babies are too. Our little girl will be like you.' She designed me as a female replica of my father, but she always wanted me to act like him too. She could never understand why I didn't follow him into a science career the way she had."

The Sleeper pointed to the paper. "You're saying their secret is hidden inside a holopic?"

"Yes. I'm afraid so. Most likely as some kind of code. She must have feared the locket would fall into the wrong hands." She turned to Senth. "And the holopic…"

He hit his forehead in dismay. "Oh no!"

"Oh yes." She crumpled the paper in her hands. "The holopic is back in the warehouse on Tarth."

Chapter Eleven

All People's Liberation Army Ship Vandal
Captain's Ready Room

Senth sat beside NarrAy, facing the Sleeper. Now that the ship had rerouted to Tarth, all that needed finalizing was a disguise.

"The best cover is to hide in plain sight." Senth swiveled his chair toward NarrAy. "They'll be looking for a Better and a HalfKin. We shouldn't disappoint them."

She rested her elbows on the arms of the chair, fingers steepled before her. "Is this more of your guild protocols?"

"No, good advice from…well, two uncles of mine. If we make it obvious what we are, then it'll look like we're obviously not what they're looking for." He tilted his head. "Does that make sense?"

"In a crazy sort of way, yes. But we'll need different IDs."

"Not a problem." The Sleeper clasped his hands in front of his mouth. "One thing is certain: Destoiya won't be expecting you to hit the warehouse again."

"Let's hope not." Senth tossed his head. "If she's

expecting us this time, we're done for."

* * *

Tarth City, Starport District
Empire Central Starport
Wintresq 14

An unmarked shuttle dropped them at the lunar station orbiting Tarth, and Senth and NarrAy took the local down to the planet. Inside the starport, they collected their bagbots as if arriving from an interstellar flight.

NarrAy more than looked the part of a Better. She had used a temporary red rinse on her hair, which she wore down over her shoulders. Unlike most Betters, NarrAy didn't flaunt her body, so when a human female officer her size offered to let NarrAy use pieces from her sexy off-duty wardrobe, NarrAy took full advantage.

Walking through the starport in stiletto-heeled white leather boots was a lot harder than she'd thought it would be. The white leather skirt *almost* covered the essentials, and only a few links of silver chain held together a plunging V-necked vest. She ignored the possibility that the vest might burst and kept moving, allowing her full breasts to sway and bounce.

She couldn't resist a peek back at Senth.

Managing their two bagbots on his own, he kept up with her like a good little pet. The streaming red silk scarf tied around his waist fluttered against tight black pants that outlined every hard curve of his thighs. His filmy, openchested white shirt managed to make him look masculine, despite the array of multigemmed necklaces he wore. Bracelets adorned one wrist, and a leather bracer, the other.

As they waited at customs, he lifted one heavily beringed hand to tuck several strands of hair back into the decorative metal clasp holding it. The gesture displayed his pectoral muscles to good advantage, and one of the agents inspecting their passcards gave him a long, speculative look.

"Tiger." NarrAy snapped her fingers.

Senth immediately played along. He came toward her, hands behind him. "Yes, mistress?"

"That agent likes your looks." NarrAy pointed to the flustered woman behind the counter. "Are you available to her?"

Senth's sexy feline smile showed itself, but he did not so much as glance at the agent. "Only to you, mistress."

NarrAy picked up one of his necklaces and wound it around her fist to drag him up against her. "See that you remember that before you decide to show off." She planted a kiss on his mouth and pushed him away.

Turning to the thoroughly embarrassed woman, she wagged her fingers. "If you're through playing with my ID?"

She slapped the card into NarrAy's hands and shot one last glance at Senth.

As soon as they were out of earshot, NarrAy whispered, "You played that perfectly."

He picked up one of his necklaces and rubbed it between finger and thumb. "Why, thank you, mistress."

"Behave." She swatted him on the rear and let her hand

linger a moment. "And wipe that smirk off your face, lover boy."

He pursed his lips and made a kissing sound.

They had reached the ground transportation mall when Senth's bagbot beeped three times and turned itself off.

NarrAy turned back when Senth stooped down to restart it. "What's wrong with it?"

"I don't know." He clicked its Reset button a few times. "It won't come on. I think maybe I messed it up when I"—he glanced up at her guiltily—"you know."

"Well, drag it, then."

"Okay. Sorry."

He extended its handle and pulled it behind him.

When they reached the limo-rental counter, the bagbot beeped and reactivated itself. "Weight limit exceeded," the bot's mechanized voice warned. "Damage not covered by warranty."

"What's this?" The rental agent peered over the counter.

"Just a little bot trouble." NarrAy pressed her foot against Senth's and plastered a smile across her face. "Turn it off, Tiger."

He knelt to take care of it.

"Weight limit exceeded. Damage not covered by warranty. Weight limit exceeded. Damage not covered by warranty."

"I said turn it off, Tiger." She smiled at the agent.

"I'm trying. It won't disengage!"

"What are you carrying in your bot, ma'am? Security

regulations prohibit overweight bots."

"Weight limit exceeded. Damage not covered by warranty."

"It's only clothing. Nothing heavy at all." NarrAy braced an arm beneath her bosom, half exposing herself to distract the agent. He never noticed. *All the rental places in here, and I have to pick one manned by an android!*

She nudged Senth's foot with her boot. "Do something!" she whispered.

"I'm trying!" Senth was tugging at the unit. "I can't get the battery out."

"Weight limit exceeded. Damage not covered by warranty."

"Ma'am, I need you to open the bot, please." The agent signaled a security officer.

Slapping a nightstick against its palm, a silver copbot glided toward them on silent, well-oiled wheels. "What seems to be the problem, ma'am?"

"Weight limit exceeded. Damage not covered by warranty."

"Our bot malfunctioned, Officer. It's nothing. Just a misunderstanding."

"Weight limit exceeded. Damage not covered by warranty."

Senth hit the bot on the side. "Shut up, you stupid machine!"

"Sir!" The copbot aimed his nightstick at Senth. "Step away from the bagbot."

"It's just"—Senth whacked it again—"stuck or something."

"Weight limit exceeded. Damage not covered by warranty."

"I said step away from the bagbot." The copbot extended another arm, and its metallic hand clasped Senth's shoulder. "Do not strike it again."

Senth shook off his hand. "Why? Are you its brother?"

NarrAy covered her eyes. *This can't be happening.*

Antennae shot out the top of the copbot's head. "Summoning backup."

Senth's fist connected with the base of the bagbot, and it beeped twice and went silent.

"Finally." NarrAy held out a placating hand to the copbot. "You see, Officer? Just a malfunction." *Please, don't let them make us open this thing. If they find Senth's cloak, we are in serious trouble.*

Senth brushed off his pants as he stood.

At that moment the bagbot emitted a shrieking alarm and started turning in circles. "Tampering detected!" it warned loudly. "Suspicious activity logged. Summoning owner."

The remote in Senth's pocket alarmed.

Frick and frack! NarrAy resigned herself to waiting for the trio of officious copbots gliding their way. *I wonder if it's too late to try to run in these heels.*

* * *

Palace District, Imperial Palace,
Conqueror's Offices

Rheyn Destoiya straightened her uniform as Alitus returned her desktop to its usual order. He gathered the completed paperwork from the floor and gave her one last kiss before he bowed. At the door he made a kissing motion her way and mouthed two words. *Thank you.*

"Mmm, thank you, darling." She blew him a kiss.

Destoiya checked herself in the mirror. She chose a different lip color from her palette and lifted the wand to her lips. Within a few seconds, they darkened to the redder shade. A few touches evened it. She stroked a hand over her upswept hairstyle.

Still more pepper than salt. Just like your love life. She smiled at the analogy. *And not a hair out of place. Why would there be? Alitus does all the work.*

With a satisfied smile, she put away the mirror and returned to her desk as Prentice entered the room.

"Your scoot has been recovered, Your Majesty."

"When and where?"

"This morning, abandoned in a dock at Sanity IV." The android handed her a notereader. "Security has been scouring the area for intruders. Nothing yet."

"Any evidence on board?" She thumbed through a few screens.

"DNA sweeps showed the usual APLA suspects, the fugitives, and one other person."

She tossed the notereader on her desk. "Who?"

"Praetorian Stealth Keheyl."

Destoiya slammed her fist on the desktop. The notereader bounced and hit the floor, and she sent it skidding across the carpet with a fierce kick.

"If Ruffhaus Fasra weren't so perfectly catlike, I would call her a bitch!"

Prentice retrieved the notereader and tucked it into a pocket.

She leaned over the wooden desk, bracing her hands against it. "I should never have crossed her, Prentice. It was a mistake to insist on possessing her brother. The Praetorian I sent went way too far."

"The other Praetorian agreed with you on that. They didn't blame you."

"Ruffhaus did." Destoiya hugged herself. "It won't matter to her that her comrades brought them all to justice. She blames me for siccing them on him. If Stealth convinces any more Praetorian to rebel, it could cost me everything."

The android made no verbal response; his expression sufficed.

"I know." She turned from him. "I had no choice, but I can't help feeling this is the beginning of the end."

* * *

Empire Central Starport, Customs Security

Under the watchful gaze of four starport copbots,

NarrAy sat beside Senth in a glass-enclosed room while two human workers went through every item in their bagbots.

Did I bring anything that could identify me? Did Senth? What about his cloak?

Senth pressed his mouth next to her ear so only she could hear him speak. "I'm your pet, remember?"

She shivered at the warmth of his breath against her earlobe. How could she forget? He was right. She could not afford to blow their cover. But touching him would have consequences for them both. With their runaway sexuality, Betters often fondled their pets in public. Though law enforcement frowned on outright sex or nudity, the outrageous behavior of Betters drew nothing more than a few curious onlookers.

NarrAy pressed her teeth into her lower lip as she raked her nails down Senth's abs. His stomach muscles flinched under the tickle in a way that made her want to scratch him everywhere.

He surprised her by scooting closer in the chair, sliding down until his cheek rested against her breast. She felt the heat of his breath on her skin where her nipple strained for release against the skimpy top.

She gritted her teeth. *It's an act, NarrAy. Only an act.* Her body wasn't in on the joke. Her clit twitched. She stretched out one leg, pressing her thighs together, and felt the seep of moisture. *He's making me so damn wet...*

Senth draped a hand over her closest leg. When he squeezed her thigh, she almost squealed. *Oh, you naughty boy. You are going to pay for this.* Twirling a length of his dark and lustrous hair around her fingers, she gave it a light tug. He grinned. She pulled harder, until his grin faded and his hand loosened. "Remember," she whispered, "who is in control here."

He patted her thigh.

"That's right."

She dragged fingertips along his jawline, down his chin, and along his throat, into the front of his shirt. When she rubbed a thumb across one of his nipples, she heard a catch in his breath.

You like that, do you? Well, well.

It had been four days since his last dose of Shackle. How much *could* he respond? She trailed her fingertips inside his shirt, beneath the waistband of his pants. His shoulders stiffened. *Wonder if anything else did?* She moved her hand along his side, up, and over his other nipple. When she brushed across it with her palm, it hardened.

Senth squirmed.

Oh yes. You like that. She cupped her hand under his chin and tilted back his head, bending to reach his mouth with hers. *Wait till you see what else I have planned for you.*

He parted his lips as he pressed up into her kiss.

So open. So willing. Oh, Senth. Her tongue explored his eager mouth. Heat pooled between her legs as she savored him.

"Ma'am. Ma'am?"

NarrAy surfaced into awareness as someone touched her shoulder.

One of the copbots offered her a notereader. "Your papers are in order, ma'am. Your bagbot seems to have malfunctioned. You should have it repaired."

"Oh." NarrAy stood, pulling her vest closed as best she could. "Thank you."

"You're free to go. One of the officers is arranging for your limo. Sorry to have kept you waiting."

"No problem."

The bagbots were turned on and activated. NarrAy went to the door without a backward glance.

"Bring those, will you, Tiger?" She headed for the exit. Neither said a word until they were seated in the limo and they'd activated the privacy screen. NarrAy sat back and sighed with relief. "I was petrified they were going to find your cloak."

"If those copbots had found it, I'd have had to prove I had rights to it or be arrested. To be safe, I left it on the ship. That officer who loaned you clothes is going to ship it home for me. The hotel is owned by the guild, so I can get anything I want by talking to the concierge."

"That was good thinking."

"Thanks."

After a few minutes Senth slid his hand under hers and squeezed it twice.

She turned to find his eyes blazing with passion.

NarrAy's breasts tingled as her pheromones let down. For the first time, she saw Senth really react. His nostrils flared. His eyes widened. When he reached for her, she climbed onto his lap, facing him, knees on the seat, arms around his neck. She claimed his mouth with hers, pulling him closer. She tangled her fingers in his hair, clutched and held him as they thrust their tongues against each other.

She pushed open his shirt and tasted his throat. "Tiger. I want you hot."

His hands heated her waist. The delicious warmth from them moved across her ribs.

She unlinked the chain holding her vest together and pulled it apart, freeing her breasts.

His mouth made an O of surprise and delight. When he reached for her and hesitated, a look of worship in his eyes, she cupped a hand under each breast and offered them to him.

"Touch me, Senth. Handle me. I want you to."

The fingers that worked such magic on impossible locks caressed her as if she were the most fragile of creatures instead of one who wanted to ravish him. His fingertips brushed softly across her nipples, his thumbs rubbing them with gentle upward strokes. The softness of his hands and his gentle touch made her want his touch everywhere. Time stopped while he fondled her with rapt adoration. Nothing existed outside the circle of his arms.

"You are so beautiful." He gazed into her eyes, amazement on his face. His touch grew more reverent. "I can't believe you're real. You...you are...an angel."

NarrAy's throat tightened. A tumult of emotion engulfed her. She cupped his hands and squeezed them before leaning forward to take his mouth. Beneath her thigh, she felt his lengthening erection.

"Oh, Tiger!" Her hand went to cover his cock at once. "Tiger, I am going to make love to you all night long." She kissed his smiling mouth.

The limo driver's voice interrupted. "We're here, ma'am."

A moan of frustrated desire left her throat. "No, wait. That's good." She scooted back enough to fasten the vest. "Once we're in our room, nothing will come between us."

They left the driver to bring the bagbots.

NarrAy and Senth hurried into the marble-floored lobby, sparing barely a glance at the high ceilings, palm trees, and indoor waterfall. Before they reached the front desk, however, a man called to Senth. They both turned as a strikingly handsome blond strode toward them.

"Who the hell is he?" she whispered to Senth. *And how soon can we get rid of him?*

Senth grinned. "Khyff! What are *you* doing here?" The two performed a complicated slap and slide of fingers and hands before gripping each other by the wrist.

A head taller than Senth, Khyff wore a dark suit that fit his muscular body perfectly.

"NarrAy." Senth took her hand. "This is Khyff Antonello, my big brother."

The one he'd told Encie about in the limo. A half brother. And one hot man. Almost as gorgeous as his baby brother. She did not offer her hand, nor did Khyff extend his. Instead he bowed in a sweet show of respect. He gave Senth's outfit a once-over but said nothing.

"What are you doing here, Khyff?"

"Saint-Cyr sent me. He gave me something for you." Khyff's smile showed pearly white teeth as flawless as the rest of him. "Senth, you won't believe it. I'm free!"

Senth slapped him on the back, and Khyff flinched and then glared at him.

"Oh, man, Bro. Sorry!" Senth clenched his hands. "'I forgot. Are you all right? I didn't mean to hurt you."

He rolled one shoulder. "I'm fine. A little tender." He spared a glance at NarrAy. "I'll tell you about it later. Right now I just need to give you something from your master. He made me promise to hand it to you the minute I saw you."

NarrAy folded her arms. *This could take all night.*

Khyff handed Senth a small box, which he opened and stared into with a look of horror.

NarrAy took Senth's arm. "What is it, Tiger?"

He snapped the box shut and handed it to Khyff. "Take it back. How could you do this to me?"

His brother held the box in front of him. "I don't have a choice, Senth, and neither do you. I owe him my freedom."

"I won't take that again." Senth took a step away. "Not now. Not ever."

Khyff lowered his head. "I'm sorry, Senth. Mr. Saint-Cyr's orders."

"What's in the box, Khyff?" NarrAy drew Senth toward her, already knowing the answer but unwilling to admit it.

The blond did not lift his gaze. "I'm sorry, ma'am. It's Shackle."

Chapter Twelve

Royal District, Royal Arms Hotel
Suite 1221

NarrAy inserted the tab of a credit bracelet into the delivery android's breastplate and keyed in the amount of his tip. When the door closed behind him, she shook her head.

"Is there anyone you don't have to tip?" She nudged Senth's bagbot with the toe of her heeled boot. "Maybe that's what's wrong with this guy. We didn't tip."

Senth and his brother probably hadn't heard her. They'd entered the room and faced off near the windows, two vigilant pagan deities—a blond god of war and a dark god of love—each pressing the other for supreme rights without a word spoken between them.

NarrAy sat down on the couch and unfastened her boots. "All right, guys. We're going to settle this my way, but first I'm going to change clothes." She arched her feet and pointed her toes skyward. "Oh, that's heavenly. Whoever made those boots should be shot."

She aimed the remote at her bot. "You gentlemen stay right here. I'll be half a minute."

Inside her room, she threw off the skimpy outfit and pulled on a long-sleeved sweater and pants. The brothers argued loudly enough to overhear. They might not look alike, but their voices were so identical, she could only tell who spoke because of context.

"I'm not spending the night in your room." That was Senth. "How did he know I'd be here anyway? I didn't even know myself until a few hours ago."

Yes, how did the Harbinger know?

"What makes you think I had the right to question him? I don't know how he knew it. But he was right, wasn't he?"

Guess I wouldn't ask either. NarrAy shivered. She brushed her hair and began putting it up.

"I'm not leaving."

"You don't have a choice. I'm supposed to keep you with me when you're not working."

NarrAy fastened a comb in her hair.

"I'm not a child! The whole time I've been on this job everyone's treated me like an adult. They've respected my abilities, Khyff. No one's questioned my decisions or told me what to do or thought I couldn't take care of myself. I've been needed! And I've done what I'm supposed to do. This job isn't over. They need me, and I'm not leaving until it's complete."

"I'm not telling you to leave. You just have to stay with me when you're not working."

"Like hell I will!"

You tell him, Tiger. NarrAy slipped on flat shoes.

"You're too young to be here with her."

She could picture Senth's outrage even before she heard the voice that went with it.

"Khyff, I do not need protecting, least of all by you!"

Silence. *That must have hurt.*

"I'd say protection is probably exactly what you need," Khyff answered levelly. "How much older is she than you? Ten years? Fifteen?"

Ouch! Closer to seven, you killjoy.

"What difference does her age make?"

That's right, my tiger. You tell 'im.

"Her age isn't the point. She's old enough to know better than to seduce a slave. It's against the law."

Senth's hearty chuckle made her smile.

"You're telling me, a professional thief, that I should worry about breaking the law?" Senth laughed again. "Maybe I want to be seduced, Khyff. Did you think of that?"

"Senth, don't do this. I know you want to stay with her, but she's a Better."

"So?"

"You're not yourself, Sen. Did you already have sex with her? What has she done to you?"

"I'm on Shackle, remember? What the fffffft do you think she did to me?"

Not as much as I'd have liked. NarrAy chuckled. *But that's about to change.*

"You're coming with me, Senth."

"No. I am not leaving with you, and that is final."

"And I am not going to tell that man I failed him!"

Poor Khyff. I wouldn't want to do that either. Neither brother had so much as said the Harbinger's name, but his authority hung over the entire conversation.

"You didn't fail anyone." The sympathy in Senth's tone sounded soothing. "Khyff, I haven't finished the job. He can't expect me to come back yet, and I don't care if you tell him that. I'll be facing him soon enough. I've always taken responsibility for my work. I don't need you to run interference between me and my Sen'dai. Stay out of it."

Sounds like they've about got this settled. NarrAy went into the adjacent bathroom and set the controls on the tub to fill at the level she wanted. She keyed in the temperature she preferred. *Mmm, this tub was made for lovers. Look at the size of this thing.*

She opened a vial of scented bubble bath and brought it to her nose. *Ooh, this smells like Senth, all woodsy and masculine and warm.* After checking the label to ensure it was pheromone friendly and wouldn't interfere with vaginal lubrication, she poured in the entire contents.

In the bedroom, she picked up a notereader from her bagbot, grabbed a pair of earrings, and opened the door. Clasping a pearl earring to one earlobe, she entered the room. Dressed like this, NarrAy became a woman instead of a sexy little creature.

Khyff's reaction to her altered upon sight.

"Sit down, gentlemen." She fastened the other earring. "We're going to decide this like adults."

"There is no decision to make." Khyff sat on the couch. "I'm authorized to take Senth with me."

"Any authority you might have is superseded by this." She tossed Khyff the reader.

He caught it in one hand. "What's this?"

"His master's contract with me. It says Senth is my responsibility until the job is complete and I'm satisfied with his performance. And I am far from satisfied." NarrAy set a hand on one hip. "Yet."

Khyff lifted his chin and threw his shoulders back.

The look on your face is priceless, O Blond One. So was the expression on Senth's, but he had the good sense not to let Khyff see it.

The elder Antonello brother thumbed through a few screens before standing. "Very well, Ms. Jorlan. Senth, I'll expect to see you when you finish this job."

"Sure, Khyff."

"I don't want this to come between us, Sen."

"No way it can, Bro."

Khyff picked up one of Senth's necklaces and smiled at him. It changed Khyff's entire demeanor, and she instantly warmed to him. "What's with all this, Sen? You trying to work my side of the street?"

Ah. NarrAy reexamined the god of war. *God of lust and anger, more like. Trying to protect little brother from your own past?* She gave Khyff a long, appraising look. *I'll bet your master made a damn fortune with you.*

"I'll explain the outfit later." Senth walked Khyff to the door, where they spoke for a few minutes.

NarrAy found the bar and poured them each a drink. When Senth returned, she handed one to him. "You like whiskey?"

"Sen'dai never lets me have alcohol." He held the shot glass up to the light. "Not much in here."

"It doesn't take much if it's good. Swallow it all at once." She tossed hers back, and he followed suit.

His eyes watered. "Wow." His voice came out a squeak.

Laughing, she took his glass and set it aside. She hooked one arm around his neck and pulled him down for a kiss. "You taste yummy."

He toyed with a necklace. "Thank you, mistress."

"You were wonderful, my tiger. I'm proud of the way you stood up to him." She placed her hands in his. "Now, it's time you and I had that talk about commitment."

* * *

Royal District, Royal Arms Hotel
Front Desk

"Your bill has already been settled, Mr. Antonello." The clerk handed a notereader to Khyff. "If you'll sign here, please. We've enjoyed having you with us, sir. Your groundcar is waiting as ordered."

"Thank you. Will you please see that the gentleman in Suite 1221 receives this envelope first thing in the morning?"

"Certainly, sir." The clerk accepted it with a polite nod of the head.

As Khyff exited the hotel, the chauffeur bowed and held the car door for him.

Saint-Cyr's pampering is going to ruin me for real work, but I sure like it.

"Starport, Mr. Antonello?"

"Yes, please." He lifted a hand as the driver began to close the door. Might as well get it over with and let the Harbinger know. "Is there a holophone on board?"

"Yes, sir, in the center console."

When Khyff nodded, the door shut. He leaned back on the leather seat, enjoying the smell of the new vehicle. Stalkos had hired a car like this to send him to certain clients. He hadn't appreciated it then, too caught up in dreading what waited for him on arrival.

He forced his shoulders to relax and spread his hands on his thighs. *Never have to go through that again.*

When the car pulled onto the street, Khyff turned on the holophone and spoke the number Saint-Cyr had made him memorize. A few minutes later, the Harbinger appeared on the seat across from him in holographic form. They might as well have been in the same room.

"So Senthys refused the Shackle, did he?"

"As you predicted, sir. But I argued with him, the way you instructed."

"Good lad." Saint-Cyr showed his teeth in what Khyff was learning was a grin. "And he wouldn't agree to stay with you."

"No, sir, and Ms. Jorlan cited contract terms and said she wasn't yet satisfied."

"Did she now? I'm impressed. What did your brother have to say for himself?"

"Senth said I could tell you whatever I liked because when he returns, he knows he'll face you anyway, and he's determined to accept responsibility for his actions."

"Excellent. The boy's become a man."

"Sir, I realize it's not my place to ask questions, so please tell me if it's inappropriate to worry about my brother over this."

"I can see why you were so popular at Stalkos's place, Khyffen. You know when to shut up, and you don't talk back." The Harbinger made a wave of dismissal. "Fact is, my young Senthys is ready to take wing. He's been scratching at the nest for months, especially since you came into his life. The way he took on the task of seeing to your freedom…" He shook his head. "I told him if he pulled off this job successfully, as his payment I'd buy out your contract and free you when he returned."

Khyff had thought he could no longer be shocked. He was wrong.

"And then Stalkos made a handy idiot of himself, and your freedom came with little help from me. Not that I wasn't prepared to do whatever I had to in order to get you out of there. I've been impressed with you since the day we met."

Khyff found his voice. "Thank you, sir."

"So as I said, I owe your brother, and he deserves a bit of trust on my part."

"Sir, he's alone with Ms. Jorlan. What if…?"

"Ah, 'what if,' indeed, Khyffen. I have no doubt about the likelihood of that what-if happening tonight." He smiled.

"Don't worry about your brother. He's in good hands. You come home, son."

The familial term tugged a smile onto Khyff's mouth. "Yes, sir. On my way."

* * *

Royal District, Royal Arms Hotel
Suite 1221

In her bedroom NarrAy sat on the edge of the bed, pulling Senth down alongside her. "Can you believe it, Tiger? Alone at last."

"Thank you for pulling rank on Khyff like that."

"Couldn't let you get away from me that easily, now could I?" When he smiled, she curled the fingers of one hand between his and caressed the back of his hand with the other. She walked her fingertips up his wrist, across a wide leather bracer with three buckles. "We really dressed you up for this part, didn't we?" She fingered one of his necklaces.

"It was fun." He cupped the beringed fingers of his free hand around hers. The chains and bangles at his wrist glinted. "You wouldn't believe the jealous stares I got from men at the starport."

"You liked that?"

He drew her hand to his lips and kissed her palm. "I liked the fact that they knew I was yours."

"Oh, Senth! That is the sweetest thing anyone's ever said to me." She reined in her emotions, refusing to let them trigger her pheromones. *Have to cool down. Have to talk to him. Control yourself, NarrAy. Breathe.* She inhaled deeply. "You have beautiful hands, Senth. You could model."

He touched her chin, bringing her gaze to his. The catlike pupils had widened. "Everything about you is beautiful, NarrAy."

She felt herself losing control—wanted to lose it—wanted to let her body make decisions for her. So much easier to let her pheromones do the thinking.

No. She stiffened her back and let go of his hand. *This is too important. He is too important.*

"What is it?" He leaned a hand on the bed.

"Senth, so far I've been the one in charge in this relationship. However I've wanted it is how you've had to give it."

"We agreed on that when you hired me, NarrAy. You were in charge."

"Professionally, yes." She dipped her head in admittance. "And I also had other things in mind from the moment I saw you. Which you've discovered."

"Yes." Senth made a purring growl that sent a shiver of excitement over her. "I have no problem with that either." He leaned over to set his nose against her cheek and nudged her like a kitten wanting to be petted. "I like it."

Her heart raced. Another touch and she'd crest. *Oh, Senth.* She positioned herself facing him, one leg folded beneath her. "Until now that's been all right. I enjoyed playing with you. But now…"

"Oh." He drew back. "I see. I thought you wanted me."

He started to rise.

"No! I mean, yes. Yes, I do. I want you." She dared a touch on his arm, where his skin was covered. Less risk of bonding, of throwing her over the edge of control.

His wounded look faded. "You're not through with me, then?"

"No, Senth, I never want to be through with you. You asked if I wanted to wait two years for you." NarrAy set a hand over her heart to keep herself from touching him. "I want you to know that I will."

His expression went from confused to pleased to worried. "We don't have to wait that long for...this." He gestured between them. "Un-unless you want to."

She swallowed, forced herself to take a breath. "Not unless you do, Senth. I want you to be ready."

"Oh, I'm ready, all right." He chuckled. "My Sen'dai told me there were terrible withdrawal symptoms from Shackle. Just now, at the door, Khyff told me that was all a lie. I hope he doesn't get in trouble for saying so. For the first time in my life, my body is in *my* control."

So is mine. She smiled. Being able to say no had never been a factor with any of her lovers. She hadn't cared. But Senth was different.

"I need you to know this, Senth. However long it takes, whatever it costs us, I only want to be with you. When you can give yourself to me freely, I'll be waiting for you."

The awe on his face sent a surge of unexpected warmth through her.

"NarrAy." He stroked his fingers down her face, leaving

a trail of heat. "I've always been free to give you my heart." He ran a finger across her lips. "It's yours. So is the rest of me. Forever."

The innocent Senth, with all his purity, his adorable charm, his beauty—hers. "Oh, Senth, yes. Yes. I want you forever." She put herself in his arms.

Senth knew the moment NarrAy came into his arms that she had yielded to him. This was so different from before, when she'd told him what to do. Guided him. Put his hands where she wanted them.

He dragged her up close to him, body to body, mouth to mouth, as he leaned back onto the bed.

"You smell so good." He bent over her, burying his face against her throat. He inhaled her scent. "Mmm, vanilla and sugar cookies and hot, melted butter."

Her soft fingers brushed back his hair. "That's my pheromones. It's called cresting. It happens when I'm turned on."

"I've smelled it before. In the elevator on the ship."

"Mmm."

"And our cabin."

"Yes." She reached up and touched his face. "Pheromones are in all my body fluids: blood, sweat, and tears. When I'm hot, they're part of the lubricant in my vagina. That's the strongest source of my pheromones. But what you smell is from all of me."

He kissed her fingers, drew one into his mouth, and sucked on it like candy. She closed her eyes, tilting her head back as she sighed.

"You like that." He licked her fingers. She moaned again. "And that too."

"Your tongue." She rubbed the tip of it. "You have a cat's tongue. All rough and scratchy. I love it. I love your cat's eyes and your fangs and your whole body. I love everything about you."

"I love you."

Her astonishment reflected his.

She brought both hands to his face and held him. "I love you too, Senth."

He propped himself on one elbow. "NarrAy?"

"Yes, my tiger?" She ran her hand across his chest.

"Will you teach me how to please you? This is my first time at sex."

Her sassy smile said she knew that. "You're doing just fine, Tiger."

"But I haven't had...you know, any kind of sex." He licked his lips. She was watching him, waiting for something—he didn't know what. He quieted himself, working up the courage to continue.

The backs of her fingers cooled his cheek. "You've played with yourself, haven't you?"

He shook his head. "I tried. It didn't do any good. On Shackle, I couldn't get hard."

"So you've never had an orgasm?"

He shook his head.

"Oh my." She set a hand over her heart. "Oh, Senth! I

feel so privileged."

"You do?"

"This is so special to you. To me. To us."

The shared wonder on NarrAy's face told him more of her love than any words.

"I don't know what it is a man does. On the streets, when Khyff…um… I was curious and I tried to watch him, but he doesn't let much show. I know there's this ache inside me and it's about to *kill* me, but I don't—you know. Oh fffffft! How do I get started and everything?"

"Oh, Tiger."

Uh-oh, she's got that "how cute" expression on her face. Is that good…or bad?

"So, um, NarrAy. Could you tell me what to do? Show me, maybe?"

When will I ever have a more perfect lover? Senth will respond to my pheromones without comparing me to other lovers or having expectations I can never meet. Far from a detriment, his virginity made Senth even more precious to her.

"I would love to." NarrAy pushed herself off the bed and held out her hands. "Come with me, pet. I think it's time I rewarded my tiger with a nice warm bubble bath." Taking him by the hand, she led him into the bathroom. "Take off your shoes and socks." NarrAy kicked off hers, unfastened her hair, and shook it loose. "No. Nothing else."

Senth had been unfastening his shirt.

"I want to do that for you."

His cheeks darkened in that innocent blush she found so endearing. *I wonder how long he'll keep that around me?* NarrAy crossed her arms and pulled off her sweater, then tossed it aside. *I'm betting it won't be long.* Her breasts tingled with the crest of pheromones. Senth's rapt gaze on them added to the feeling of fullness as her nipples stiffened to rigid points. She longed for his touch to ease them.

She unfastened the waistband of her pants and let them drop.

He bit into his lower lip, a big grin on his face. "You were naked under all those clothes."

She giggled. "I didn't want to waste any time once your brother left."

He dropped his gaze only for a second. "You weren't surprised when I wouldn't leave with him."

"I was counting on it." She went to stand in front of him. "Finding out you're a complete virgin—that's a surprise. A pleasant one. One I'm never going to forget."

When he touched her, she arched against his hand.

"You're so soft."

"Mmm." NarrAy closed her eyes briefly as he cupped her breasts. He moved his hands across them slowly, as if memorizing their contours. When he rubbed his palms across her hard nipples, she gasped in delight. "Oh, I like that, Senth."

"Your breasts are beautiful, NarrAy. All of you is beautiful."

She brought her hands under his. "I'm yours to touch, Senth. All of me. Before the night is through, I want you to touch every single part of me." The thought of that evoked another crest, and she and Senth shivered at the same time.

He made a little sound in his throat, like a growl crossed with a cry. Her inner muscles clenched.

NarrAy took his hands, brought them to her mouth, and kissed his knuckles. "Let's get into the water." She stopped him from removing his shirt. "No. Not yet. I want you fully dressed for a while."

"In the water?"

"Yes. It will help slow me down."

He grinned. "What if I don't want you to slow down?"

She swatted him playfully on the rear and squeezed his butt cheek. "I'm in charge this time. Next time, you get to be the boss. Now get in the water."

"Yes, mistress." He stepped into the tub, his smile sparking with mischief.

"You can keep calling me that, you naughty boy. I may let you come first if you do."

"Ooh, nice reward!" Senth sat and leaned back against the wall.

Climbing into the tub, she faced him and put her knees on either side of his hips. The water rose to just below her breasts. She picked up a large natural sponge and dipped it in the soapy water before handing it to him.

"Bathe me, Tiger. Make sure you don't miss anything." She placed her hands on the edges of the wide tub.

He set about thoroughly obeying her.

His exotic gaze fastened on her as he worked. Seeing him

between her thighs, all wet, so serious about pleasing her and making her happy, shot heat through her. The open white shirt clung to his skin, showing off his abs and the definition of his arms. Droplets of water sparkled on the array of necklaces and darkened the leather bracer on his wrist. Surely Senth was a fantastic creature from an erotic dream, a man conjured up from too many nights with no one in her bed, a phantasm of lust made flesh.

She relished the feel of the sponge against her skin as he worked his way down from her shoulders, across her breasts. The trickle of warm water and the pressure of his hands delighted. She gasped as the sponge brushed between her legs.

"Did I hurt you?" Concern knit his brow.

She placed her hand over his. "No," she whispered. "Good."

He raised both brows. Experimentally he slid his fingers between her labia. "You feel wet here. Not from the water. It's thicker."

One of the advantages of being a Better. Only the fact that he was fully dressed kept her from taking him inside her. "When I'm aroused." She nodded jerkily. "Hot."

"Touching you here makes you hot?" Gently he wiggled his fingers and smiled at her reaction.

She moved his hand. "My turn."

"For...?"

"To bathe you." She took the sponge.

"But, mistress, I never got to wash your legs."

"You can wash those later, Tiger. Any more of those

magic fingers of yours and you won't be the one coming first."

He grinned at her. "I don't really care, you know."

"I do." She tapped his nose with the sponge, leaving bubbles. She laughed and tried to wipe them off but left more in their place.

Senth shook his head and tried blowing them off, to no avail.

"Here, let me." NarrAy rose on her knees and reached for a towel. She squealed as the slippery bottom of the tub made her fall against Senth's chest, splashing water onto the floor. Holding on to him to keep her head above water, she ended up taking Senth with her. She came up sputtering, wiping at her eyes.

Soapy water dripped down Senth's face as he sat up, his hair coated with bubbles. He slicked it back. "You're all bubbly."

"So are you." NarrAy scooped up a handful of bubbles and arranged them on his head in a crown shape. "King Senth."

"Have to make one for you, then. Here." He piled on the bubbles. "Okay. That looks right, but it needs a few jewels." He pulled off a necklace and draped it over her hair. "There, a lovely crown for my queen."

When she made a mock bow to him, the necklace slipped off and hung on the end of her nose. Laughter burst from both of them.

He hung the necklace around her neck and wiped at the bubbles on her nose. He brushed both hands across her face and leaned back. "There. That's better."

NarrAy took Senth's face between her palms. His sincerity and trust made her even more naked before him.

"NarrAy." He caressed her bare back. "I love you."

All the passion she'd felt for this man flooded her at once, and her pheromones kicked down all resistance to desire.

Senth's pupils dilated so fast, his eye color went instantly to black. Nostrils flaring, he bared his fangs and tugged her down against him.

At the scrape of his tongue on her throat, she clutched the edges of the tub and threw back her head. He laved her skin and pushed her back from him to capture one nipple between his teeth.

She splayed a hand behind his head and clutched him against her. His scratchy tongue wrenched a sob from her throat. Exquisite rawness. Her clit twitched and throbbed.

"I have to have you. Now." NarrAy reached beneath her, fumbling in the water for the fly of Senth's pants. Her palm found his erection, felt it jerk when she touched him. "I need you inside me, Senth, now."

He helped her, both of them hurrying to unfasten his wet trousers. She pushed them down far enough to straddle him.

She wrapped her hand around his rigid length; her fingertips could not meet. Rising over him, she placed the tip of his shaft at her entrance. NarrAy seized his mouth with hers and plunged her tongue inside. She impaled herself on his cock.

Senth's cry of pleasure escaped into her mouth as she took him.

She wrapped her arms around his neck, clung to his mouth with hers, and rocked her hips forward to bring his fullness all the way into her. She moved aside to let him breathe, heard his cry of lust as she pushed her way down, taking every bit of his hard male heat inside. He filled her, stretched her, and made her knees widen to accept him.

When his eyes rolled back, NarrAy licked her lips with pleasure.

A deep rumble sounded in his chest.

She pushed Senth back against the tub and moved up the hard length of his cock. At the top, she paused. He watched her, his burning gaze as powerful as a touch.

When she slid down his rigid shaft, he cried out—the howl of a beast, hungry and wild.

"Now you're going to come for me, my tiger."

She made frantic circles with her hips. Her body hummed with desire as Senth writhed beneath her, lost in bliss. Seeing his pleasure increased her own.

Senth braced against the sides of the tub and thrust up against her, his thighs parting her legs as he drove into her.

Water sloshed over them, wet slapping noises mingling with their panting cries as they both plunged into the depths of ecstasy.

Chapter Thirteen

Starport District
Empire Central Starport

Killing time before boarding the sleepliner back to Kelthia, Khyff ambled along the length of the secured area of the port. He'd already checked out the entryways and ramps to the ship and acquainted himself with landmarks surrounding the area, so he wouldn't get lost.

He caught sight of his reflection in the shop windows as he strolled past. Saint-Cyr had tricked him out in new clothes, treating him empire-class all the way. Smoothing a hand down the finest coat he'd ever worn, he smiled at his image. Shaking his head at his vanity, Khyff continued along the concourse.

He passed a children's store, another for sporting goods, and one with an android hawking duty-free liquor imported from the far side of the empire. Across from him, an elderly cyborg with metallic arms demonstrated restored weapons from the Badledeerin War. He steered clear of a shop filled with Androg-designed sex toys. Double-ended phalluses, jointed female couplers, and their various combinations held no novelty for him.

Khyff stopped in front of a jewelry store displaying Kyrenie fire crystals ranging from clear to the finest-quality ice blue.

The pictures in the background showed the Great Kyrenie Desert stretching from horizon to horizon. A full two-thirds of the world, its golden landscape broken and pocked by black craters. Shallow pits less deep than the height of a man, quarried in an instant by firestorms.

No one had ever seen a firestorm up close. No one had filmed one of the instantaneous orbs of lightning that melted sand and fused it into fire crystal. The electromagnetic pulse unleashed by a firestorm disrupted all power around it.

But as soon as a pit cooled enough to enter, miners went in after the crystals. Miners younger than age ten. Older slaves could not stand up inside the mines. Older slaves too often fainted from the heat.

Khyff pressed his fingers against the glass of the window and remembered the scrape of jagged crystals splitting open his scalp. The blinding sting of stitches in raw skin. It was the only time anyone had held him as a child, to keep him from thrashing too hard while they had sewn him up. They didn't waste anesthetics on a slave. He winced at the memory of cramps in his neck, back, and legs from long hours hunched over or squatting, laboring in the dim light reflected from uncut gems. The burn in his arms from reaching overhead with a drill, sweat stinging his eyes behind dirty goggles.

Sometimes when he closed his eyes at night, he could still smell the sweat of the other kids, feel the grit on the floor where they slept in a huddle. They took turns being at the center, so everyone got a chance to be warm once in a while. Even now, when he showered, he washed and rinsed again and again, trying to erase the memory of the black crust of dirt and sand in every pore.

Khyff turned and walked past a bar without slowing. The storefront was genteel enough, but adult patrons could enter stand-up booths in the back and choose any of a dozen or more slakes for a few minutes' mouth-pleasure. Stark black-and-white symbols on the door showed it also catered to travelers desiring fetishes he preferred not to contemplate.

An identical facility across the lobby had icons in one window that meant they rented beds. In the other window sat a pair of scantily dressed twin boys younger than Senth. Just barely legal.

Khyff strode in the other direction, trying to put distance between himself and his memories.

A light in the window of a bookshop drew his attention, and he stepped into a recessed foyer in front of a display of open volumes. He'd learned to read schematics when he worked jump-port maintenance at age eight but, aside from that, had no schooling until prison.

His last year there, a guard had taken it on himself to teach Khyff letters and numbers and enough words to read two complete children's books. The man had shown him how to apply for parole and coached him until he'd gained a hearing and then release.

Into Stalkos's custody. Stalkos, who had laughed at the idea of an educated slake. Stalkos, who had addicted him to Thrust and kept him chained for days on end.

He shook his head, forcing back that memory. *You're*

free, Khyff. Don't think about him.

The reading lessons had been less than a year ago, but Khyff could no longer recognize even one word on the pages showing in the window.

When NarrAy tossed that notereader at me, I thought I'd die. What's Saint-Cyr going to say when he finds out I have no idea what it said?

Movement reflected in the glass, but the warning came too late.

Khyff ducked. The syringe forced against his neck connected and stung. The reflection distorted into darkness.

Firm hands supported him when he fell.

* * *

Royal District, Royal Arms Hotel
Suite 1221
Wintresq 15

Senth woke without opening his eyes, content in the warm luxury of NarrAy's arms. She lay behind him in bed. Her body fit perfectly, all along his length.

He snuggled into the pillow and lifted his lashes. The sodden heap of his discarded clothes rested on the tiled bathroom floor. A trail of necklaces and rings lay scattered across the carpet, hastily discarded on the way to the bed.

Cool morning air chilled his skin, and Senth twisted toward NarrAy, reaching for the sheet they'd cast off during their love play a few hours ago. He stopped at the sight of her bare breasts.

He caressed them with his fingers, remembering the feel of them on his tongue. The wide, dark area that pebbled when he aroused her was now smooth and plump. When the tip of her nipple stiffened under his touch, a spike of hot pleasure pierced his groin, jerking his cock to throbbing life.

He rose above her body, moved to ease into position between her thighs.

She did not stir.

Senth spread the fingers of one hand between her legs. Wet and sticky evidence of the night's lovemaking still drenched her labia. He pushed his cock between her swollen nether lips and paused inside the moist mouth of her heat.

NarrAy gasped. Her eyes fluttered open and her gaze focused on his. "Tiger…" She opened her thighs for him.

Hands beneath her hips, he drew her toward him, up the length of his hard cock.

Her arms went wide; her fingers clutched the bedclothes. Eyes rolling back in her head, NarrAy arched her neck and opened her mouth in a soundless cry of desire.

Senth nudged against her and gave one small thrust. He withdrew the full length of his shaft and plunged it into her again, treasuring her magnificent passion.

NarrAy tossed her head, moaning, hoarse from so many pleasured cries during the night.

Her vagina quivered all around his cock. Pulsed, throbbed. Sucked like a hungry mouth. He pulled out and slammed back into her.

All through the night NarrAy had taught him how to

appease both her lust and his, and he had not wanted to sleep until he'd learned every lesson.

Senth stopped before the head of his shaft left her slick pussy lips. He pressed the heel of his palm over her mons and rubbed it across the hard nub of her clitoris.

Eyes squeezed shut, she panted. "Please… Senth, Tiger, please. Beg you!"

But did she beg him to stop? Or give her more?

He lifted her hips and rocked into her.

A frenzied and rough cry wrenched from her throat.

"I love you!"

Senth could not tell whether his mouth had formed the words or hers. It was simply the truth.

Where their bodies joined, straight, dark pubic hair met golden brown curls. He brought NarrAy's legs to his shoulders and held them there, turning her inner grip on his cock into a glorious vise of heat.

With a shout of joy, Senth thrust once, twice, and then pumped into her and emptied himself into her wet sheath.

* * *

The chill of a stone floor against his cheek jerked Khyff awake. He lay flat on his stomach, hands crossed and bound behind him. The memory of his capture swept over him with humbling clarity.

Careless! Never turn your back on the street. Never!

He tested his bonds. Wide leather cuffs linked his wrists. Khyff pushed himself to his knees and took stock of his situation. Steel bars, stone passageway, low-level lighting, no windows. No way to tell the time of day. The cell had a metal cot suspended from the wall by chains, but no mattress. Metal rings and a leather collar hung on the opposite wall; against the third sat a metal sink and toilet.

Great. All the comforts of prison. Where the hell am I? He walked back through every word the Harbinger had said, searching for any clue. *Finally free and the first job you get lands you here. Damn it, Khyff. Now what have you done?*

His thoughts shrank from the possibility that Stalkos had arranged this side trip. Worse yet, that Saint-Cyr might abandon him.

Down the passageway, metal hinges shrieked. Footsteps echoed: three people. Khyff lowered his head enough to shield his face but still see. A guard uniformed in black unlocked the cell. The bars clanged open, and three sets of boots entered.

Even without a glimpse of her face, Khyff had seen enough pictures of the empress to recognize her. Medals covered the scarlet sash across her chest.

Khyff bit back the string of curses that hurried to mind. *What the hell did Saint-Cyr get me into?*

One guard raised a leather quirt. "Eyes down before the Conqueror!"

He had not lifted them, but Khyff lowered his head more. When the guards yanked him to his feet between them, he made no move to resist.

Stalkos had taught him one lesson well. Survival outweighed pride.

The guards shoved him against the wall so hard, it robbed him of breath. They separated Khyff's bound hands and refastened them to heavy rings at his sides. His fingers tingled from blood rushing back to them. Metal cuffs clamped around his ankles.

Ignoring his gasps for air, the one on his right gripped him by the throat and shoved back Khyff's head while the other buckled a leather collar around his neck. It trapped him against the wall like a bug pinned to a board.

"Not too tight, gentlemen." The Conqueror folded both hands in front of her, a notereader in one. "No need to hurt him. You may leave us."

The guards backed out of the cell and clanged the bars shut.

"You may look at me." The empress moved up close to him.

Growing up, Khyff had seen newscasts of the Conqueror but never perceived her as a flesh-and-blood woman until now. Her pictures didn't show how much silver laced her hair or the depth of her quiet beauty, more from presence than perfection. Her face was angular; her nose, narrow. Khyff knew all about mouths, and Destoiya's showed no hint of her legendary ruthlessness, but her eyes…her eyes bore all the metallic glory of a stormy, threatening sky.

"So you're Khyffen Antoncllo." She gestured with the reader. "From the length of this dossier, it's hard to believe you're so young. When were you born?"

"Birit 82, 4642, Your Majesty."

"Not even twenty-one." She cast him a doubtful look,

then shook her head and perused the notereader. "Because you intrigue me, Khyffen, you may refer to me informally as 'Majesty' unless I direct you otherwise. You may answer my questions without fear of reprisal." She looked at him. "Is that clear?"

Intrigue her? Khyff hid disbelief behind lowered lashes. "Yes, Majesty."

"Your dossier says you were abandoned in a day-care facility at the starport on Felidae. Hmm." She gave him a sympathetic glance. "You were four. Mother's whereabouts unknown. No father listed on your birth certificate. When no one claimed you, you were handed over to slavers. You've been on your own since?"

"Yes, Majesty."

"It doesn't say what the slavers did with you that first year. Care to tell me?"

"They tried adopting us out when we first got there."

"Us?"

What is she up to with these questions? "Five and younger, Majesty."

"I see."

He waited, not knowing what else to say.

"And no one wanted you?"

Blunt and cold, but fact. When he swallowed, the leather collar chafed. "I was human."

"They left you on Felidae?"

"Yes, Majesty."

"That was foolish of them. On Tarth you'd have been

adopted right away. I have your picture here. You were a beautiful little boy." Destoiya sent an exploratory gaze down his length. "You're a gorgeous man. I imagine you get plenty of attention now."

Don't let it go to your head, Khyff. He bit the inside of his cheek. *She can see what you're good for; that's all.*

"You worked the Kyrenie firestorm mines from age five to eight, then the jump ports on Porosen'la until you were thirteen." She paused. "Why didn't they keep you in the mines?"

"I got too tall, Majesty."

"And the ports?"

"Too tall for them too."

"Hmm. I have a feeling you fought them too hard to be worth the trouble. Did they molest you in the ports too or just the mines?"

Khyff focused on the iron bars, more aware of his tight bonds than his own breath.

"Both, I see. Don't worry; it's not written on your face. I have experience with pretty young men. Sad to say, Khyffen, your story isn't the first."

Before now, only the Harbinger had ever used his full first name, but many called him *pretty*, a vile word that haunted his memories.

"Your first slave master on Tarth licensed you as a slake at fourteen. The legal age is fifteen." Destoiya studied the reader a moment before looking over at him. "You might like to know this. According to my assistant's notes, the man is in prison. A sting operation caught him doing the same thing."

Don't let this woman play you, Khyff. Think! What does she want?

"Should I assume he prostituted you even before you were fourteen?"

Khyff nodded, his neck rubbing against the collar.

"You'd been passed to seven more masters by the time you were sixteen. They all cited attitude and aggression. You attacked one of your masters, and when arrested, you reported him for abuse and claimed self-defense. He later lost his license when other slaves reported the same thing. I don't suppose you were too popular with slave masters, were you?"

Don't let her make you hope. Hope can break your soul.
"No, Majesty."

"You were sold twice more before being shipped off world, where you worked for one month before being arrested for assault, battery, theft, and violating your license. You spent three years in prison, then were returned to prostitution because the time you spent in jail and on probation doesn't count toward your freedom." She tapped a finger on the reader. "By law anyone enslaved prior to age five must be freed at twenty. You would have been freed this year on your birthday if you'd behaved yourself. Did you know that?"

"All too well, Majesty."

"About a tradestandard month ago, one of your clients reunited you with the half brother you thought had died at birth."

It's Senth. Khyff stilled his body, praying Destoiya could not hear the sudden pounding of his heart. He felt it in his ears. *Or it's NarrAy. Breathe, slake! Now you know what she wants. Just like prison. No slips. Give her the face. Nothing behind it. Pure face. Let her tell you what she knows.*

"You recently gained your freedom through court action due to another run-in with a slave master." The Conqueror ran a finger down the reader's front. "How accurate is all this?"

"Completely, Majesty."

"Your brother and a Better broke into a government building. Did you know that?"

Khyff waited, chest aching from a held breath.

"We didn't catch them."

Relief and gratitude tumbled together in his mind, but he fought not to let one glimmer of emotion make it to his eyes. He forced air into his lungs, slow, easy, hiding the terror for Senth behind a face devoid of passion.

"The Better is known as NarrAy Jorlan. She's involved in what a few rebels frivolously call 'the resistance.' Were you aware your brother consorted with enemies of the empire?"

"I'm sure my brother is innocent, Majesty."

"Hmm. So you say." She tucked the reader in a pocket. "You can see I already know quite a bit, Khyffen, so it isn't going to matter if you tell me a little more."

Here we go. He wet his lips. *Would she torture him herself? Or bring back the guards? Did Senth really get away? I was tortured in prison. If I had to, I…*

Her gentle touch scattered his thoughts. She was unfastening the collar.

"There. More comfortable?" She cupped his chin and

directed his face toward her.

Her eyes were the color of an ice-laden storm in winter and equally dangerous. All at once their coolness warmed. A smile crossed her face.

"Why did your masters sell you off so many times, Khyffen? You're attractive enough to please any slaver's clientele."

She turned his face to one side, then the other. She stepped back and, with a quick motion, tore open his shirt and pushed it aside to survey him.

He suppressed a shudder. *Come on, slake! Don't shame out now. They used to put you on display in less than this at work every day.*

"You have a magnificent body." The empress pulled a tuft of his chest hair between her fingers. "Soft, not coarse. Mmm, I like that. Tell me, Khyffen. Are you this tan all over?" She opened his trousers and pushed them down his hips to his knees. "This is nice. Nothing underneath."

Ice jabbed into his heart. *Stop it, Khyff! Toughen up. This is for Senth. It's not like you've never been raped.*

Destoiya spread her warm hands across Khyff's bared chest and dragged them down his abs, slowing to trace their defined shape with her fingertips before trailing down the path of hair to his groin. She closed one hand around his cock.

His limp cock.

The empress glanced down, then back into his eyes. "You don't like being touched." She let go of his penis and leaned into him, angling his face toward her. "Or being forced."

He closed his eyes. Her warm breath heated his skin, and an answering heat stirred inside him. *Stop it, slake. Just because she makes you want it doesn't mean it's not rape. Don't let her get to you.*

"Or do you hate being touched"—she brushed her lips across his—"because your master sold you not to women, but to men?"

Khyff fought his instant reaction of anguish and fury, but she caught it. Now that she knew what he hated most, she'd use it to break him. He cringed inside.

Destoiya soothed him with a caress of his cheek. "He wasted you, Khyffen. It's obvious you were meant for women only."

She drew his head down to capture his mouth, and any resistance he'd thought to offer disintegrated. His mind insisted on denial, but his body responded to the onslaught of her tongue. The tangy scent of her arousal filled his nostrils.

His cock hardened. Lifted. His testicles tightened.

Both male and female clients had tied him like this. Forced him to accept their will. They had paid his master— but they'd *raped* him. Destoiya made it sweet fire.

The final, lingering dregs of Thrust coerced him into enjoying the heat coursing through his body. When she pressed one thigh against his cock, he arched into her touch. So erotic—bound, helpless to forbid anything. She was making him want what she did to him.

Destoiya moved back and smiled with satisfaction. "Guards!"

They hurried into the cell.

Khyff's heart cried out, knowing what they'd do to him. He stood there, manacled and helpless, half stripped. Exposed. Erect.

"Remove his bonds." The Conqueror's heavy-lidded gaze returned over Khyff. "Take him to the Stable. Let him bathe and dress himself in private."

Her next words heated his blood and rocked him to the core.

"And then bring him to me."

Chapter Fourteen

Royal District, Royal Arms Hotel
Suite 1221

NarrAy tipped the hotel android and tucked the note he'd delivered into the pocket of her robe. "Senth?" She walked back into the bedroom, heard water running, and poked her head inside the bathroom. Steam frosted the glass-enclosed shower. "Senth, honey, there's a—Whoa!"

Senth was pressed against the glass from his firm buttocks all the way up to his shoulders.

NarrAy gulped against a rush of pheromones. "Uh, there's a…a note."

"What?" Senth stepped away from the glass and came to the opening, both hands in his soapy hair. His thick cock swayed with the movement as he worked lather into his scalp. "I couldn't hear you, sweetie."

Shampoo bubbles trickled down his upraised arms, onto his shoulders, and down across his chest. Senth's nose wriggled. He'd done that several times during the night, inhaling her scent. It shot a tinge of warmth from her nipples down to her clit.

NarrAy let out a long sigh. *What is it about bubbles, a little-boy smile, and a great big dick that I find so endearing?* She cast off her robe and stepped into the shower, right into Senth's slippery, soapy, slick, sexy, and open arms.

* * *

Senth initiated the holophone link to Saint-Cyr from a conference room on the third floor of the hotel, far from NarrAy's presence and the hard-on she always inspired. When a chime announced his Sen'dai was at last online, Senth stood.

Saint-Cyr's image sparkled into being before him.

He made a deep bow. "Good morning, Sen'dai."

"You're late, Senthys."

Late? For what?

The Harbinger motioned with one hand. "Turn around, slowly. I want to look at you."

Uh-oh. Senth obeyed. *Where's this going?*

"So this is what a thief looks like who thinks he's independent of his Sen'dai."

"Sir?"

"Don't play coy with me, Senthys." Saint-Cyr seated himself. The background of the room did not appear, nor the chair he used. His image floated. "Sit down. We need to talk."

"Yes, sir." He pulled a chair away from the table and plunked himself in it.

"And sit up straight."

Senth bristled, but he straightened in the chair.

"Now what is this about Ms. Jorlan not being satisfied?"

She seemed pretty satisfied when I left the room. Senth masked a grin with a cough. "She discovered that the item we recovered indicated a related item with more significance."

The Harbinger's perfect white teeth showed in a wide smile, and he nodded. "Well put, son. I understand. You're staying with her until the new item is recovered, then?"

"Yes, sir."

"Guild protocols require additional payment for extended services. Is she aware of that?"

"Yes, sir."

"And what is the nature of these extended services, Senthys?" He paused. "Anything else I should bill her for?"

Senth's cheeks burned. He cleared his throat. "Nothing billable, Sen'dai."

The Harbinger chuckled throatily. "She should be glad I don't charge the way Stalkos does, son. I have a feeling I'd get rich off you if I did."

What's that supposed to mean? The burn in his cheeks turned to flame. He turned his head. "I found out Khyff checked out last night, sir. Did you send for him?"

"No need to keep him there if he isn't babysitting."

Senth's mouth popped open. "Babysitting!"

"Just a phrase, Senthys. Think nothing of it. I'm well aware you're a man now."

You don't know the half. "Yes, sir."

"What equipment do you need?"

"Only codes, sir."

"Consider it done. See the concierge when you leave." He added, "That *is* a billable expense, by the way. And let me know if you do anything else that we should charge for. Personal work, that sort of thing."

Senth cleared his throat. "Of course, Sen'dai."

"Have a safe trip. Oh, and Senthys." He smiled. "Good job, son. See you at home. I owe you one."

* * *

Namalia District

Imperial Armada Military Storage and Weigh Facility Tarth-F

"Shh… Don't argue." NarrAy kissed Senth to quiet him.

She had him up against the wall in a shadow-filled alley near the storage facility, a hand on either side of his head, her legs between his outspread ones. His stance put his mouth a little lower than hers. His lips were swollen and dark from kissing—among other things.

"I don't care what your services cost. My time with you was more than worth every drak I paid for the late-checkout fee at the hotel and whatever else Saint-Cyr wants to charge me. We couldn't come here until nightfall, and I didn't want to waste half a day when I could spend it in bed with you."

He circled her waist with both arms and pulled her against him, lifting his mouth to hers. His rigid cock pressed against her thigh. Once un-Shackled, her tiger knew no bounds. He'd been teasing her for hours and following through with the stamina of a true wildcat. No man had ever worn her out before.

"You know, Tiger, from the moment I saw you, I wanted you."

He nipped her chin with his teeth. "You did not. You thought I was a child."

"That was a test."

He looked skyward. "Sure."

"It was. You can ask Brox."

Senth regarded her for a moment, head tilted back. "Hmm."

"You don't believe me?" She dragged her fingertip across the edges of his teeth. He bit her finger, held it tightly. Low in his throat, he growled. She crested at once, gasping with the sudden heat of arousal.

Senth chuckled, released her, and set his head back against the wall. He watched her through lowered lashes. His nose wriggled. "You smell good."

"I do?"

"Like fresh-baked cookies. I like making you hot. It's so easy."

She drew back. "I am not easy."

"What?" Senth straightened. "I didn't mean to be insulting."

NarrAy frowned at him.

"I'm sorry, sweetie." He gave her his innocent smile.

"Forgive me?"

She kissed him. "Of course."

"It's shift change." He nodded toward the storage building behind her. "Just you and me this time, so we've got to be extra careful. I wish you didn't have to go with me."

"I'll be careful."

"Oh, I know." Senth pushed away from the wall and brushed himself off. "I just don't want you to lose control in there. I'd hate for one of the guards to smell you and come looking."

She blinked. "Excuse me?"

He turned both hands up. "What did I say now?"

"Smell me?" she prompted.

"Well, I know I can smell you when you're hot. I don't want anybody else to; that's all."

She tugged her clothes into place. "Senth, it's not like I can't control myself. I only crest when I'm alone with you."

"Oh, so you *can* control it?"

"Of course I can."

He grinned. "Like you did on the ship out from Kelthia in the elevator? And then in your bedroom?"

"That was different."

"Oh. What about the *Vandal* and the limo and the bathtub and the—"

"All right!" She swept her hands down and out. "Enough. You've got the picture entirely backward. I was seducing you."

Senth placed the tip of a finger under her chin, leaned

forward, and smiled into her eyes. "Sure you were, sweetie." He tilted his head in the direction of the building. "Come on. Time to get going. And remember, no cresting till we're through." He walked away from her.

With a grunt, NarrAy folded her arms, tapping one foot. *Men!*

* * *

Inside the storage facility, Senth rubbed his fingers together and withdrew the lockpick from a pocket. It had passed through customs as nothing more than a fancy data pen, a simpler version of a notereader. Until it lay in the hands of a trained thief.

The slim shaft thickened and elongated between his fingers. The double meanings of those words almost made him laugh. Until NarrAy, he'd rarely given sex more than a passing thought; now everything made him aware of it.

He shrugged. *Women.*

The Vassindorf codes flickered into life as he programmed the lockpick and held the tool out in front of him.

NarrAy's shadow on the wall nearby caught his attention. The image of her in the shower with him came to mind, lathering her skin with soap while she…

Focus, Senth! He shook his head. *Where the fffffft was I?*

He brought the lockpick up closer to check the settings. *Might as well reset and start over.* He thumbed the appropriate controls.

Can't be thinking about naked women and showers.

Especially NarrAy naked. Reality blurred around the edges. *Especially in the shower.*

She had bent over at the waist and braced her hands against the wall as he took her that morning standing up. And then he'd lifted her into his arms, face-to-face, and held her while...

"Senth?"

Her voice next to his ear made him jump.

"What's wrong, Tiger? You were just standing there. Are you okay?"

"Ffffftt! I was concentrating." He adjusted the front of his trousers where they'd got tight all of a sudden. "Don't interrupt me."

"Fine!" She stepped back peevishly. "Sorry."

He rubbed his eyes. *What the ffffftt was I doing? Start over again, Senth, and this time pay ffffftting attention.*

The Vassindorf cycled and reset. Senth timed it to give them an hour of uninterrupted searching.

Upstairs, he removed the bar from the door of the shipping container and stood guard while NarrAy explored.

She emerged a short time later with a small album of holopics. "Got it!"

Now this is more like it. In and out, like it should be.

Senth returned the locks to their original positions and led the way out and back to the alley. Once there, NarrAy threw her arms around his neck and kissed him.

She gave a happy squeal. "We did it! Now let's get out of here."

"Ready if you are, sweetie."

"Oh, wait a sec, Senth. Do you have anything that'll mark on brick?"

He drew back. "My lockpick works like a stylus. Why?"

"We always write *APLA was here* everywhere we go. It drives the armada soldiers crazy. They have no idea how few of us there really are."

She looked so pleased, Senth couldn't refuse. He set the lockpick to stylus mode and wrote the phrase on the wall. "There. How's that?"

"Perfect, Tiger." She kissed him. "Congratulations. You just became an honorary rebel."

He laughed. "I think I earned that honor the *first* time I broke into this place."

Holding hands, they set off for the starport.

The Harbinger's words echoed in Senth's thoughts. "*Good job, son. See you at home.*" In the past he'd lived to hear those words. They spoke of pride, a job completed. Reward. Fulfillment. Satisfaction. That was before he'd made love. Before he'd tasted freedom. Before he'd been at NarrAy's side.

Now those words meant only one thing. Slavery.

* * *

Imperial Palace, Stable—Sample Level
Pleasure Room Three
Wintresq 16

By the time the Conqueror arrived, her newest prisoner was asleep. The golden-haired Khyffen lay stretched across the foot of the bed, one arm over his head, a hand on his chest.

Destoiya smiled in satisfaction with the stable groom's choice of rooms. None of the bondage gear showed in this one, all of it hidden behind discreet panels or in drawers. Far different from Khyffen's cell, the room also had a fireplace, seductive lighting, a massive white-draped bed piled with beige and brown pillows, and a private bath.

Like all the bathrooms in the Stable, it had an oversize tiled shower affixed with an overhead chain and padded manacles, designed for administering discipline.

Destoiya dropped her uniform jacket across the back of a chair and opened her blouse. After stepping out of her shoes, she slipped off her trousers and hose, laid them next to her jacket, and crossed to the bed.

The play of shadows across Khyffen's deep-set eyes and high cheekbones made a dramatic impression. He was almost too beautiful for a man. Spiky lashes lay against his cheeks. A lock of fair hair spilled over his forehead. He wore it above his ears, barely touching his collar in back. Much shorter than most slakes'.

Of course. You're free now. The first thing most men did when freed was cut their hair. Grooming cost money and bit into profits, so most masters never bothered with regular haircuts. *Well, gorgeous, I'd prefer your blond locks long enough to grab a fistful when I held you down and had my way with you.* She licked her lips and let her gaze slide down him.

The Sample level in the Stable contained closets full of clothing, all in charcoal gray, but with varying detail, style, and expense. He'd dressed himself in simple, tailored quality. She nodded in approval.

Destoiya sat on the end of the bed beside him. Khyffen might have been a prince awaiting a kiss from his empress, his lush mouth open ever so slightly. She bent down and pressed her lips against his. He responded with sleepy ardor, humming against her mouth.

When she lay down, he nuzzled her throat drowsily. She felt him go completely still, as if taking stock of his surroundings, and then he pitched backward and leaned on one hand.

"Easy." Destoiya stroked his face. She smiled up at him. "It's just me."

His gaze darted around the room before coming to rest on her face. "I'm sorry, Your Majesty." He rubbed the back of a hand across one eye. "I didn't mean to fall asleep."

"Majesty," she corrected gently. "No need to apologize. I was much later than I thought I'd be. I'm glad you rested. Do you go by Khyffen?"

"Just Khyff, Majesty."

"You look so serious." She brushed back a lock of hair over his brow. "Do I make you nervous?"

"I want to please you."

"Relax, gorgeous. Don't think of me as someone you want to please." Twining his hair around a finger, she tugged it gently. "Think of me as someone you want to enjoy."

His smile gratified her.

"I'm going to enjoy taking you, Khyff. You make me smile."

"I'm glad."

"That you make me smile? Or that I'm going to take you?"

He studied her for a moment before answering. "Yes."

"All right, gorgeous. Let's enjoy ourselves, shall we?" She drew him down alongside her on the bed and rose over him. *Ah, the luxury of indulging in lust for the first time with a new lover.* With one hand, she caressed his face and hair. "I don't need to go anywhere until morning, so we'll take our time. Let's start by exploring this sensual mouth of yours. Part your lips for me, Khyff." She stroked the corners of his mouth with her tongue.

"I'll want you aggressive later, darling. For now just let me have you." She gave another lick. "Yes, like that. Passive." She caressed his lips with one finger. "Perfect, perfect."

The Conqueror stroked the inside of his mouth with her tongue, relishing the heat of his breath on her skin. Beneath her, his erection throbbed against her belly.

"Open wider, love. I want to taste you for a while."

She rubbed his tongue with hers, under, over, along the side, flicking against the tip. Letting him know what else he'd have done to him. Khyff's breathless groan of desire elicited her own pleasure.

Something about this one made her feel like smiling all the time. His instant sexual response in the cell told her Khyff would respond to interrogation much faster through pleasure than pain.

If only she needed him for information instead of as a hostage. At any cost, she had to obtain the item his brother now possessed.

Destoiya drew her fingers along Khyff's jaw and tilted his face upward, deepening her kiss. Magnificent man, talented, aware. Right there in the moment with her, a willing participant in lust.

It would be such a damn shame when she had to kill him.

Chapter Fifteen

Tyran Sleepliner Manc'eor Neth'e
Business-class Berth Sierra Forty-one

Wait till Senth sees this. Standing in the door of their cabin, NarrAy turned back to her lover. "Remember that closet on the other ship? I think it has this cabin beat."

He stepped over the threshold and looked around. "Oh fffffft! You weren't kidding. Think the bagbots will fit in here with us? Where's the bed?"

She pointed up at a handle on the wall. "I think you pull that and it drops down. Is the bed all you're interested in, my tiger?"

"As long as you're in it, I am." He leaned over her shoulder and kissed the corner of her mouth. "I'll see if I can get the bagbots in here."

Senth turned toward the automated suitcases, affording NarrAy a great view of his lean backside.

Honey, when I can't keep you naked, I am going to dress you in the tightest pants I can find. Mmm, mmm, you are one fine hunk of male.

Bagbots anchored in their slots on the wall, Senth

stretched both arms over his head. He hissed when the backs of his hands brushed the ceiling. "This is low. Khyff would dust this ceiling with his head."

"Khyff." NarrAy set a hand over her heart. "Oh, Senth, I'm so sorry. I forgot." She aimed her remote at the bagbot. "The hotel sent up a note Khyff left you. I was going to give it to you, but you were in the shower."

"You could have at least told me. That note might be important."

"Senth, you kind of distracted me, remember?"

"Oh yeah." His eyes glittered. "I do remember that. Really well."

She stooped to unlock the bagbot. "It's in my robe pocket." When the suitcase deployed itself into closet form, she rummaged through the clothes piled in the bottom. "It's in here somewhere."

"What a mess." Senth went down on one knee to unlock his bagbot. "Why don't you fold your things before you put them away?"

"Excuse me? We were in a hurry, as I recall, because someone wanted to do it in the shower one more time before we left." She pulled out several items and dumped them on the floor. "I don't see my robe in here."

I hardly wore any of my other clothes. She grinned. *Senth didn't need many of his either.*

"Oh wait!" She touched her mouth. "Maybe I put my robe in your bagbot."

"You packed *your* stuff in *my* bagbot?" He gestured to himself.

"What? Is your bot sacred or something? I ran out of room."

Senth's bagbot deployed. "You ran out of room because you cram stuff instead of folding your clothes neatly. You can fit plenty in one of these if you're careful."

NarrAy gave him a sarcastic smile. "Oh, you mean like your entire body?"

His cheeks turned a bright pink.

"My, my," she simpered, "hasn't it gone quiet?"

A low rumble sounded from his chest. He gestured to the bot. "Have at it."

NarrAy opened the bottom compartment and reached inside, feeling for the soft texture of her robe. *I know it's in here. I checked the hotel room twice and didn't—*

"Eww, ick!" She removed her hand and shook her fingers. "There's something wet in there." NarrAy pulled out the compartment. "It's that outfit you had on in the bathtub." She picked up the see-through bag, and water sloshed out of it and across Senth's thighs.

He hissed like a mad cat and swatted it away. "I didn't pack that! What the ffffftt did you do? Everything in my bot is sopping wet!"

"I thought this bag was waterproof." She held up the sack to see the underside of it. More water rained on Senth.

"Hey!" His wet pants clung to muscled thighs. "You're getting me all wet."

Look who's talking. NarrAy grinned and angled the sack a little higher, soaking the entire front of him. The solid outline of his thick shaft showed against his upper thigh.

"Quit foolin' around, NarrAy." He grabbed the sack and stood. "That water's cold."

Couldn't tell by looking at any part of you, hot thing.

Senth carried the sack to the tiny sink in the corner of their cabin. "You've ruined my stuff."

"I did not. You're overreacting."

He grabbed a towel and rubbed it across his pants. "Just find the note, will you?" He knelt on the floor beside her and mopped up spilled water.

She dug through the layers of clothes. "Here's my robe." She fished in the pocket. "Sorry. It's a little damp."

Water dripped from the envelope. Senth growled, snatched it from her, and laid it on the floor. He pressed the towel against it.

"I hope I can still read this." He tore open the envelope and removed the heavy paper inside. "Oh kkkhh. This is my Sen'dai's handwriting."

"What's it say?"

"'If you're reading this, you've refused to accept the Shackle I sent your brother to administer. I'm sure he told you he's been freed, which may lead you to believe the deal we made is no longer valid. When you get home, we'll see how well you honored your word.' Oh ffffftt, ffffftt, ffffftt!"

"Deal?"

"He made me swear I wouldn't have sex."

"What? He pumped you full of Shackle *and* made you promise?"

"Like either one did me any good around you!"

Speechless, NarrAy moved back a bit. *I guess I did come on pretty strong.*

"He said if I obeyed, he'd buy Khyff and free him. What was I supposed to do? I had to put my brother first. Besides, I didn't even know you then."

"But Khyff's free now."

"Well, I'm not." Senth threw the note aside and pushed to his feet. "And when my Sen'dai finds out what I've done, he *will* punish me."

She climbed to her feet. "Senth, I—"

"He threatened once to apprentice me to another Sen'dai. Or sell me."

"I don't want to lose you, Senth. I'm sure we can work something out."

"Work something out?" He laughed ruefully. "With him? Are you crazy! You don't work things out with that man. You obey him. Or else."

"But, Senth, he'll listen to reason. We—"

"Reason?" A muscle in his jaw flexed. "Do you know what happens to people who defy him?"

NarrAy thought back to the dossier Broxus had given her. *No one speaks up against him... Never tied to murder... Police can't get a snitch close.*

Senth leaned toward her. "There are reasons no one talks, NarrAy. Most of the time they don't even say his fffffftting name!"

What have I done? If that man so much as touches Senth... "He can't take you from me, Senth. I won't let him."

"No one stops him from doing anything he wants to do." He turned away, shoulders hunched, defeated.

"I won't abandon you. I swear it! No matter what Saint-Cyr does." She reached for his hand.

He stepped back, angling away from her touch. "You don't understand. You don't know what he's capable of. Your glimpse of him was all business and propriety. He was in a good mood because he got what he wanted."

"It doesn't matter. I swear we'll be together. We'll get through this. I love you, Senth. Saint-Cyr can't do anything about that."

"I shouldn't have complained, NarrAy." His eyes were wide; the fear in them, real. "It always gets back to him if I do anything wrong or say anything I shouldn't have. I don't know why I thought I could get away with anything."

"I'll never say a word, Senth. Trust me. I won't tell him."

"No, it's all right." His pupils had dilated. A false smile crossed his weary face. "I have to tell him myself. I have to tell him when I've disobeyed."

At the sound of Senth's flat voice, NarrAy shivered. Brox's warning came back to her: the effects of Shackle and Senth's overdose combined with the possibility of mind control.

"I don't want to displease my Sen'dai. I know what happens when I displease him."

His glassy-eyed expression made her flinch inside. "Senth, sit down, and let's talk about this."

"No, I want to obey him, NarrAy. I know what his rules are, and I feel good when I comply. This job has to be a success. I don't want to anger him."

The chill running up her spine had nothing to do with the room temperature. "What does that monster do to you, Senth?"

"I'm his slave. He has every right to discipline me."

"I won't let him hurt you, Senth. He's not going to hurt you again. I promise."

He shook his head. He backed toward the door and paused. "I need to think, NarrAy. I'm going for a walk."

"I'll come with you."

"No, I need to think."

"But I—"

He shut the door in her face.

* * *

Tarth City, Imperial Palace, Stable—Sample Level
Pleasure Room Three

Destoiya kissed each spot of Khyff's bared chest as she pushed his shirt aside. They'd kissed for the last hour, tasting each other's mouths in every way possible. She never hurried with the new ones.

Anticipation made even straight sex a feast.

Khyff shivered beneath her touch.

"I know what you are, love." She pressed her lips against a tiny white scar. "What you've been trained to do." She kissed another scar revealed when she peeled back his shirt farther. "This time it's all for you. I want to give you pleasure."

She moved so he could look into her eyes when he lay back. A pillow cradled his head. "I love seeing a man writhe beneath me. Watching him give up his will when passion overtakes him."

Khyff squirmed but obeyed her previous command not to touch her.

"You're doing so well, Khyff. I love making you act docile when I know you'd rather tear off my clothes and thrust into me."

He agreed with a heated whimper.

"In time, love. You'll love having that long, thick cock of yours inside me." She stroked a finger down his jaw. "Into my heat. And I am going to milk you so dry, your balls will ache for days." Destoiya took his mouth in a hot kiss.

Khyff relaxed his tongue, accepting her dominion over his mouth. His submission jolted heat down to her toes. She dragged her tongue down Khyff's chin and licked along his arched throat, across his chest, and down the hard ridges of his belly.

You're quivering from my touch, aren't you, my fine Jade? Mmm, all this luscious skin, mine to taste. I'm going to lap you up.

She dipped her tongue into his navel, then licked her way toward his broad shoulders. When she set her lips over one of his nipples and sucked it into her mouth, he gave a strangled cry and clutched the bedsheets on either side of him.

Oh, yes, my beautiful Jade. Show me your strength. Show me how much you ache to get inside me.

His labored breathing and clenched fists spoke eloquently of denied passion. Most of her Jades would have spurted their seed by now. This one mastered himself, submitting to her every demand.

You'll soon be begging to thrust that hard rod inside me. She smiled down at him. *I always make my Jades beg. It reminds them who's in charge.*

If she but touched his quivering shaft, he'd come in her hand. Jades always did after being teased this long. Destoiya pressed her mouth against his and held her cupped fingers above his rigid sex, close enough to feel his heat through his clothes.

He whimpered into her open mouth, his cry a wordless plea for release. When she drew back, Khyff begged with his eyes.

"Get them off." The Conqueror made a laconic gesture, indicating her soaked bikini panties, and lay back against the bed pillows. "No hands."

He rose on his knees, braced his hands on either side of her waist, and stroked his tongue up under the side of her panties.

"And, Khyff...?"

He looked up at her with expectation in his gaze, the bikinis held between his teeth.

She smiled. "No rush, love. I'm far from done with you."

Khyff groaned. *Demon! You hot, cock-teasing...* His

throat ached with pent-up frustration. His balls drew up hard against him, shaft throbbing. "Yes, Majesty."

He clenched his teeth over the elastic band of her white panties and tugged. The scent of her arousal, a woman's carnality, shot through him. He wanted to bury his face against her curls, inhale her womanly fragrance, lick up the taste of her with his tongue.

With a taunting smile, she gestured him to continue.

Think I'm tame, do you? He dragged her panties down one hip, then moved to clasp the other side with his teeth. *Wait till you get my cock in you. You won't want me docile then.*

Khyff inched the panties down her shapely legs, then dropped them over the side of the bed.

Destoiya sat up cross-legged and made a circling motion with one hand. "Turn around. Sit with your back to me."

He obeyed, his head halfway turned toward her.

"I know you don't like being forced." The heat of her fingers on his shoulders sent shivers over him. "I could restrain you, Khyff, bend you to my will."

Before he could respond, she pulled his shirt down his arms and back, capturing his hands behind him.

"But I'd rather you submit on your own."

She held him there, imprisoning his hands with no more than a piece of cloth and the knowledge that Senth's life might lie in his ability to please.

He knew she was looking at his scars. The fresh marks of Stalkos's rage.

Would she send him away? Or mark him more herself?

He'd seen the manacles and chains in the bathroom. No illusions about her desires.

She'd already chained and used him against his will in the cell.

Please don't touch me where he hit me. Please don't— He jerked as if burned when she touched the fresh stripes.

"You enjoy this." A long pause. "It's all right to admit it, Khyff. I can already tell."

His clients always wanted him to say that. Wanted him to declare his recoil meant lust instead of anger.

"Tell me how it makes you feel, Khyff." The tip of her tongue teased his sensitive flesh. "Talk me through your pleasure."

He ground his teeth together. *Come on, slake. Put on your street face and let her use you.* "Your touch is hot, Majesty. It scorches me."

"Good. That's an excellent start." She gripped his crossed hands, still bound with his shirt. "Tell me more. Tell me what your body's experiencing right now."

Khyff sucked in a harsh breath, fighting fury. "Fire." He gasped. "Erotic fire."

She licked and then blew on his damp skin.

He whimpered, unable to speak. *Please, please stop.*

He knew she wouldn't. No client stopped when he begged. No client had ever stopped, no matter how much he'd fought. He'd long since stopped fighting. They hurt him less when he just let them use him.

"You like this, don't you?"

Khyff jerked and shuddered under the relentless, gentle, wet strokes of her tongue. He bit his lips.

"Talk to me, love. What do you feel? I want your voice."

"My cock." He forced the words out. "Pulsing. Throbbing."

"Good, Khyff. Tell me more." While he talked to her, she handled him less.

"Everything feels tight. My balls. My ass. My skin's on fire, everywhere. Everywhere you touch me, it burns."

"More."

"You want me to talk to you?" Was this his way out? A way to keep her from fondling him? "You want to know everything I would do to you?" Khyff turned his head toward her, waiting.

"Everything." She placed both hands on his shoulders.

"It pleases you to have a man describe how he'll satisfy you."

"Yes."

"You want to hear every delicious way he'll tease your body."

"Oh yes, Khyff. That's exactly what I want."

He turned to the front, his back fully to her. Her body radiated heat. "I'd start by surrendering my mouth."

"How?"

"Your tongue would be my master. My lips would be your slave."

She hummed against his skin, laving his back with her tongue.

He jerked forward. "I'd submit to your kisses as if they were wine and I wanted to drink them."

Destoiya's breath came fast, wet, and hot.

"Your body would become my temple. I would worship you with my mouth and my tongue and my hands."

She used the tip of her tongue on his neck, a wet lick of heat.

"And every bit of my long, hard cock."

Destoiya pressed her lips against his nape and drew in air, cooling his skin.

Khyff gasped. "Free my hands, Majesty. Let me take you in my arms."

"What would you do?" Destoiya held his wrists together, her mouth pressed against his shoulder. "Tell me."

"Bury my cock inside you. Deep."

"I like that. How deep, Khyff?"

"All the way to your heart. So deep you will never get me out."

The vibration of her moan tickled. "I *like* that. Go on."

"I would thrust into you until you begged me to let you come. And then I would make you come until you begged me to stop."

Her arms wrapped around him from behind, hugging his neck. "Tell me, Khyff," she said, her voice feather soft against his ear, "can you outlast me?"

He turned his head toward her. "I will try, my fallen angel."

She laughed with delight. "Fallen, am I?"

"If you were an innocent, you wouldn't want the things I'll do to you."

She played with his hair. "But you did call me an angel."

"That was wrong of me." He lowered his head. "You are a goddess, Majesty."

She kissed his cheek. "And you're sumptuous, Khyff." Destoiya's fingers trailed across his back. "Your last master… Did he give you these scars?"

"Most of them."

"Who else?"

"Clients."

"I'm so sorry, Khyff."

Brutality, he could handle. Her gentleness unnerved him. "Some of them paid him extra so they could mark me."

The bed moved when she knelt behind him. She set her mouth near his ear. "What a small-minded idiot he was."

He was unable to speak with her so close to him.

Destoiya combed her fingers through his hair, pulling his head back against her shoulder. "You're priceless, Khyff. A rare and valuable prince of a man."

He soaked up the words, even if she didn't mean them.

She leaned over his shoulder and covered his mouth with hers, and he pressed his lips up against hers, surrendering himself.

She released his mouth, pulled away the shirt binding him, and scooted back on the bed. "I want you inside me."

Khyff stood long enough to drop his pants, then turned around.

Destoiya leaned back on her elbows, legs apart. "Now."

He wedged himself between her willing thighs.

Pearly liquid coated her labia, drenched her curls. He angled his shaft against her and, with one thrust, entered the fist-tight heat of her dripping sheath.

Destoiya lay back, taking him in with body and eyes. "You may touch me."

He set her knees across the insides of his elbows and pistoned into her, rocking his pelvis hard as he slammed against her.

He reached around her legs and pulled her labia wide apart, exposing her clitoris to his gaze. It peeked from its hood, glistening and erect.

She gasped when he withdrew his cock.

He read the surprise in her eyes when he knelt between her outstretched legs. She'd thought he'd come the moment he got inside her. She knew what he could do, all right, but not what he could keep from doing. Khyff lowered his lips over her labia and pressed a soft kiss on her steaming skin.

Destoiya wriggled toward him, opening her legs wider.

He placed both hands under the small of her back and lifted her toward him. He stroked his tongue across her clit's hood, teasing her. She flinched up against him. A pleasure sound escaped her.

Khyff set his pursed lips over her clit and sipped. He laughed to himself when her back bowed as she arched up into his mouth. Her legs trembled.

"You are delicious, Majesty. Salty. Sweet."

He settled onto his stomach, his erection an agony of

sensation against the sheets. He brought both hands back to her labia. Khyff held her lips between forefingers and thumbs, alternately pulling them apart and pressing them together.

She clutched the pillow beneath her head.

He let the tip of his tongue dart up under her clit while he stretched her labia. He wagged the flat of his tongue across her lips, spreading her open, and stroked upward, coming up under her clit and flicking it with the tip of his tongue as he completed the movement.

Destoiya moaned. "Khyff."

He pressed up against her, tilted his head, opened his mouth over her...and hummed.

She clasped both hands in his hair to hold him in place. He stayed there, humming, while she climaxed.

Khyff slid a finger inside her, moved it out, then pushed in two. He tapped her clit, using only the tip of his tongue, then forced up the swollen member, sliding it under its hood. She arched against him, shoving herself against his mouth. He tongued her swollen clit, let it fall, and then lifted it again. And again.

She thrashed on the bed.

He grinned. Added a third finger.

Khyff hooked those three inside her and pressed up, dragged them toward her opening. She convulsed around his fingers, head thrown back. He did it again. Flexed them while she came some more.

A fourth finger stretched her.

Destoiya grabbed the headboard and levered herself

harder against his hand, her quivering slit milking his fingers. Her clit twitched against his tongue. He sucked the jerking nub into his mouth.

"Khyff," she demanded hoarsely. "Khyff! Put it in me. I want your cock in me. Now!"

He withdrew his fingers and rose over her, then slid his shaft into her open slit. Gripping her buttocks, he tilted her body and rode into her hard, fast. The quake of her vagina clutched him. Milked him. Slick. Burning. Raw. He pounded her. Rocked her. Jarred her body. Her breasts bounced. He rubbed a palm against one of her nipples, and she exploded around him.

Frantic panting. His, hers. Release. Relief... Rest...

Khyff remained inside her while he rolled over and drew her on top of him, into his arms. He dragged in a breath. He was still hard.

When his cock had pulsed against the mouth of her womb, he'd dared hope for a moment that Destoiya loved him. But she lifted her head and looked at him now with the same expression of rapturous satisfaction he'd seen on so many of his clients' faces. In love with what he could do to them, not with who he was. He turned his head away.

"If you let me rest a moment"—he cupped her hips and held her tightly against him—"I *will* make you beg for more." He let out a sighing, shuddering breath.

Destoiya did not reply, just draped herself over him, her head on his shoulder.

"Unless you'd planned to kill me." Sudden anger coarsened his words. "Now that you've fucked me."

"You're more to me than a good lay." Destoiya lifted her head to look into his eyes. "If you can make me beg for you to stop, I give you my word, you will never die because of me."

Her gaze held when he studied her. *Now. Ask her now.* He nodded. "And my brother?"

Silence stretched between them like a taut string on the verge of breaking.

"Very well. I will give the same vow of protection to your brother."

Before Khyff could rejoice, she added, "If you make me beg twice."

Chapter Sixteen

Tyran Sleepliner Manc'eor Neth'e
Business Class, Promenade Deck

Senth did not wander long before a wheeled porter-droid intercepted him.

"Excuse me, sir." The android rolled in front of him. "Will you be returning to your quarters to sleep for jump, or may I provide a jumpdrug for you?"

"Drug, thanks." Senth shrugged out of his jacket and pulled back a sleeve. *How many times have I done this with Shackle?*

"Do you have a drug preference, sir?" The android's right wrist rotated. The skin of his index finger dilated open on the tip like a data pen and emitted a syringe.

"Holiday, please."

"Very good, sir."

The android supported Senth's arm with his left hand and set his right forefinger-syringe against the inner elbow.

The sting of Holiday was nothing compared to the scald of Shackle. The syringe withdrew, and the droid's finger rubbed across the entry point, covering the skin with clear sealant.

"Will there be anything else, sir?"

"No, thank you."

The android made a slight bow and then rolled off in another direction.

Senth rubbed his thumb across the fading yellow bruise from his last dose of Shackle. He pulled on his jacket and fastened it.

The observation area lay ahead. He turned down an alternate route to avoid the view of soul-sucking darkness during jump.

Too much like my life. Saint-Cyr's obedient little thief. Controlled. Never arguing. Never questioning. Taking what he gives me and keeping my mouth shut. All those warnings from my master. All lies. Thanks to Khyff, I know the truth.

NarrAy had no poison kisses. She tasted of vanilla and warm sugar. Her saliva didn't let her control his mind. She listened to him and sought his advice. Trusted him to do his job. His heart only pounded when he thought about making love to her. And it wasn't his head feeling like it was splitting apart.

It was his heart.

He had to grin. *Although the part about having a semipermanent erection and the touch of her hands driving me insane was certainly true.*

He strolled without thinking and ignored the jump alarm when it sounded. Lights in the corridor dimmed briefly in warning and then brightened.

I can't run from my master any more than Khyff could

run from his. If I do, I'll never be free. I have to go back. Is love supposed to hurt? He stopped in the center of a hall that branched in four directions. *Maybe I'm addicted to her.* He chose a hallway and entered it. *No. I'm in love. I love this woman! So what am I going to do?*

Gift shops came into view. He wandered past the bright windows and holovid displays.

Face my master and admit the truth; that's what I'm going to do. He said he owed me one. Khyff is already free. Maybe Saint-Cyr already knows what I've done. Maybe he was trying to get me to admit I had sex with her.

He stopped again, noticed he was in front of a jewelry store, and stepped back before the face-recognition software could identify him as a guild thief.

Shopping, he could do. Loitering, no.

I have to make this decision—not Khyff, not my Sen'dai, not even NarrAy. Me. I have to make it. I have to face Saint-Cyr and tell him the truth. If he punishes me, fine. I'm a man. I can deal with whatever I have to so I can be with my woman.

In two years I'll be free; then I can be with NarrAy, and no one can stop me. His shoulders relaxed. *I need to tell NarrAy everything will be okay. We will be together.*

Senth let a smile break loose as he headed back toward their cabin. *Wait. Wasn't there a chocolate shop near that jeweler?*

He searched his pockets as he turned and rounded a corner. Accidentally he brushed against the shoulder of a youth going the opposite direction.

"Excuse me."

"Hey!" the boy shouted. "Watch where you're going!"

Oh kkkhh, this could be profitable.

A hand reached out to shove him, and Senth turned aside to soften the blow but let the boy's palm connect with his shoulder.

He turned to face three human boys dressed in fake Kin leathers edged with fringe. No Kin wasted hard-won leather like that, and the bright orange beads in their hair represented none of the sixteen clans on Felidae.

Senth smirked as he stepped past them.

A pair of hands grabbed the back of his jacket, yanked him off his feet, and slammed him against the wall.

He did nothing to resist.

These little phonies have less total power combined than Khyff does in one hand. Okay, boys, show me what you've got.

"Look at his eyes," one of them sneered. "He's a half-breed freak."

As opposed to you, dressed like a species you're not?

Well versed in the game, he waited for the comment he knew was coming.

One of the others poked a finger into Senth's chest. "Why don't you watch where you're going, freak?"

"Oh fffffftt." Senth gave them the most bored expression he could muster. "And here it's been at least five days since anyone called me a freak. Thank you, boys. I was starting to think I'd blended into a piece of kkkhh like you."

The hard jab into his stomach almost made Senth retch. Before any of them could get in another punch, two porterdroids wheeled into view. The boys shoved Senth to the floor and ran down the hall.

The droids sped toward him, one chasing the boys. The other helped Senth to his feet. "Do you need medical assistance, sir?"

"No. I wasn't hurt." Senth finger combed his hair back into place.

The android inserted a hand into an apron pouch and withdrew his arm with a brush attached instead of a hand. He began dusting off Senth's clothes.

"I'm fine." Senth waved off further help. "Really."

The other android returned and skidded to a stop beside him. "Assailants recognized as passengers. Event logged. Do you wish to file charges, sir?"

"No, thank you. Not necessary. The incident was a misunderstanding." Senth spread his arms, ignoring the dull pain in his stomach. "See? No harm done."

The two androids bowed. "As you wish, sir," they chorused and then rolled back toward their original direction.

Senth patted the pocket where he'd dropped the drakloaded debit bracelets the boys had been wearing.

Freak, huh? Look in the mirror. Well, at least now this freak has some spending money. And I doubt your mommy and daddy are going to hear how you lost your debs, are they?

I wonder what kind of flowers NarrAy likes? Now where

did I see that chocolate shop?

* * *

Tarth City, Imperial Palace, Stable—Sample Level

Destoiya shared a quick shower and a light meal with Khyff, then led him by the hand to a pool. She stretched out full length in the shallow end, nestled in a place sculpted to fit her body. Heated tiles beneath her radiated warmth into her back, soothing muscles tired from exertion.

Khyff lay in a similar support next to her, eyes closed, arms floating in the water.

What a perfect body he has. The water glistened on his ridged abs, filled his navel. She licked her lips.

As if Khyff felt her gaze on him, he turned his head and looked over at her. "This feels wonderful, Majesty. Thank you for inviting me."

Only the newest pleasure slaves entered the Sample level of the Stable. It afforded the most privacy.

The better to accustom her Jades to sharing later.

She stretched out more fully. "Khyff." She drew up her feet and spread her legs wide apart, making room for his shoulders. Motioning for him to face her feet, she patted her belly. "Lie down between my thighs and put your head here."

He arranged himself in the long shallows. Her thighs rested on his shoulders, her mound against the back of his neck.

"That's good, Khyff. We'll relax a moment before we play again."

He chuckled. "You think lying between your legs will *relax* me?"

She tugged a lock of his hair. "I'm counting on no such thing."

"Then you won't be disappointed." He placed his hands on her ankles. "May I please you with a foot massage, my goddess?"

"A foot fetish, Khyff?"

"I have a fetish for all parts of you, Majesty." He massaged her arches, stroking firmly with his thumbs.

"Mmm. I think I like 'goddess' better. You have strong hands." Destoiya closed her eyes, relaxing into his touch. "Where did you learn to do that?"

When he laughed, his shoulders pressed into her thighs. "If you knew, you might not want my hands on you again."

"In that case, never tell me."

The Conqueror let herself rest, opening herself to Khyff's hands. He massaged the balls of her feet, swept his fingers across the insteps and up over the tops.

"Turn over, Khyff. I want that wonderful mouth of yours on mine for a while."

He twisted around and slid up into her arms to obey.

The Conqueror caressed the length of his chiseled torso with both hands.

Water slapped the edges of the pool.

Khyff pulled back and looked down at her with a sensual

grin. He shook hair out of his eyes, a few blond strands clinging to his brow. Trickles of steaming water shone on his chest and arms.

She inhaled his scent and almost moaned in pleasure. The smell of a clean, fresh, and healthy man was as heady as pheromones any day.

I love what this one makes me feel. She dragged her gaze down the wet length of Khyff's magnificent body. *And he's all mine.* She cupped her hands around his firm rear and pulled him upward, guiding his cock into her. "Slowly," she whispered. "Take your time."

When he moved to his knees and leaned back, he drew her hips with him, angling his penis up into her at the perfect depth to inflame her. Water sloshed onto the floor.

Destoiya cried out when he rocked from side to side. Warm water trickled into her ears. The hard ridge of his cockhead massaged the hollow spot just inside her vagina. Her second-favorite site of pleasure.

As if he walked into her thoughts, Khyff placed one hand over her outer lips and squeezed them together over her favorite site. The hard nub of her clit jerked and twitched under his continued caress.

The fullness of his cock inside her, rubbing against her pleasure spot, made Destoiya moan. He kept up his firm caress on the outside of her labia.

She wrapped her legs around his waist and braced her arms against the floor of the pool. Water splashed over her face and into her eyes as he rocked against her. Her crotch rubbed hard against Khyff's. Up. Down. After hours of lovemaking, the brush of his pubic hair against her skin made her so sensitive, she bit back a cry for mercy. He'd said he could make her beg him to stop—she would not give in so easily.

Her wetness drenched her labia. He held her hips out of the water as he rode her. Destoiya shuddered and shook, trying to catch her breath, but could hold back no longer. The orgasm tore through her like fire through paper. She collapsed, sobbing for breath.

Khyff still held her. Still stroked into her. Soft, easy, slow.

She knew then he was far from through with her. Destoiya's breath caught in her throat. *He really will make me beg.*

Khyff brought her legs up, placed her ankles against his shoulders, and did not move. After a moment, the gentle twitch of his cock inside her declared his intent.

Tightening and relaxing his inner muscles to tease her sensitive vagina, Khyff brought the unconquerable Conqueror to another searing climax.

Destoiya lay still, amazed, while Khyff rocked relentlessly in and out of her vagina. Far from weary, he stroked into her with vigor.

She relaxed against the floor of the pool and held out her arms.

He lay atop her, weight on his elbows, and brought his mouth to hers. Khyff supported himself above her, trembling on the brink of release.

She played with his blond hair, her dripping hands clutching the wet, silky strands. *I wish you hadn't cut this. I love long hair on my men.* The pictures of him in her notes showed his hair shoulder length.

She clenched around him and smiled, enjoying his cry of lust when she made him come.

Inches above her, water dripped from his brow. Or sweat.

Time to test him.

She pulled him close and took his mouth with gentle ferocity. He lost his breath, and she kissed him harder, forcing a cry from him when she bit cruelly into his lower lip.

When she released him, Khyff panted, his lower lip already bruised and swelling. A drop of blood rose to the surface. Destoiya licked it away.

He had not fought her or even questioned her with his eyes, accepting her abuse of him as her right. If ever a man had redeemed himself from death, Khyff had.

But Khyff's brother need not know he'd be spared. Young Antonello would do anything to save his older brother.

Docile, obedient, full of lust. Such a perfect hostage, this young blond god in her arms. Destoiya stroked her fingers through his hair. *Maybe I'll make him grow it out again, since I plan to keep him.*

His cock twitched inside her, still hard. Destoiya sucked in a breath in awe and held it. *I'm going to have to beg, after all.*

"Khyff, darling." She caressed his face. "I absolutely love you."

He looked down at her through thick lashes, gave her a wicked smile, and began once more to thrust.

* * *

Tyran Sleepliner Manc'eor Neth'e
Business-class Berth Sierra Forty-one

NarrAy paced the tiny cabin, awaiting a response from Broxus. When her comm chimed, she grabbed it off the top of her bagbot and turned it on.

Her security officer's image shimmered in front of her.

"Sorry it took me so long, ma'am. I—"

"Fine." She motioned him to hurry. "I need to know what that man does to Senth."

She had sent Broxus on a research mission to discover exactly what kind of punishment Saint-Cyr meted out that caused Senth so much fear.

"I found no emergency-room records or doctor's visits for injuries, unexplained or otherwise. Nothing in the police files. Saint-Cyr keeps a tight lid on everyone in his employ, which seems to be about half the city."

"So you're telling me we've got nothing?"

"Afraid so."

NarrAy folded her arms. "A lot of good you are."

Brox raised both eyebrows. "Sorry. I did the best I could. There is one account, but it's about someone else."

"Go on."

"Does Senth have scars anywhere?"

She'd touched and kissed every inch of his body. "No, I don't think—Wait. Yes. On his right hand." She studied her own. "On the back and palm, like stab wounds. Think that's significant?"

"About six years ago a thief named Rokko died in prison before he could testify against Saint-Cyr. Rokko said James Stalkos, one of the Harbinger's former partners, paid him to steal something from Saint-Cyr, but the Harbinger caught him in the act. Rokko had a stab wound on one hand that he said Saint-Cyr ordered as punishment." Broxus held up a hand. "He nailed Rokko's hand to a table and then beat him."

NarrAy laid a hand over her heart. *Did he do that to my tiger?*

"How did the man die?"

"Autopsy says he choked to death on a piece of food in the prison cafeteria. Don't find that believable, do you?"

"No. What about the treatment of his slaves, Brox?"

"No abuse reported, but then, who'd dare? The only slave Saint-Cyr has ever had is Senth. There are five professional thieves whom he adopted the same way he did Senth, but they weren't slaves. They're all registered with the guild. Naturally everyone's happy as can be when it comes to Daddy Harbinger."

"The man scares me, Brox. And he scares Senth."

"Surprise! He scares everybody."

NarrAy shivered. The heat of tears stung her eyes.

"Anything else you need from me, ma'am?"

"No. Not tonight. Thanks, Brox."

He gave her a loose salute, and his image faded from sight.

Pacing, she reviewed her options, ticking them off on her fingers.

Buy him from Saint-Cyr. No, what if Senth felt he owed her?

Beg Saint-Cyr to forgive Senth, swear it was all her fault. No, that would take authority away from Senth. He needed her to believe in him.

"How could I be so selfish? He was a slave. This is all my fault."

Senth had been drugged, forbidden to touch her, and forced to swear he wouldn't. She'd made him do it anyway.

She pressed her palms over her eyes. "What have I done?"

NarrAy licked her lips. "Maybe it's not too late. If I don't touch him, he can break away from me." She nodded, an idea forming in her mind. "All I have to do is resist touching him. He can go back to his master with a clear conscience. In two years, when he's free, we can be together."

She pulled down the wall-enclosed bed and stripped off the blanket. She folded it lengthwise and laid it down the center.

"Now all I have to do is make sure I don't touch him."

She set her hands on her hips.

"I can do this. I can keep my hands to myself, for Senth's sake. I have to keep Senth safe. I have to give him up."

She forced herself to nod agreeably. "You're more than human, NarrAy. Remember that. You can do anything you decide to. You're a Better. Act like it. Put him first!"

This is going to work.

This is going to fix everything.

The door opened, and Senth walked in smiling, a bouquet of roses in one hand and a box of chocolates in the other.

This is going to kill me.

Chapter Seventeen

Tarth City, Imperial Palace, Stable—Sample Level

Khyff awoke in bed alone, stretched, and remembered Destoiya's rich and throaty cries. He *had* made her beg.

Twice.

To protect his brother, he would use every nuance and artifice gained from half a lifetime of whoring and depravity. Endure any perversion she asked for, perform any self-defilement she liked. He rose and tried one of the doors.

Damn it! Khyff leaned back against the wood. He sighed. *What did you think, Khyff? She was going to invite her newest whore to wander through her palace?* The window was sealed and, at an angle, revealed the same fibrous reinforcements as the windows in prison. The portal overlooked an inner courtyard six floors below. Except for the flowers and statues, the area was no different from the exercise yard in jail. *If I had Senth's skill with locks, nobody'd ever hold me prisoner again.*

The second door connected to a blue-tiled bathroom. Khyff relieved himself, then went to the mirror and examined the gash in his lower lip, a souvenir from Destoiya's teeth. *Ball-busting, power-hungry bitch.* He splashed water on his face and patted it dry. The towel in his hand was just like the ones Stalkos kept in the expensive suites. *This place is nothing but a glorified brothel.* He reached for the bottle of lotion on the sink and only just stopped himself from hurling it across the room. Like the slakehouse, no doubt spyware watched his every move. He pumped lotion onto his palm and rubbed it into his skin.

Stop brooding like a stupid whore and start thinking of a way out of here. Exhaustion dragged at him, a narcotic he couldn't shake. Unsure when he might get more, he drank as much water as he could and hauled himself back to bed. He pulled a pillow beneath his chest.

His sexual exploits last night would have netted Stalkos a small ransom in coin. Khyff tried to summon gratitude that even though the Conqueror had locked him up, at least she hadn't chained him to the bed.

Sometime later, the sound of running water woke him. Khyff struggled to a sitting position in the middle of tangled sheets.

Dark-haired male twins dressed in black exited from the bathing room.

"Who the hell are you?" Khyff worked at unwrapping the sheets from around his legs.

"I'm Triss." The one on the right walked toward him.

"Stay away from me!" Khyff got up on the opposite side of the bed, grabbed the sheet, and wrapped it around himself. "What do you want?"

Triss held up both hands. "Her Majesty assigned us to serve you."

Both men were handsome and muscled. Absolutely identical faces. Gold tags sat on the upper right of their chests. The other twin threw open the heavy drapes. "I'm Trey."

Khyff shielded his eyes from the sudden light.

"Triss will never give you details, which is how you can tell us apart. Or just look at our name tags." Trey tapped the gold tag and smiled. "We promise not to switch them."

"We started running water for your bath." Triss gestured toward the door that led to the bathroom. "We're here to bathe and dress you."

"I'm a big boy, thanks. You can go."

The twins grinned at each other, then turned back to Khyff.

"All the new guys say that. You're no less macho because servants shave you or give you a manicure."

"Some other time." Khyff tossed one end of the sheet over his shoulder.

The twins shared another glance, and Triss deferred to Trey. "The men in the Stable are Her Majesty's personal favorites, Khyff." Trey leaned against the open door. "If we touched you without your consent, we'd be sold within the hour. Believe me, we're not here to hurt you."

"I'm in Her Majesty's Stable? *The* Stable?"

"Yes. At dinner, you're being promoted to Toy, one of the highest levels. Your rank provides you with two servants." Trey gestured between himself and Triss. "If we fail to care for you in a manner befitting your station, we'll be disciplined."

"I can still bathe myself. Thank you."

"As you wish." They inclined their heads.

Khyff grunted, but he padded into the cool blue bathroom. Triss turned off the water in the marble tub. Khyff ignored him and relieved himself first. When he at last stepped into the steaming water, he peeled off the sheet only after he was submerged. He handed the dripping cloth to Triss, who carried it to another part of the room.

The heat pampered Khyff's overworked muscles, and he sank into it, stretching out his legs and leaning back. Triss pointed out an array of icons on a panel at the edge of the tub.

Khyff touched the neck icon. Hot, pulsating water pummeled his neck and shoulders, stroking his muscles. He sighed audibly and tapped every button on the panel. Powerful streams of water shot all around him, massaging every point of his body, churning the water into a froth of white.

Heavenly. He closed his eyes, opened them again swiftly, and checked the location of the twins.

Triss was pulling towels from a closet while Trey laid out grooming tools near a barber's chair.

"Tell me more about this level stuff." Khyff spread out in the water to reap the effects of the massage.

"Sample level is a test of personality and skill." Trey paused in his work. "Novice is training, and Toy is for the experienced. If you earn Her Majesty's highest favor, you move to Keeper. Inside the Stable, everyone nicks the terms. Right now you're a sip. Novice is slurp. Tonight you'll be promoted to swig, and Keeper is swallow."

Khyff smiled thinly at the obvious references. *Tell me where my brother is, and I'll be impressed with your knowledge.*

Triss handed him a natural sponge and offered the choice of two white bottles of soap with fancy lettering on the labels.

Khyff examined the sponge. "Do you stock Her Majesty's favorite scent?"

Triss hesitated, returned the bottles of soap to a shelf, and offered another, identical to the first two.

Had Triss thought to trick him, or was this a different scent in a similar bottle? He pushed the sponge underwater and squeezed the air out of it. Bubbles fizzed to the surface.

Triss sighed and held the soap out at arm's length. "Alitus uses this one."

Khyff made him wait a moment while he considered it. He took the soap and inspected the label as if he could read it, then flipped open the lid and sniffed it.

A smooth blend of citrus and amber, the same fragrance he wore when meeting female clients for the first time. They must have repackaged it for the Stable. How would he ever recognize his when all the bottles looked the same?

"Who is Alitus?"

"A favorite."

"Free or slave?"

"I'll answer that." Trey motioned Triss aside and sat beside the tub on a low stool. They were eye to eye. "What you really want to know is whether you're a slave. This morning, when she assigned us, Her Majesty made it clear we're to treat you as a highly favored guest."

Khyff gave him a prison face, revealing nothing. "So I'm free to go."

"No." Trey smiled. "She was quite clear about that too. She has plans for you. The other members of her stable are curious as hell."

I'll bet they are.

"Her Majesty's never installed a free man in her stable before."

"And what happens when she tires of me?"

"Many a man's fortune has been made by his association with the Conqueror."

Which tells me nothing about my fate or Senth's. All right, let's find out what else you know. Khyff nodded. "So tell me more about this Alitus person and why I should care whether Her Majesty prefers the scent he wears."

"Alitus is Her Majesty's highest favorite, her personal assistant. He has his own staff, an enormous budget, his quarters take up an entire floor of the Stable, and it's no secret he has the Conqueror's heart as well as her ear."

Great. Competition for a prize I don't even want.

Trey stretched his legs and crossed his ankles. "Would you like to know about the sex toys he uses on her and the flavors of lubricant he stocks too?"

Khyff drizzled soap onto the sponge and lathered it. "I'd like to know what tales you'll tell the others about me."

"It's my job to answer questions and take care of *you*. No one else."

"Uh-huh. And the Conqueror was a virgin last night."

Trey laughed. "Believe what you like, Khyff, but we're here to serve you. Whether that means answering questions, explaining the use of new sex toys, finding a special book on positions for intercourse—anything you want. Just ask."

"Why don't you start by telling me about those flavored lubricants." Beginning with his arm, Khyff scrubbed, cleansing his body of the Conqueror's touch. "I'll jump in with questions as I think of them."

* * *

Tyran Sleepliner Manc'eor Neth'e
Business-class Berth Sierra Forty-one

Senth went still when NarrAy turned to look at him. In that moment, with her hair down and her face so full of concern, she took his breath away.

It was more than her incredible beauty or her lush curves. More than her perfect mouth or sweet lips. NarrAy herself. Her loving acceptance. Her willingness to trust him.

The woman owned his soul. All he wanted to do was give her the rest of his life.

Senth held out the red roses, and she accepted them without looking into his eyes.

"These are for you too." He offered the box of candy. "They're dark chocolate. Your favorite."

"Thank you, Senth." She took them from his hand.

The brush of her fingers against his electrified his senses.

She jerked back at the touch.

"I shouldn't have walked out like that, NarrAy. I was wrong not to talk to you." He stepped closer.

She flinched back, her lowered lashes covering her eyes. She set the chocolates on the small desk.

"I'm so sorry, NarrAy. I'll never do that again. I promise."

He reached for her hand, but she turned aside, shoulders slumped. "Senth…"

"Aww, sweetie, I'm so sorry! I was a slack-minded, stupid ass to treat you that way." Senth shifted from one foot to the other and rubbed the back of his neck. "Please forgive me."

NarrAy brought the flowers to her nose and inhaled their fragrance. A little smile played at the corners of her mouth.

Fftt-fftt sha kee! A purr rose up in Senth's chest, blocking words. *If it makes her smile, I'll buy her roses every single day for the rest of my life. Mercy, she's beautiful.*

"I…I was…um…" Words faded as his purr took over. "NarrAy." Senth shook his head, trying to stop purring and control his breathing so he could speak. "Petals." He gestured blindly. "Scatter. On the bed."

"Oh, Senth!" NarrAy clutched the roses to her breast and turned her back on him.

His purr ceased, and he hurried toward her. He took the roses from her, set them beside the candy, and drew her into his arms.

"What is it, sweetie? What's wrong? Tell me."

NarrAy's body conformed to his as if he'd been made to be a part of her. The way her head fit against his chest, below his shoulder. The way her arms reached all the way around his waist—surely his body had been designed to comfort her. Love her. Take her.

"Whatever I did that hurt you, baby, I swear I won't ever do it again. I'm so sorry, NarrAy. I love you, baby. Please, please, talk to me."

"Stop." Senth's tenderness almost undid her resolve. Before her desire could sweep them both into passion, NarrAy pushed her hands against chest, forcing herself out of his arms.

How am I ever going to get through this?

"NarrAy—"

"Don't touch me, Senth."

She stumbled back a step, not allowing herself to meet his gaze. If she saw his desire, she would drown them both in lust. Her pheromones were already rising. She had to put distance between them, or she'd lose control. She'd give in to what her body craved instead of doing what was right for Senth.

He reached out with both hands, inviting her touch.

She forced herself to focus on the scar on his hand. Made herself picture him with a knife impaled through his flesh, suffering a beating while Saint-Cyr watched and approved.

NarrAy turned her back. *No! Not my Senth. Not my tiger. I'm not going to let that monster hurt him.*

"Senth." She hugged herself, trembling with the desire to

let down her pheromones. "Senth, you c-can't touch me anymore."

"What?" He moved closer. "Why, NarrAy?"

She crossed the room. If she said it was for his own good, he'd convince her otherwise. She *wanted* him to convince her.

"I—You…" NarrAy fought to control her shaking. "You're too…" She bit her lips, unwilling to hurt him even a little, but it would save him from worse pain later.

"I'm what, NarrAy? Tell me. Please. Whatever it is, I'll change it."

How can I do this?

He came toward her, and she held up a hand to stop him. "No, Senth! I mean it."

She backed away, still not letting herself look at him. She did not want to see the hurt her words inflicted. If she let him see her pain, he might discern her true motives, and Senth would never knowingly let her protect him from his master.

"You're too young."

When he did not respond, she let herself glance in his direction.

He was standing with his head down, expressionless, hands at his sides.

"Young?" He echoed the word as if it were foreign. "I thought age didn't matter to you. It doesn't matter to me."

"A lot of things don't matter to you."

He frowned, lifted his head to stare at her. "Like what?"

Hating herself, NarrAy gestured to the flowers. "Stealing expensive roses to impress me."

His mouth dropped open. "You think I stole those?" He gestured to himself. "I bought those flowers with money I earned."

"Earned how, Senth?"

He looked away.

"I see. You stole the money too."

"Believe me. I earned every drak." His pale eyes narrowed at her. "I did not steal your gift, NarrAy. You mean more to me than that."

"If that's the way you see it, Senth, you don't know the difference between right and wrong."

He sputtered. "You hired me because I was a thief. It's a little late to complain because I am one."

"I hired you for a job paid for by the resistance. The job is over, Senth. It's finished."

He stared at her. The hurt of her words flashed a grimace of pain across his face.

NarrAy made herself say the rest.

"And so are we."

Chapter Eighteen

Tyran Sleepliner Manc'eor Neth'e
Business-class Berth Sierra Forty-one

"NarrAy, I love you." She could not mean they were finished. It could not be over between them. "I thought you loved me."

"It could never work between us, Senth. O'Venna promoted me, and I don't have time to play around anymore."

"I don't understand."

"As soon as I get back, I'm taking a new position. The prototype will go into production, and there's an influx of new leaders. I'll be in charge of hiring and training an entirely new staff." She folded her arms. "I've had a lot of fun with you, but I can't wait around for you to grow up."

Those words punched him like a fist to the chest.

"You were good, Senth, and I enjoyed you, but I don't have time for boyish games." She flipped her hand in the air. "And I certainly don't have time to bail you out of whatever scrapes your hyperactive inner child gets you into."

He couldn't breathe. His vision swam. With effort, Senth

walked to the door and pressed his forehead against it.

"I'm sorry, Senth, but that's the way it has to be."

I swore I'd never walk out again without talking it through. He remained there, frozen, rooted to the floor. *A man keeps his word.*

He could not bear it if she laughed. Senth turned and leaned back against the door, slid down it, and laid his arms across his upraised knees.

Disjointed images flickered through his mind. NarrAy in stiletto heels, mincing ahead of him in the starport. Saint-Cyr and his predatory raven's eyes. NarrAy, covered with bubbles. Khyff's face caught in a silent scream in an alley. NarrAy sleeping in his arms, sharing his pillow. NarrAy spurning him.

When he got home, Saint-Cyr would know immediately that he'd had sex. He'd see every guilty secret. NarrAy had changed everything about him in a fundamental way.

I don't walk the same, don't talk the same, don't think the same. His chest ached with pent-up emotion. *Don't hurt the same.*

The punishment he knew was coming would have been worth enduring with NarrAy as his reward when it was over and he was finally free. *Now? How can I endure punishment now?*

The sound of NarrAy's movements drew his attention.

She switched off the light, plunging the room into darkness. "Good night, Senth." The strain in her voice cut through the dark, spearing his heart like a shard of ice.

A moment later a pillow whumped the floor near his

feet, and a blanket followed.

Senth dragged them closer and lay down. Wetness pooled against his lashes, and he dashed it away, refusing to succumb to the tears of a boy.

She doesn't have time for a boy? Fine. I can be the man she wants. No more games. No more making life fun. I don't have to enjoy my work. I can just do the job, think of everything as a chore the way everyone else does, and never play again. I know the rules. I can comply. I can be a success. Touch all the bases, obey all the rules.

His disclaimer of a few hours earlier came to mind.

Saint-Cyr's obedient little thief. Controlled. Never arguing. Never questioning. Taking what he gives me and keeping my mouth shut. Guess that will be my life after all.

NarrAy tossed on the bed, and he listened to the sound of her breathing until it slowed and she fell asleep. A sobbing sigh left her throat, like a child weary after a bout of crying.

Senth braced one arm beneath him, grimacing at the spasms in his stomach. The boy's fist might have bruised him, but the pain of a beating was trifling compared to the agony of NarrAy's words stabbing through his heart.

He lay in painful silence a long time before sleep overcame him, his senses drowning in the smell of roses and the memory of sweet, warm vanilla on his tongue.

* * *

Tarth City, Imperial Palace, Stable—Sample Level

After his bath, Khyff wrapped himself in a thick terry robe and nodded off in the barber's chair while Triss shaved him. He flinched awake when a cool towel wrapped around his face.

"Easy." Trey patted Khyff's hand. "I'm almost finished with your manicure. Nice hands, by the way. A lot of men never care for their nails."

Khyff grunted in thanks. Stalkos had made them all stay clean, especially the ones who earned him the most money.

Triss unfolded a massage table, and he and Trey covered Khyff with a light blanket. They exposed only the part of him they worked on at that time, and once he trusted their touches would not turn sexual, he relaxed beneath their capable hands. In no hurry, they lavished attention on each muscle group, paying as much time on his fingers and toes as they did his abdomen and chest.

A man could get spoiled here in a big hurry. I'll be useless the rest of the day after this massage.

Khyff lashed himself mentally for his complacent thoughts, steeling himself against the seduction of such indolent pleasure. Before long, though, that same pleasure soothed him to sleep.

When it was time to dress for dinner, the twins woke him and escorted him back to his room.

Trey held out a charcoal, floor-length tunic. The high collar, shoulders, and long sleeves were a solid piece, but the rest consisted of narrow strips.

"I'm not wearing that."

"They always say that," Trey told Triss, who nodded

agreeably.

Khyff folded his arms across his chest. "There is no ffffftting way I'm walking around wearing a bunch of fluttering ribbons."

The twins laughed.

"It's your costume for the induction ceremony," Trey explained. "Everyone wears one."

Khyff gauged their expressions against his limited time with them. "If you two are setting me up, I am going to break you in half."

He pulled on the tunic and fastened it. When he stood still, the gray strips covered him completely, but one step and he exposed his entire body.

"Where are the pants?"

"They always ask that too," Triss commented. "There are none."

"Forget it. I'm not going anywhere dressed like this." He started unfastening the collar.

"We could escort you naked," Trey said, "but Her Majesty wants you to wear that."

Khyff hesitated. The twins were his height, no more muscled than he. He could take them in a fair fight.

"Her Majesty wants me to wear this? You're sure?"

"Positive." Trey smiled.

Damn it! With a small shake of his head, he refastened the tunic. No point arriving bruised and beaten.

Triss held out a man's gold ring set with onyx and circled with diamonds. "Put it on the first finger of your left hand."

Khyff complied and held out his hand to examine the ring. He brought it closer and smiled. The letter *K* was carved into the onyx. "This is the first letter of my name."

"Jewelry shows Her Majesty's favor."

"Oh, so everyone gets a ring."

Trey gave him a knowing look. "No. No one starts out with anything. Her Majesty will give you a ring shaped like a fist at the ceremony tonight, which goes on your right hand. That's the first jewelry most Jades receive. The fact that you're wearing jewelry in her colors won't go unnoticed by the others."

"Jades?"

"Stable members."

As in jaded. Khyff rubbed his thumb across the ring. *Or slaked.*

Triss opened the door. "Shall we go?"

Khyff glanced down at himself. "Don't I at least get shoes?"

Triss shook his head.

Khyff counted doors and memorized turns. Signs on the wall were no help. Triss and Trey stayed on either side of him through a maze of corridors that soon had him panicking, checking over his shoulder.

I'll never find my way out of here.

"Relax." Trey patted him on the shoulder. "We're assigned to you, so we won't leave you anywhere. Besides, you'll be in new quarters after this."

Prison face, Khyff. You're giving yourself away. The

tunic fluttered around his legs when he walked, exposing every part of him. Would Destoiya be there? His cock thickened at the thought, and he raised a hand to his forehead in dismay. *Talk about giving yourself away...*

They entered a dining area with one large table set with candelabra, a white tablecloth, china, and crystal. Seven men stood around it, all decked out in black formal evening clothes.

Khyff froze to the spot, fury rising in his gut.

"You lied to me," he whispered furiously. "No one else is wearing one of these things."

"We didn't lie." Trey smiled. "Every one of them wore a tunic like this at his induction."

The seven other men had been talking among themselves, and they turned as one to stare at Khyff.

He covered his cock with both hands.

One of the blonds walked toward him. The others resumed talking as if nothing had happened.

Tall and slender, the one approaching wore his hair as short as Khyff's. The beauty of his perfectly symmetrical features marked him as a Better.

"Alitus Vivaldi." He extended a hand. "It's okay to touch me. I'm totally attuned to Her Majesty. I can't addict you." They shook hands. The man had a firm grip.

"Khyff Antonello."

"Welcome to the Stable, Khyff. Also known as the male harem, the lair, den, corral, and kennel. Or as we like to call it"—Alitus quirked one brow—"the cockpit."

Khyff smiled. "I hear you're the favorite around here."

He chuckled. "Depends on what day it is." Alitus made a dismissive gesture to Triss and Trey, and they bowed before leaving. Alitus reached into a pocket and withdrew a sheet of paper. "Here. You'll need this."

Khyff unfolded it. Black marks trailed down the page. His name was at the top, and a list of numbers on the left side. A prickle of sweat broke out under his arms.

"Those are your vows."

What am I going to do now?

"I know you can't read," Alitus said without condemnation or ridicule. "Her Majesty knows too. It's okay." He nodded toward the others. "They never have to find out. I'll coach you on what to say." He handed Khyff a bud no bigger than the end of a stylus. "Put this in your ear."

When he did, the tiny device melted and flowed into the ear canal. Khyff rubbed the outside area. "What's it doing?"

"It's liquefying. It's a temporary listening device that'll evaporate before dinner's over." He adjusted a pin on his evening jacket. "Can you hear me?" Though he whispered, Alitus's voice came through distinctly.

Khyff nodded.

"Good." Alitus looked over his shoulder. "The servants are entering. That means Her Majesty's here."

A dozen or more male servants in black uniforms filed through the door. They lined up around the outside area next to Triss and Trey.

Khyff blinked. Every one of the servants in the room had the same face. Triss and Trey were not twins. They were androids.

"They look real, don't they?" Alitus adjusted his cuffs. "Appearances only. They'll lay down their lives to protect you. Enormous physical strength. Any one of them could pick us both up and walk around without straining a muscle. They're incapable of sex in any fashion, and though I doubt you care, some of the others do. Friendly, warm, comfortable to be around. Easy to confide in. They'll laugh and joke with you, but never let yourself forget they are one hundred percent loyal to Her Majesty. They don't."

Destoiya entered the room, and the other men gathered around her, bowing and then kissing her on the lips when she greeted them one at a time.

Destoiya wore a black evening gown, sleeveless and strapless. Her hair was up. Ice blue fire crystals glittered at her throat, ears, and wrists.

Alitus sighed, watching her with open longing. "She's fabulous, isn't she?"

Khyff murmured a response he doubted Alitus even heard, so taken was the man with Destoiya. *Was that part of the addiction?*

Alitus blinked and shook his head. He turned to Khyff. "Her Majesty will come and lead you to the stage in a moment. This ceremony gives everyone else a peek at the competition. You'll feel naked as hell, but resist the urge to cover yourself. I remember how I felt." He chuckled. "All I could think about while I stood up there was that I hoped my dick was covered."

Khyff swallowed.

"You don't have anything to be ashamed of, believe me." Alitus grinned. "We all share the same pool and gymnasium, among other things. You'll get your turn to check us out, whether you want to or not, I'm afraid."

Before Khyff could ask about that cryptic comment, Destoiya walked up to them, and they both bowed to her.

"Good evening, Majesty." Alitus leaned forward and kissed her on the mouth. "You look radiant this evening."

"You always say that, Alitus." Destoiya smiled up at the man like a young girl newly in love, not a thing false about her expression.

Khyff smiled in appreciation. *He really must be good.*

"You're always beautiful to me, Majesty." Alitus picked up her hand and bowed over it, then pressed his lips against her fingers. He inclined his head to Khyff and returned to the group of men who were seating themselves around the large table.

Destoiya turned to Khyff. "You shook hands with him, didn't you?"

"Yes, Majesty. He said it was—"

He broke off when Destoiya laughed.

Damn. "He addicted me, didn't he?"

"Don't take it too hard. Making people like him is part of what he is. Alitus will never know a true enemy. He'll have foes, yes, and people who want to displace him, but it's impossible not to like him once he touches you. I've never seen it wear off either. One of the finest Betters ever made. I count myself fortunate to have him. I'm sure I waste his talents by not making him an ambassador or politician, but in truth, I can't bear to part with him for any length of time." She looked Khyff up and down. "You look good enough to eat."

"Thank you. This"—he gestured to the tunic—"makes me uncomfortable."

"Good. I want you squirming." Her gaze slid down him. "Did Alitus tell you what to do?"

Khyff touched his ear. "He said he'd coach me and that you knew…"

"I do." She took his hand. "We'll go up on the stage in a moment. I'll say your name, then go through your vows. You'll respond to me as Alitus directs you. You're not my slave, Khyff. I want you to understand that."

He swallowed, his throat so tight, he could not speak even if he knew what to say.

"Your vows are those of a free man. I'll ask if you're willing to stay with me. But until I have the item your brother now possesses, you have no choice about leaving. Afterward, if you decide you want to stay, the choice will be yours."

"You gave me your word that Senth—"

"I will keep it. No harm will come to your brother. But until he delivers the item to me, you're my hostage, and I have every intention of enjoying your services while you're here." She dragged a fingertip down his chest. "Exclusively. I'll pay attention to the others when I've had my fill of you." She smiled. "To that end, my Jades are all hoping you drop dead onstage tonight."

"Thank you. I feel so much better now."

She laughed. "If your brother doesn't deliver as well as you do, Khyff"—Destoiya's mouth twitched into a sultry smile—"the Jades in my stable may be hating you for a long, long time."

* * *

Kelthia, Miraj City
Starhaven Leojnimaj
Wintresq 17

NarrAy wore a midlength, plain red dress with long sleeves and a white lace collar. Red boots rose to her knees. She'd tucked her hair up and pinned it and didn't bother with makeup, trying to blend in. Men stared at her anyway. All of them except Senth.

He walked beside her in silence all the way through the starport, dragging his bagbot behind him, never once glancing in her direction.

She'd asked for his scorn. Telling him they were over, that he was a child, that he meant nothing to her. The grief at losing him washed over her, and her step faltered, one foot twisting.

Senth immediately supported her arm. "Are you all right?"

NarrAy brightened at his concern, then withdrew her arm and nodded soberly. *Can't let him touch me. Have to let him get my influence out of his system.*

Senth glanced at her several times while they made their way to the nonsecured area.

A driver in black opened the door to a hoversine when

she and Senth exited the terminal. No doubt the shuttle was sent by Saint-Cyr and would be billed separately. NarrAy sighed.

Senth sat on the far side of the seat, gazing out the window, his profile serene. The energetic youth who'd slid on stocking feet across the floor, locked himself in a bagbot for fun, and brought her candy and flowers might never have existed at all. Judging from his expression now, he might be older than his brother. Khyff, the blond god of war and lust and anger and ancient, lonely eyes.

The car came to a stop outside a hotel, and Senth set a hand on the door handle. "My Sen'dai will want you to imprint the contract." He did not look her direction. "He'll want to know I satisfied you."

Those words dug into her heart.

NarrAy followed Senth into the hotel. A uniformed servant bowed to him as if he were royalty, then led the way to a private elevator. On the fourteenth floor, Senth stepped out and gestured NarrAy to precede him.

The suite on this level occupied the entire floor, and a doorman swept a deep bow before opening double doors. The room beyond was open and spacious, far grander than the one they'd occupied on Tarth. Pale paper lined the walls; gilded tables and oversize couches and chairs filled the huge space. A massive marble fireplace sat center stage on the far wall.

The Harbinger and a Praetorian faced each other on opposing couches.

NarrAy halted. *A trap. I should have known.*

But she'd passed the holopic containing the data to a resistance operative long before they left the ship. It was already on its way to another starport and, eventually, the rebel ship. Destoiya would never get her hands on it.

Saint-Cyr came to his feet. The Praetorian followed suit.

"Senthys!" The Harbinger strode forward. "I thought you'd never get here. Ms. Jorlan. Please be seated. I assure you this is not what you think."

"I'll stand." NarrAy eyed the Praetorian before turning her attention to Saint-Cyr. "Suppose you tell me what it truly is, then."

Saint-Cyr inclined his head to the Praetorian. "Sir, if you please."

Coming to attention, the Kin clicked his boot heels together and made a slight bow. "Lieutenant Tahll Jhareen, at your service. Her Majesty Empress Rheyn Destoiya directed me to obtain the data that your late parents hid within their belongings, Captain Jorlan." He held out one hand. "If you would be so kind?"

"You expect me to hand over what my parents spent their lives working on? What they died for? Give it up like that?" NarrAy snapped her fingers. "You must take me for a fool, Lieutenant."

"Not at all, Captain Jorlan. Her Majesty expected your response. Therefore I've been instructed to deliver this note to Mr. Antonello."

"Me?" Senth had been standing at one side, arms folded tightly across his stomach. He accepted the envelope Jhareen offered.

Saint-Cyr gestured for him to hurry and moved to stand beside him.

Senth read the enclosed paper. His face went white.

"Let me see." NarrAy took the paper from his hands.

It bore the Conqueror's seal and promised that, unless Senth delivered the data for the jump prototype to Destoiya, Khyffen Antonello would die.

Chapter Nineteen

Kelthia, Miraj City, Holding District
The Holding Suites

Even if NarrAy wanted to, she could not grant Destoiya the data, since it was already out of her hands. If her parents had died rather than surrender it to the empress, she could do nothing less. But did that give her the right to end Khyff's life as well?

She waited for Senth to plead for his brother's life. How could she bear it when she had to turn him down? What could she possibly say that would make him understand her parents' technology must never fall into Destoiya's hands?

Billions of lives were at stake, as well as the freedom of planets not yet discovered. With this technology, Destoiya could send in one lone assassin behind enemy lines, or an entire army. The Conqueror would not stop until she ruled a thousand worlds.

But instead of pleading, Senth sank into a chair in silence, leaned forward, and buried his face between his hands. Saint-Cyr laid a hand on Senth's shoulder.

Neither of them looked at her.

The Praetorian spread his hands. "Your response, Captain?"

"I need time to consider it."

"Not good enough, Captain. Her Majesty wants your answer now." Jhareen tapped a wristband communicator. "She's waiting to decide Mr. Antonello's fate."

Senth clutched his hands together as if he was praying. Still, he did not lift his head.

He trusts me. Even though I hurt him, he trusts me. How could she let him down? He sat there in silence, waiting for her to do the right thing. *This is what a true man does. He loves his woman enough to trust her, even with a decision like this. This is the kind of man I've waited for my entire life.*

"Mr. Saint-Cyr? How can the empress have Khyff? I thought he came home."

The Harbinger's whiteless eyes gave no indication of emotion. "According to the starlines, Khyffen checked in at the gate on Tarth, but he never boarded the ship. I've had locals searching for him."

"Lieutenant Jhareen, I want proof Khyff is safe before I even think about complying."

Senth's head jerked up, hope and pride clear on his face. He turned to watch the Praetorian.

Jhareen produced Khyff's work ID, a small lock of hair, and a flatpic. In it, Khyff stood against a stone wall, bound at wrists and ankles, a leather collar around his neck, his shirt torn open. The Conqueror stood beside him, one hand on his bare chest.

Prurient, whoring bitch.

NarrAy showed the pic to Senth and Saint-Cyr.

Senth made a low growling sound. Saint-Cyr turned aside but gripped Senth's shoulder more tightly. Not at all the response that NarrAy expected. They were waiting for her to respond.

"I'll need five days."

A whispered prayer left Senth's mouth.

Jhareen shook his head. "You have two."

"Five, or no deal." NarrAy held her arms out at her sides. "I no longer have possession of the data. I need travel time, time to retrieve it, and time to get it to Destoiya. That's going to take five days."

"No." Jhareen shook his head again. "The most I'm authorized to allow is three."

NarrAy rubbed her chin. "If I can get Senth's help..."

Saint-Cyr tapped him on the shoulder.

Senth stood.

"And," NarrAy said, capturing Saint-Cyr's immediate attention, "assurances Senth won't be punished for anything he might have done while with me." She added, "Or will do in the near future."

Darkened cheeks revealed Senth's embarrassment.

Saint-Cyr's eyebrows shot up. He turned to Senth, appraising him head to toe. "Very well, Captain Jorlan. Done."

"Where is Khyff now, Jhareen? Is he being cared for?"

"Oh, he's quite safe, Captain." The Kin's mouth twisted

in a sarcastic smile. "Her Majesty admitted him to her stable last night. I imagine he's happy to wait for the three days."

"You bastard!"

Saint-Cyr brought Senth up short with one hand. "Son, don't."

He shook off the man's touch and took another step toward Jhareen. "You don't know anything about my brother. Khyff's not a piece-of-kkkhh whore like you!"

Jhareen sidled away from him.

"Take your answer to the empress," NarrAy told the Praetorian. "We'll deliver the goods in three days on Tarth. And if she lays one hand on Khyff…"

Jhareen smirked. "I suspect it's a bit late for that requirement."

Senth roared like a jungle cat and lunged for the Praetorian.

NarrAy threw herself in front of Senth, dug in her heels, and pushed back on his chest with her full weight. She slid backward on the floor, unable to slow him down.

"Take it back!"

"Senth, no!" NarrAy wrapped her arms around him. "He's a Praetorian! He'll kill you."

Senth's chest vibrated against her hands. A series of deep, booming growls rose from his throat. Fangs glistened in his mouth. He roared again.

The Praetorian backed toward the exit.

Senth roared and lunged.

The Praetorian fled without looking back.

NarrAy nearly fell trying to keep Senth from following, but Saint-Cyr stopped Senth by slipping a leather loop around his throat from behind.

"Down!" Saint-Cyr commanded.

"Stop it!" NarrAy pushed at the Harbinger. He ignored her.

Senth hissed and yowled and twisted like a mad cat, clutching the collar with both hands.

"I said down!" The Harbinger dragged hard on the collar with one hand. With the other, he jammed a short prod against Senth's back.

It emitted a spark of voltage that forced Senth to his knees.

"Stop it!" NarrAy threw herself between them. "What are you doing? Stop it now!"

Senth choked against the collar, his lips blue. Still, he twisted and fought.

"Let him go! He can't breathe."

Saint-Cyr grimaced as if he'd jabbed himself, but then zapped Senth again.

This time Senth hit the floor and lay twitching.

NarrAy punched Saint-Cyr square on the jaw and sent him reeling across the room. She knelt and loosened the leather from around Senth's neck.

He gasped for air, a dark line of bruises already appearing around his throat. She drew his head onto her lap and stroked hair away from his face.

"When he turns feral like that, it takes violence to bring

him out of it." Saint-Cyr rubbed his jaw. "I assure you, he needs a strong hand to rein him in. He's a HalfKin. Senthys is hardly the domesticated kitten you think he is."

"Is that how you punish him? Tie him up and shock him? Is that why he's so terrified of you?"

Seeing Senth was all right, NarrAy eased his head off her lap and rose. When she advanced on the Harbinger, he took one step back.

"I warn you, Ms. Jorlan—"

"That's *Captain* Jorlan, and you'll warn me of what?" She jerked the prod out of his hand. "Think you're fearsome when you're holding one of these?" NarrAy turned it on. It arced in her hand. "So am I."

The Harbinger retreated a few more steps. "You don't know what Senthys is like when he's feral. It takes everything I have to control him."

NarrAy thrust the prod at him, and Saint-Cyr jerked back.

"Is that why you drug him?" She set the prod on a higher setting. "What is it you say to control his mind? Do you tell him he's feral? That he needs you? What is it, Saint-Cyr?" She swiped at him again. "Do you tell him to fear you?"

Saint-Cyr bumped up against the wall, both hands lifted. He twisted his head, avoiding the prod.

"Don't, NarrAy." Behind her, Senth sounded weary and weak.

She never took her gaze off Saint-Cyr.

"I deserved it," Senth admitted, still on the floor. "I'd've killed Jhareen if I'd gotten my hands on him. My Sen'dai has to punish me. I deserve it. I need him to keep me out of trouble."

"No, you don't." NarrAy turned off the prod and hurled it at the wall. It broke into pieces. She walked swiftly away from the Harbinger. "He controls you so you won't leave him, Senth. You bring in a huge amount of income for this man, and you don't need him. The truth is, he needs you."

Senth shook his head, eyes down. "I have to obey him. I know the rules. I feel better when I do what I'm told."

"No!" NarrAy stooped beside him and stroked Senth's face. "That isn't feeling better, my tiger. That's feeling owned."

He lifted his pale blue gaze and held hers a long moment before he turned to Saint-Cyr, who still stood across the room.

NarrAy stood. "I want Senth's freedom, Saint-Cyr. I know his contract's almost up. Name your price."

"You don't want him, Captain Jorlan." The Harbinger straightened his jacket. "Truth is, Senthys has already grown too strong for me to control him much longer. To manage him I had to use his desire to help Khyffen."

Senth accepted NarrAy's hand for balance as he stood, and then drew her close to him.

"You used my brother to control me?"

Saint-Cyr made an offhand gesture. "I didn't buy Khyffen's freedom, Senthys. It was handed to him in a legal decision against Stalkos."

Senth flinched at the name. He looked down at his right hand and covered it with his left.

"Did you tell her how you got that scar, Senthys?"

"What did you do to him, Saint-Cyr?" NarrAy stepped in front of Senth.

"That scar is from nothing I did, Captain Jorlan. It's from what Senthys did."

She turned back to her young lover, but he refused to look at her.

"Shall I tell her, son?"

Senth remained quiet.

"I suppose I have to, then. She needs to know what you're capable of."

"Sen'dai, don't. Please. I'll stay with you."

"No." NarrAy wrapped an arm around Senth's waist. "Let him tell me. I want to know."

Senth stood so still, she could hardly tell he was breathing.

"A former partner of mine named James Stalkos sent a petty thief to my house one night. I had something that belonged to Stalkos, and he wanted it back. Senth heard the thief downstairs and went after him."

"A thief named Rokko. The way I heard it, you had his hand nailed to a table and beat him. Did you have him killed? There's no way I'll believe he died from choking on food."

"You've done some homework. But that story about Rokko dying in prison was an elaborate ruse and completely false. We gave it out to protect Senthys. He attacked the man and killed him with his bare hands, and the scar on his hand is from Rokko trying to protect himself. Senthys took the knife away from him and plunged it through Rokko's hand, pinning him into place. He then cold-bloodedly tore out the man's throat with his fangs."

NarrAy set a hand over her heart. Beside her, Senth tried to draw away, but she tightened her arm around him.

"The only way I could pull him off Rokko was by shocking him until he let go. He was drenched in blood, gnawing the man's throat." He added, "Senthys was fourteen years old. Kin males only get more aggressive after that age. I've kept him on Shackle since he was fifteen, but he's already on the highest dose he can take."

She clasped Senth's right hand in hers. "You can't control him forever, Saint-Cyr!"

"I'm not trying to control Senthys, Captain Jorlan. I'm trying to protect him, as well as everyone else, from what he might do." He brushed at his jacket. "That innocent-looking young man you're holding hands with can be a merciless killer."

NarrAy brought Senth's hand to her mouth and kissed the scar. "I think the only one here who's merciless is you, Saint-Cyr."

Senth came to fierce attention, his gaze riveted on her.

The Harbinger narrowed his predatory eyes.

"All these years you've let Senth think he was some kind of animal you had to control, instead of teaching him how to overcome his aggression. I've worked around Kin most of my life. I know how territorial they are. A HalfKin child who's never been taught how to use his strength can be dangerous, yes. But he doesn't have to be. Senth was protecting his family when Rokko broke in, wasn't he? No one else came to help. When Rokko stabbed him, *that's* when Senth attacked, wasn't it? When he was hurt and afraid. He thought if he didn't protect you, you'd suffer like he did."

Saint-Cyr's nostrils flared. His mouth tightened.

"Isn't that what happened?" NarrAy waited.

Beside her, Senth huffed in his throat like a caged tiger, his body humming with restrained growls.

"You made me lie," he told Saint-Cyr. "You said I could never tell anyone what happened. You said that was the only way you could make sure no one took me away from you."

The Harbinger hesitated.

"You said they'd kill me for slaughtering a human."

"I wanted to protect you, son."

"Don't call me that!"

NarrAy drew closer to Senth.

"I've never been your son, and you sure as hell aren't my father."

Go, Senth! NarrAy smiled with pride.

"I won't let you drug me anymore. I owe two years on my slave contract, but when that's over, I want my freedom. And if NarrAy will have me"—he met her eyes, drawing their joined hands to his mouth for a kiss—"I want her too."

NarrAy put her arms around his neck and kissed him. "I want you forever, my tiger. I was trying to protect you from being punished when I attempted to end our relationship. I couldn't stand the thought of him hurting you."

"Nothing *he* could ever do to me could hurt as much as

losing you."

"Oh, Senth!"

He hauled her halfway off her feet and devoured her with kisses.

Saint-Cyr coughed.

They turned toward him.

"I had already told Khyffen I owed you your freedom." Saint-Cyr withdrew a notereader from an inner pocket and tossed it to Senth.

He caught it.

"That's your contract. I've already marked it 'paid in full.'"

"What?" Senth flipped open the reader and thumbed through it. He looked over at Saint-Cyr. "Then why did you do that to me? Shock me like that?"

"I couldn't let you risk your freedom attacking Jhareen. Not when your brother's life is at stake."

Senth gave NarrAy a tremulous smile. "I'm free."

"I'd like you to consider working for me, Senthys." The Harbinger cleared his throat. "At guild wages, of course."

"Fffffft that, Tiger. I have a better offer. The resistance could really use a thief with your talents." NarrAy fingered his shirt collar. "And to tell the truth, I could use a husband, if you're interested in the job."

Saint-Cyr's mouth dropped open.

Senth laughed. "Fftt-fftt sha kee!" He whirled her around. Letting her slide down the front of his body, he drew her tighter for a long kiss.

When he released her, NarrAy ran a finger along his lips. "I love you, Senth."

"I love you, NarrAy."

"Ahem." Saint-Cyr interrupted. "I hate to break this up, but don't you have something to deliver on Tarth?"

"Deliver?" NarrAy shook her head. "You think I'd actually agree to hand over my parents' work to the Conqueror?"

"But"—Senth paled—"you said... But she'll kill my brother."

"Oh no, she won't, Tiger. I'm not leaving my future brother-in-law under that bitch's control, but we're not handing over the prototype for perjump technology either."

"Then what do you have planned, Captain?" The Harbinger took a step closer.

NarrAy slid both arms around Senth. "We're going to go visit with the Sleeper and offer to test the prototype for the resistance."

"Test it how?" Senth asked.

NarrAy grinned. "We're going to go get your brother out of there."

Chapter Twenty

All People's Liberation Army Ship Vandal
Officers' Quarters

NarrAy lay in bed, propped on pillows so she could feast on the sight of Senth shaving.

He used the same kind of razor her father had favored. High-tech devices might have ruled in her father's lab, but at home he'd liked the simple luxury of a good lather and a sharp blade.

Naked from the waist up, Senth had his thighs braced against the sink while he leaned toward the mirror. The muscles in his arm flexed and relaxed when he dipped his razor underwater. He shook off the excess and raised the blade to his face again. He dragged it slowly up under his chin.

NarrAy used to love watching her father shave. He'd made a game of it. He'd try to soap her nose, and she'd dance out of his reach, giggling. She listened to the scrape of Senth's razor across the stubble on his chin, remembering the sound when her father shaved.

He used to pick her up after he'd shaved and hold her in his arms to let her touch his smooth face. So many memories, even more precious now that he was gone forever. She flicked away tears, wiping aside melancholy thoughts with them. Time to get back to business.

O'Venna had been more than happy to agree to testing the prototype with a real jump, especially when NarrAy pointed out that her parents had designed the device using her DNA for all the initial runs.

"*It's still only a prototype*," O'Venna had cautioned. "*Perjump could be dangerous.*"

Perjump, short for personal jump technology. She already knew some of its dangers.

"*It's all we have*," he'd warned. "*If anything happens to the prototype, there's no way for us to come after you. It could take years before we could reverse engineer what your parents built.*"

Wearing the prototype on her belt, she and Senth would disappear from the *Vandal* and reappear inside the Stable. If everything went right, they'd disable security, grab Khyff, and be back on board in no time. *If* everything went right.

How did Senth put it when I first hired him? Oh yes.

"*Count on it. Grab and go. Just like that.*" She snapped her fingers the way he had.

Senth turned from the mirror, razor in hand. His lazy smile promised paradise. "Impatient, love?"

"Sorry." She smiled at him. "I was thinking of something. Not snapping my fingers at you. Take your time. I wouldn't want a cut on that baby face of yours."

His peevish grimace at that comment made her giggle.

"I wouldn't have minded staying in that little room they

gave us before." Senth finished the last few strokes on his chin. "Though it's great to have some space to stretch."

"My promotion warrants it, according to O'Venna. I'd have been happy in a bunk bed with you. As long as we shared the same bunk."

"Me too, sweetie." Senth splashed water on his face and dried it, then tossed the towel aside.

He unfastened his pants while he padded toward the bed. He let them drop to the floor and reached to pull down the blanket.

"Oh, Senth. Stay right there a moment, love." She sat up in the bed. "Let me look at you."

"Whatever you say, mistress." His smile teased.

Senth let her look her fill. He had promised not to cut his hair now that he was free, because she loved it long. She slid her gaze down his defined abs, to his narrow hips, down along the corded muscles in his legs.

"Mmm, mmm, mmm." NarrAy shook her head in awe. "I can't believe you're finally all mine, Tiger."

His shaft stiffened while she watched, and she trailed her gaze along its length, giving it all the attention it seemed to crave. Thicker than her wrist and longer than her hand even soft, his cock ended in a plum-shaped head the color of dusky roses. It lifted, engorged and dark, pointing at the ceiling, the tiny slit at the opening glistening with precum.

"I'm going to keep that big, hard cock inside me all night, Senth. But right now I want to taste it."

His cheeks turned a bright pink, and he held his lower lip between his fangs.

She drew back the blanket and sheet. "Get in this bed and come over here, you hot man. Get on your knees in front of my mouth and show me how lucky I am."

She sat up in the bed slightly, propping pillows behind her to be at the correct level to take Senth into her mouth. He straddled her on his knees.

"Perfect, Tiger. Put your knees farther apart. Yes, like that. I want you totally open to my touch. My mouth."

She fanned out her fingers across his smooth chest and traced a mark on his abdomen, near his ribs. "Have you been in a fight recently?"

He covered the bruise with his hand. "It's nothing. Pissed off the wrong person; that's all. It's fading. Almost gone."

"I noticed you haven't eaten much since we left Kelthia. Are you sure you're okay?"

"Hey." Senth took her face in his hands and kissed her. "Forget about it. It's no big deal. Believe me. I'm fine."

"Good." When she rubbed her fingers across his nipples, they hardened. "Lean forward, Senth. Put your hands up high on the wall behind me, wide apart."

The position arched him over the top of her and gave him balance while she explored him with her hands and mouth. He shivered. The touch of her tongue and fingers on the hard muscles of his chest and ridged abs raised goose bumps on his skin. She trailed a finger from his navel down the fine line of hair to his groin. His straight pubic hair felt like a kitten's fur.

"NarrAy, I feel more than naked posing like this."

She chuckled. "Better get used to it, Senth." She stroked his lower back and the rounded cheeks of his hard ass. "I love putting you on display. Looking at you. I can't get enough."

"I hope you know you're next."

"Ooh, is the big, scary tiger going to eat me too?"

He chuckled. "You're damn right I am."

She leaned forward and licked his flat stomach, gripping his hips to hold him still when he shrank back.

"Come on, NarrAy. You're driving me crazy. Let me touch you now. Please, baby."

"Not yet, Senth. Your body's so open in this position. I really like it." She ran her hands down the insides of his thighs.

He jerked under her touch, sucking in a harsh breath. "NarrAy, please, let me touch you."

"After I've tasted you awhile, love. I want you ready."

"I'm ready now."

She tilted back her head so he could see her eyes. "No begging or I won't take you inside me until I've looked at you for another hour."

He closed his eyes, a flicker of pleasure-pain crossing his features. He arched his neck, head back.

NarrAy caressed Senth's thighs, scraped her nails over the sensitive skin of his hips, and cupped his buttocks. She pulled him toward her, opened her mouth, and breathed against his cock.

He sighed, the sound deep and harsh.

"I love making you lose control, Tiger. I want you wild.

Feral." She licked his cock tip, loving it when he hissed. The hot shaft throbbed with a life of its own. "This part of you is for my pleasure, Senth." She kissed the tip. "No other woman is ever going to get your cock in her mouth. Or in any other part of her. Is she?"

"Never, NarrAy." His eyes blazed with passion as he looked down at her. "I swear it. Only you."

"Good." She kissed the wet tip, licked it once. "Do you want me to make love to you with my mouth?"

"Yesss!"

"Then I want you to roar when I make you come, Senth. I want you feral."

Eyes wide, he shook his head once. "I can't, NarrAy. It's not safe."

That was Saint-Cyr talking. She knew that look. Limitations. Boundaries. Fears.

"Senth, you never have to be afraid of who you are again. I want you to let go."

"I might hurt you, NarrAy."

"I can take anything you dish out, Tiger, and then some. Now I mean it. I want you to let go. Be wild for me, Senth. I want it."

She parted her lips over the huge cockhead, taking the tip into her mouth. She licked the underside, lapped along the crown. His legs jerked.

"NarrAy, oh, that feels so good!"

She couldn't take his huge cock fully into her mouth, so she licked all the way down its underside. Senth's strangled cry of lust mixed with hoarse Kin curses.

NarrAy slid her hands down his wide shaft and squeezed the base. Senth made guttural noises, and his hands slapped the wall. If he'd had claws, he'd have torn holes in it.

She lapped and sucked him, sliding back so she could flick her tongue against the tip and then take as much of his erection into her mouth as she could. His masculine scent enticed, excited, filled her as much as his cock. NarrAy pressed her legs together as wetness seeped onto her thighs. Her clit ached for release. Her nipples tingled, wanting the rough scratch of his tongue.

A purr resounded through his chest, vibrating his entire body.

Yummy.

She cupped his balls, weighing them on her palm. She slid two fingers from just below his anus all the way down to his testicles. Inarticulate cries erupted from him.

Having him on his knees, displayed so appealingly, his cock in her mouth, and hearing him purr sent an orgasm fluttering through her. She let his engorged cockhead pop out of her mouth and cupped one hand between her thighs.

Opening herself with two fingers, she gripped his cock with the other hand. "Put it in me, Senth." She stretched out on the bed. "Take me."

Senth maneuvered himself between her thighs. He lifted one of her legs and slid into her pussy. His width stretched her so far, she had to wiggle her hips to get him all the way inside.

He gave a languorous stroke, withdrew halfway, and plunged in again slowly. Such exquisite torture.

"Harder, Senth. Deeper."

"Whatever your heart desires, mistress."

He pushed her knees wide apart with his shoulders and withdrew all the way. He rocked the bed with a hard thrust that made her sob.

NarrAy arched herself up against him, milking his penis as he drove into her repeatedly. She twisted her hips, pulling her legs wider apart.

Senth growled, fangs bared. He dragged her up hard against him.

"Yes, Senth. Show me how wild you are. Take me, Tiger. Make me yours."

His unrelenting cock opened her wide with each hard thrust. Filled her.

NarrAy's breasts bounced. Senth palmed them. Kneaded. Squeezed. Rolled her nipples between fingers and thumbs.

She cupped a hand beneath one breast and offered it, and Senth scraped his cat's tongue across the nipple. When his teeth tightened over it, NarrAy panted hoarsely, lost in heat. She dug her fingers into Senth's buttocks. Ground herself against him.

His fangs gleamed. Head back and mouth open, he gave a tiger's snarling roar—savage, barbaric, free.

He held her down while he thrust into her, claiming her, taking her with unleashed passion. Senth pumped his cum into her. Drenched her with liquid satisfaction while he purred and purred and purred. He rocked gently into her while she came down from—

"Senth! Oh, oh!"

He stilled at once, his eyes huge. "What is it, baby? Did I hurt you?"

"No, no, Tiger. I didn't do it!"

His confusion showed. He pulled out of her. "Didn't what, baby?"

Tears blurred her vision. Inside, her body still fluttered from her orgasm.

Senth lay down next to her and drew her into his arms. "Baby, don't cry! What's wrong? Please, talk to me. Don't shut me out."

She turned on her side, grinning at him. "Senth, this is the first time I've ever had an orgasm without my pheromones taking over. I didn't crest at all."

His nose twitched, making her giggle. He was smelling her.

"Is this a good thing?"

She nodded, too contented to speak.

Senth brushed aside the tears on her cheeks. He rubbed their wetness between fingers and thumbs. "So these are happy tears?"

"Yes."

"Why, baby? I don't understand."

NarrAy slid her arms around his waist and drew Senth close. He cuddled her into him, her head on his shoulder, strong hands holding her protectively against his body.

"It means I came because of you, Tiger. I didn't need anything but you." She pressed a quick kiss against his chin.

"I'm happy because it means I'm really, really in love."

"Will your pheromones come back?"

"They're still there, Tiger, but from now on I'm not ruled by them. Your love set me free."

Senth looked long and deep into her eyes, adoration in his gaze. "You set me free first, NarrAy. You loved enough to let me be whole."

He purred again, making NarrAy melt into his arms.

"Oh, Senth, I want to stay in this moment forever. Safe in your arms, lost in your love. I never want it to end."

She snuggled close, listening to the sound dearest to her in the entire world. Her tiger's purr of love.

* * *

Tarth City, Palace District, Imperial Palace
Wintresq 17

NarrAy expected queasiness when her body reassembled inside the palace. Instead it was like she'd closed her eyes in one place and opened them in another.

Instead of the *Vandal's* Ready Room, they stood in a utility room stocked with linens and deactivated housecleaning droids.

The swift disorientation of different surroundings startled but didn't hurt.

Senth, on the other hand, dropped to his knees at her side and doubled over.

"Tiger!" She knelt beside him. "Didn't the jumpdrug

help? Are you sick?"

He braced one arm across his stomach. "I got punched." He grimaced. "The night we broke up. Been hurting ever since."

"Why didn't you tell me?"

"Because you'd worry like you are now." He was ashen and shaking. Moments ago he'd been fine.

"I have good reason to worry, Senth. My parents knew perjump couldn't be used by an injured person."

He looked up. "Why not?"

"When there was an injury, perjump accelerated the damage." She laid her hands on his shoulders. "They wanted to use it to move casualties off a battlefield or accident victims to a hospital, but in every test, it made the injury worse. You should have told me!"

Senth grunted, still on his knees on the floor.

"We have to get you back on board." She reached for the perjump controls.

He grabbed her hand. "No! Not without my brother."

"Senth, I—"

"No." His grip tightened on her hand. His pale eyes were flinty, hard, determined. "You said there was only enough power for one jump here and back. I'm not leaving without my brother!"

"And just how are you going to work in your condition?"

"I can make it." He clenched his teeth. "Help me up."

"Senth—"

"NarrAy, I need you to trust me. Let me do my job." He

rubbed his thumb across the back of her hand. His innocent blue eyes pleaded with her. "Please. Help me save my brother."

"All right." She let him lean on her arm and helped him rise, supporting his weight as best she could. "If we landed where we thought we would, security should be through that door."

She put her left arm around Senth's waist. With his right arm draped over her shoulder, she helped him into the security room.

A wall of lights, switches, and monitors glowed in the eerie dark. How would he ever know where to find his brother with all those indicators?

Grimacing, Senth dug his left hand into a pocket and retrieved his lockpick. With his arm still over her shoulder, he used both hands to set the lockpick's controls and held the unit up in front of the panel of lights. He passed it slowly across each row, then down and back in the other direction.

The pick bleeped, and Senth turned it off and slid it back in his pocket.

"This is the last room locked, so I'm betting that's where she's keeping him."

"And if you're wrong?"

"Then we're about to pay a visit to a total stranger." He moved his arm off her shoulder. "Can you hold me up on the other side instead? I need my right hand for this."

NarrAy slid around and took her place on his left. "What if someone comes in?"

"Guild intel says all the security is automated." He

touched part of the panel and then worked so quickly, his fingers blurred. "Done." He motioned to the door. "Let's go get Khyff."

"Are you sure it's safe now?"

He gave her a perturbed smile. "What's that supposed to mean?"

"That was awfully quick. Are you sure it's—"

"NarrAy, never think about the importance of a lock. Just pick it." He jerked his head toward the door. "Come on."

They entered a lushly appointed bedroom complete with canopied bed and fireplace. Upon finding it empty, they looked in on the tiled bath and a separate sitting room leading to a balcony.

"No sign of him, Tiger."

Senth stumbled, and NarrAy helped him lean against the wall. His mouth made a harsh line of pain.

"I'm taking you back to the ship, Senth. Your face is white. This is—"

"No." He pulled free of her grasp. "Not without my brother."

"You stubborn—What can we do, Tiger? He's not here."

He nudged his chin toward a red door with a lock on the outside. "Let's check there."

He took only one step before collapsing. NarrAy almost couldn't stop his fall. She clung to him, using his momentum to turn his body and ease him to the floor. His lips were bluish, and the veins beneath the skin of his face showed.

"No." His fingers closed over hers when she reached for

the perjump controls.

"Senth! You're seriously hurt. I—"

"If you love me, NarrAy, find my brother."

He watched her while she weighed the risks of complying. She relented at the naked plea in his eyes.

"All right, Tiger. You rest here."

He nodded, eyes closing.

If Khyff isn't in that room, like it or not, I'm taking Senth back to the ship. She turned the bolt on the door and pushed it open. Red light similar to night ops glowed from indirect sources. Odd-shaped furniture covered with leather surfaces and straps filled the room. She swallowed, seeing the items for what they really were.

Swings, slings, tables, scaffolds—all structures enabling different positions and angles for whatever person might be strapped into or on them. Whips and canes hung on the walls beside manacles and long links of chain. She searched beneath tables and behind scaffolds. The smell of sweat and sex filled the small area, mixed with the coppery tang of blood.

She found Khyff huddled in a corner, naked and shivering, arms wrapped around his knees. He turned away from her.

She stripped off her coat and went down on one knee beside him, offering the garment. "Here, Khyff. I know it won't fit you, but you can wrap it around your waist."

Braced against the wall, he rocked his head back and forth. "Go away."

Even in the red light, she could see he was bloody. His

eyes were swollen half-shut. Fingernail scrapes lined his chest and arms. The bruises ringing his wrists and ankles told her he'd been bound, abused and abandoned, locked up and forgotten.

I hope Destoiya rots in hell for this.

NarrAy kept her gaze on Khyff's face. "It's all right. You have nothing to be ashamed of. I'm here to help you."

He shook his head. "Let me die."

Untreated, he'd suffer from loss of blood and infection, but his wounds didn't look that severe. It hit her all at once that the death he referred to wouldn't come from his injuries. He meant to take his own life.

What did that monster do to you?

"Khyff, I'm not leaving you here. You're coming with me, and that's an order, Mister." She shoved the coat against his hands. "Now you take this. Right now!"

He reached out a hand that shook violently, dragged the coat back, and held it next to him. "She said she shares her toys. Gave me to three women." His voice sounded like concrete dragging on steel: hard, rough, threatening. "They forced Thrust into me." He clutched her coat to him. "Still hurting."

He was still erect, he meant.

"Oh, Khyff. I'm so sorry."

No wonder he didn't want to move. He was hiding himself. Hiding a body that had betrayed him.

"Three governors. Her *friends...* No one thinks a woman can rape a man." A single tear streaked down his face. "She can," he whispered.

NarrAy had to get him out of here. What would she do if it were a woman who'd been raped?

Thankful she'd worn a bra, NarrAy untucked her shirt, stripped it off, and moved closer to him. "I'm not going to hurt you, baby. It's all right."

Khyff flinched when she wiped his face with the shirt, but he didn't resist.

"I'm going to tie this around your waist. It's okay. Let me help you." Gingerly she reached around him and tied the sleeves behind his back. His skin felt hot, feverish.

She'd used her pheromones to question prisoners. It made them open up and trust her. She concentrated on that now, crested willingly, letting the powerful chemicals down to influence Senth's brother. She put her arms around him and hugged him, and he let himself be held. His skin was wet—some of it sweat, most of it blood.

Too late, she realized he'd made physical contact with her pheromones through broken skin. Right into his bloodstream. Khyff sighed, sank wearily against her shoulder like a child, and pressed his cheek against her. She'd addicted him in a flash.

Damn. She let out a long breath. Nothing to do but deal with weaning him later. At least now he wouldn't try to kill himself. "Come on, Khyff. Let me help you stand. We've got to help Senth. He's been hurt."

"Senth's hurt?" He sat up. News of his brother mobilized him. "Where? Take me to him."

How am I going to get these guys back to the ship in one piece? Please don't let the perjump kill them both.

She helped him to his feet. She bit her lips shut to keep from exclaiming over the stroke marks and bruises all over him. He'd been flogged, every bit of his legs and torso marked. Blood streaked his thighs. *What did they do to him? What kind of monsters did Destoiya set loose on this man?*

Back in the outer room, Senth lay unconscious on the floor. Khyff squatted, lifted his brother into his arms, and stood.

She blinked. He'd been tortured and whipped, yet he picked up his adult brother as easily as if Senth had been a child.

"How do we get out of here?"

"Like this." NarrAy stood beside him and activated the perjump unit.

The next moment a room full of APLA officers surrounded them.

One woman spewed her drink, no doubt at the shock of seeing a naked blond god appear out of nowhere, whipped bloody and fully erect, holding another male beauty unconscious in his arms. NarrAy covered herself with her arms.

O'Venna charged to his feet. "Medical emergency! Med team to the Ready Room!"

Everyone sprang into action at once. NarrAy helped Khyff ease Senth onto the conference table.

Someone grabbed blankets from a storage closet and handed them out. Khyff spread one over Senth. NarrAy wrapped hers around Khyff and maneuvered him into a chair before he fell.

He took Senth's hand in his, resting his forehead against his brother's arm. NarrAy stood beside them, one hand on Senth's shoulder, the other on Khyff's. No point in avoiding touch when she'd already addicted them both.

Eyes closed, O'Venna laid his hands on Senth's chest. When he opened them a few seconds later, he smiled at her. "He'll be fine, Captain. He has minor internal bleeding, but he's suffering withdrawal from Shackle, if I recall his file." He removed his own coat while he was talking, unfastened his shirt. "Any type of bleeding during that time can cause dizziness and fainting. He's going to be all right." He offered her the shirt, and she yanked it on and tied it in front.

NarrAy stroked Senth's hair and shared a relieved smile with Khyff.

"No offense," O'Venna told the elder Antonello brother, "but you look like you've been through hell." He offered him a bottle of water.

Khyff hesitated before taking it. He opened the bottle and drank deeply. "I've been living there for years." He wiped a hand across his mouth. "Think it's about time I moved."

NarrAy grinned at him.

O'Venna took her hand, held it in both of his. "You can debrief later, Captain. It looks like you'll have quite a report."

"You don't know the half of it, sir."

"Hand off the prototype to engineering, and then go to sick bay. I want you checked out thoroughly."

When the med team bustled in and surrounded Khyff and Senth, NarrAy headed down the corridor, entered a lift, and got off on the level designated engineering. Outside the main office, she opened a hatch labeled *Armory* and withdrew a quasi-burn rifle.

Setting the perjump prototype on the floor, she stood back. Her parents' lifework. Every dream they'd shared, every goal they'd reached. The only copy of everything they'd accomplished. The gateway to a different kind of hell, where no walls kept the enemy out and no one slept secure in the quiet night.

"I'm sorry, Dad. Mom. I can't let anyone control this kind of power."

NarrAy released the gun's safety, set it against the unit, and fired.

Epilogue

All People's Liberation Army Ship Vandal
Sick Bay
Wintresq 18

Purplish bands of light-rails surrounded Senth's hospital bed. The innocence of his face in sleep made NarrAy sigh. *You'd think I was a lovesick girl.* She rested her elbow on a light-rail and propped her chin on one hand. *Fffffft. Guess maybe I am.*

Since his surgery two days ago, Senth had recovered enough to eat solid food, but the doctors weren't releasing him for a few more days. It would be longer than that before his abs were up to any kind of exercise.

Any kind, damn it. The perjump had turned a simple bruise on Senth's abdomen into an internal laceration the size of a fist. All because of one unguarded moment and a punch thrown by a bigoted kid. A moment Senth leveraged into money to buy roses and chocolates for her that she had refused to accept. *Never again. I will never let anything come between us again.*

Khyff dozed in the next bed, blankets pulled up around his ears. His physical trauma warranted surgery and extensive rest. Combined with the massive dose of Thrust he'd received and the emotional consequences of his assault, it was a miracle he hadn't completely withdrawn from reality.

The doctor had warned them of depression signs to watch for, but so far Khyff had been nothing but quiet. Too quiet. And annoyingly protective of his little brother.

"Hi." Senth smiled up at her. "I like waking up and seeing your face."

"Good thing, sweetheart." She brushed back his hair and caressed one of his ears with her fingertips. "You're going to be seeing it every morning for the rest of your life."

"I like that even more." He leaned his cheek against her hand.

"You look better."

"I thought you were the Better." He hissed playfully when she tugged a lock of his hair and then grinned at her. "I love you."

"I love you too."

She leaned over the light-rail and kissed him.

"Oh please." Khyff pulled the blanket over his head. "Get a room."

Senth and NarrAy laughed.

"Quit complaining," Senth told him. "You're the one who wants us to wait two years to get married. If I'm going to live with you, you'd better get used to seeing me kiss NarrAy."

She leaned her elbows on the railing, hands relaxed. "I think Khyff's right. You've only known me a short time.

Marriage is a permanent thing. You should be positive it's what you want."

"Fffffftt Khyff." Senth squeezed her hand. "I do know what I want."

She giggled. "I know what you want too, you bad boy."

"Yes, you do, sweetie, and that is a fact." He drew her hand to his mouth and kissed her palm. "I don't see why we have to wait."

"I'll tell you why." Khyff pushed back the covers and leaned on one elbow. "Because you're going to get taller over the next two years—probably top me in height. You'll put on weight and fill out. I want you to let your body catch up with your emotions. You have plenty of time for these decisions. You need to finish growing up before you—"

Senth interrupted him with a growl.

"Let your hackles down, little brother. I meant physically. I know the routine by heart. You're a legal adult, you can join the armada and vote, and blah blah blah. But you still have to wait."

"But—"

"No." He held up a hand, stilling protest. "Because I said so, and that's the end of it."

Senth looked up at NarrAy. "He thinks he knows everything. Are all brothers this bossy?"

"I don't know. I was an only child, sweetheart. I never had a brother."

Khyff snorted.

She added, "Until now."

Her future brother-in-law rewarded her with a heart-melting smile. And then stuck out his tongue at Senth.

"Oh yeah"—Senth pouted—"now there's an example of maturity."

His brother let out a belly laugh and lay back down.

Senth started to laugh, grabbed his stomach, and groaned. "Ow... It hurts when I laugh."

Khyff pulled a face, sticking his thumbs in his ears and wagging his fingers.

Laughing and whimpering at the same time, Senth curled into a ball.

NarrAy shook her head, grinning. *Life around these two will never be dull; that's for sure.* She turned when O'Venna knocked on the open door.

He spoke briefly with Khyff and Senth, asking about their health, and then asked NarrAy to walk with him. Once in the corridor, the Sleeper drew her aside.

"Let's get right to it. The governing council has reviewed your destruction of the prototype. Frankly, only the fact it was your parents' technology and that I intervened on your behalf kept you out of the brig."

"Thank you, sir."

"They've agreed to retain you in the APLA, but you'll be demoted to second lieutenant."

Only two pay grades down. Much less severe than I expected.

"You're still assigned to Ruffhaus Fasra. Stealth Keheyl contacted us this morning. He's on his way back with her. A med team's meeting them later tonight."

"Is she all right?"

He gave a small shake of his head. "She was Destoiya's top Praetorian, and the Conqueror didn't take kindly to her rebellion. Ruff was tortured. Stealth says it'll be weeks before she's up to speed. She's going to need your expertise."

"I'll do whatever's necessary, sir."

"The council also considered your recruitment of Senth Antonello. We believe he'll be a tremendous asset to the resistance. We'd like you to place him on your staff. That's assuming he'll have no problem reporting to you."

"Thank you, sir. I believe Senth will go along with that. Anything else?"

The Sleeper resumed walking, and she kept pace beside him. "Khyff and Senth have a visitor. I want your approval. How he got here is off the record. You can assume I cleared it. There are people working on our side whom you'd never suspect of being rebels."

O'Venna stopped outside the Ready Room.

"Due to his history with the two men, I declined to admit him without your okay." He opened the door for her.

A man in black turned toward her, revealing his whiteless eyes. None other than Luc Saint-Cyr.

* * *

Tarth City, Imperial Palace
Conqueror's Offices

Alitus knocked on and then opened Destoiya's office

door. He stepped inside and smiled at her, warming the room just by his presence. "Please excuse the interruption, Majesty."

She set down her stylus and leaned her chin on one hand, enjoying the view of her blond assistant. He wore a dark business suit, conservatively cut, the jacket short enough for her to see the shape of his tight butt when he turned around and shut the door. The pants showed off his long, powerful legs.

Does he ever tire of my lusting after him?

Alitus faced her and dropped his blue-eyed gaze briefly before meeting her intense scrutiny. His cheeks colored, and he licked his dark lips. His pheromones wafted to her, a clean scent of apricots and healthy male.

He wants me. I must be living right. She smiled. "Yes, Alitus?"

"The guest you were expecting is here, Majesty. The side door. Shall I admit him?"

"No, thank you, love. I'll get it." She stood. "I'm going to want absolute privacy for a while. See that my door is locked. Post a Praetorian on your outer door, and admit no one to my office. I'll need you later."

"Yes, Majesty. Understood." He bowed.

When the door shut behind him, she cleared the massive wooden desk by sliding the notereaders and paperwork into a drawer carelessly. Alitus would sort them out later. She slid her palm across the dark, polished surface.

Only two hours ago she'd perched on its edge while Alitus serviced her. Her nipples tightened at the memory, and the dampness between her legs increased.

After adjusting the angle of the wingback chairs and plumping the pillows in them, she smoothed her uniform, then crossed the room to the side entrance.

Luc Saint-Cyr stood there, cold and hard like a statue carved from coal. His onyx-colored gaze met hers without blinking.

She stepped back and beckoned him inside. Shutting the door behind him, she gestured to the chairs. "I expected you an hour ago."

"Security issues on the *Vandal* took more time than we thought. For some reason they didn't trust me. Imagine that." He leaned back in the chair and gave her a wry smile. "Otherwise it all went as planned."

She sat across from him. "Did you verify the prototype was destroyed?"

"It was."

"Excellent. That's what I wanted in the first place. O'Venna was a fool to think anyone would use perjump for good. It nearly destroyed civilization thousands of years ago. The Forgotten Technologies Arena is only supposed to make sure the different technologies *can't* be used until we decide it's time for them again. The Jorlans' political wavering toward rebellion is what got them killed."

"The rebels demoted NarrAy Jorlan to second lieutenant, but she's still assigned to Ruffhaus."

"Demotion won't hold her back long." Destoiya crossed her legs and leaned back. "She's powerful. And my dear Ruffhaus. If I ever get my hands on Stealth Keheyl, I'll kill him for stealing her from me. A little bit longer and I'd have broken her. Ruffhaus is dangerous out there working against me."

Saint-Cyr steepled his fingers. "O'Venna and Jorlan recruited Senthys right out from under my nose. I had the boy in complete thrall until that Better got her hands on him. You owe me for that. He'd have made me rich."

"I'll give you a hundred times what he'd have earned you. You more than deserve it for masterminding this entire theft. It was brilliant, Luc. Confiscating everything and then letting Jorlan steal back the important piece." She swung one foot. "How is my beautiful Khyff?"

The Harbinger blinked his whiteless eyes like a bird of prey. "He's agreed to work for me at For Women Only. I let it drop that you'd arrested the three governors who abused him."

"They were only supposed to share him. I never gave them permission to mistreat him. His blood was on half the toys in that room! You're sure he's all right?"

"He needed surgery."

"Those animals! Believe me; I'll make them suffer for what they did to him. I already refitted his androids. Khyff would have been one of my keepers if not for them. I should never have shared him. He was too good to waste like that. If I had him back..." She hit her fist against the arm of the chair. "You knew Jorlan was coming for him, didn't you?"

"Sorry, love. All's fair. Nothing in the rules says I have to warn you."

Destoiya chewed the inside of her lower lip, gauging his

expression. *Cold, heartless, icy bastard. Fine. I can play too. You'll need warning one day, and I won't give it either.*

She smiled. "I expect you to be good to him. I want the boy well rewarded. He deserves it."

"Stalkos always said he was good."

She dragged the toe of one foot up his right leg, all the way to his knee. "Damned near as good as you."

His sly smile warmed her in all the right places. How long had it been since she'd had him? The thought of his smooth, dark skin pooled heat between her thighs and drenched her panties with moisture. "Khyff let me rule him. He didn't take charge like you do."

"No one else ever takes you in hand the way I do. They see the uniform; I see the naked woman beneath it."

"What can I say? I'm a hopeless testosterone junkie, and you have an overabundance of it."

The Harbinger inclined his head in agreement.

"Did you tell him about the new law?" Destoiya had signed the Khyffen law into being that morning, a bill requiring the education of child slaves and proof of their ability to read and write before businesses owning them would be eligible for government contracts.

"I did. The boy actually smiled. He never smiles. He's worse than Prentice."

"He'll learn to eventually." She kicked off her shoe and slid bare toes under the hem of his trouser leg. "He has his whole life ahead of him."

She reached over and tapped the pad connecting her to Alitus.

He answered immediately. "Yes, Majesty?"

"Cancel all my appointments for the rest of the day." Destoiya started unbuttoning her jacket. "I'm going to be in conference until I tell you otherwise."

"Yes, Majesty. Consider it done."

"Tell me, Rheyn." The Harbinger rose, unfastening his coat and opening his shirt. "Will Alitus be able to hear what I'm doing to you behind these doors?"

"Of course." She stripped off her uniform and stood before him naked.

"And am I enough, or will you go to him after I'm finished with you?"

"Sorry if it damages your ego, love." Destoiya knelt to unfasten and help remove his shoes. "But I end every workday with Alitus. Sometimes he's lunch too. And then I go home to the Stable and enjoy the evening."

He extended a hand and helped her to her feet. "So"—he dropped his pants and stepped out of them—"you're still an insatiable nymphomaniac."

"Why, thank you." Destoiya gave him a tiny curtsy.

"I pity Alitus. If he's like me, he'll get hard as stone when he hears you coming. You have a luscious scream when you come. Deep and hoarse. I intend to listen to it for a while."

Laughing, she wrapped her arms around his neck. "I look forward to that."

Saint-Cyr plunged his tongue into her mouth. He crushed her against him while his kisses plundered her.

She leaned against him, savoring the warmth of his body

all along the length of hers. She caressed his dark, velvet-textured skin. No man ought to have skin that soft and not have to work at it the way a woman did.

Pressing a kiss against the corner of her mouth, he slid his fingers between her legs and stroked her. "Let's see if we can't get a scream out of you right away."

He moved to his knees before her. Hands around her buttocks, he pulled her forward and buried his mouth between her thighs. He licked between her soft folds.

She melted against the Harbinger, hands braced on his shoulders, legs straining. Trembling, she rocked against his commanding tongue. Little cries left her throat as he mastered her.

Saint-Cyr had always dominated her with his mouth. Demanded she yield to his gift of pleasure. Forced orgasms from her even while she fought to remain in control. He knew all her secret places, all the spots she liked being touched. Caressed. Licked. Sucked.

The Conqueror suddenly capitulated without reserve and cried out in release.

ᘐTHE ENDᘓ

Kayelle Allen

Science Fiction Romance author Kayelle Allen's heart-age is slightly above 21 (more like 12, actually), and she's married to her own personal hero. She believes that Romance Lives Forever, and uses that theme on all her sites. She loves heavy metal and hard rock, never misses *24*, *The Unit*, action movies, or good SciFi. Kayelle's gadget-happy. She loads up her cell phone, iPod, PDA, DS or PSP, and says she needs a larger tote that hovers and follows her around. She's a new addict to Sudoku and confesses she's started dreaming rows of numbers.

Kayelle developed a sweeping ten-thousand years of future history, wrote a feline language, and created tradestandard laws. A reader said of her surprising twists, "Think you know what'll happen next? No way! It's by Kayelle..." She authored two romance series, and is writing two new ones. Her 130-page website features a tour of worlds where her stories are based. She coordinates multi-author online promos, and founded Marketing for Romance Writers to help authors of all genres learn about promotion.

She hosts authors on her personal site Romance Lives Forever. Writers are welcome to post contest info and excerpts, share news, and schedule chats upon request. It's open and diverse with content that runs the gamut from sweet romance to hot ménages and GLBT.

LaVergne, TN USA
11 July 2010
189058LV00001B/42/P